GET OUT OF OUR WAY

GET OUT OF OUR WAY

BIRTH OF HEAVY METAL™ BOOK 5

MICHAEL TODD

MICHAEL ANDERLE

DISRUPTIVE IMAGINATION

LMBPN Publishing
PMB 196, 2540 South Maryland Pkwy
Las Vegas, NV 89109

First US edition, May 2019
Version 1.05, December 2025
eBook ISBN: 978-1-64202-290-2

GET OUT OF OUR WAY TEAM

JIT Readers

John Ashmore
James Caplan
Nicole Emens
Kelly O'Donnell
Diane L. Smith
Peter Manis
Dorothy Lloyd
Jeff Eaton
Micky Cocker

Editor
Skyhunter Editing Team

DEDICATION

To Family, Friends and
Those Who Love
to Read.
May We All Enjoy Grace
to Live the Life We Are
Called.

CHAPTER ONE

There were a myriad reasons why someone would choose to live in Europe instead of the States— better infrastructure, healthier food, and more pleasant climates. Something could also be said about the cheap healthcare and the fact that you didn't have to deal with some kind of natural disaster or another tearing you and yours a couple of new assholes every few months.

There was a deal-breaker, though, that had persuaded Smythe to move to the New England area once he'd finished his time with the Royal Marines. There was more than enough work in the US for a man like him, especially with all the security contracting companies, so he didn't lack for money. That aside, the largest crime of the Old Continent was its lack of muscle cars. He'd spent a couple of years restoring a '69, and once he'd finished it, a friend had connected him with a classic Shelby Cobra 427 that needed to be rebuilt. He would probably sell it to a million-aire down the line, but he could drive it around the circuit near his house and put a few laps in simply to enjoy it first before he parted with it.

Of course, with all the new environmental laws the EU had passed, classic muscle cars were no longer allowed on the continent's roads, and the few that were imported were only allowed on tracks and circuits. Fair enough, they did all that to save the planet—undoubtedly a noble cause—but at what price? What good would saving the planet be if muscle cars were forced into near mechanical extinction?

Common sense asserted that it would be extremely good, but the no doubt substantial rewards would be negated by the fact that a piece of the collective soul of humanity would be missing.

Andy Smythe stepped out of the environmentally conscious vehicle he'd been allocated by the rental agency and inspected his surroundings. He'd been given an address for a property just outside Hamburg which was, apparently, a huddle of old coal manufacturing plants that had been closed for a long time.

As far as investors were concerned, places like these were almost radioactive for anyone who had the money to sink into them. Leaving them vacant for the decade and a half since they'd been closed had forced the prices down. He had heard that many companies were, very quietly, buying up the real estate in the area, merely waiting for it to regain its value. Things like this always swung around and, in a few years, this entire area would bustle with activity and prices would sky-rocket.

That was what his investment banker friend from work had told him, anyway. The people managing his considerable monetary gains were far less enthusiastic about the idea and chose to go with low-risk, low-yield opportunities instead. He had no objection to this, of course. While he wasn't doing too badly financially, he didn't have five or six million to drop on a gamble like real estate.

He moved closer to the building marked on his GPS and noticed one other car already parked there. A couple more cruised up the deserted access road. The chances were that these were the people he'd been told would join him on this high-price operation.

"Smithy?" a man asked tentatively as he stepped out of the parked car.

Smythe narrowed his eyes and it took a second or two for him to recognize the man. "Holy shit snacks—Dylan Dutch. How the hell are you doing, Double-D?"

The tall, powerfully built man chuckled at the old nickname. "A lot better for seeing you, fucker. Now that they brought you in, I can't imagine they have something too difficult for the money they're paying."

Andy chuckled. "Yeah, well, they had to make it easy for your training wheels to get through. Do you know who else they brought in?"

"No, but they did say they were mining talent from the Brigade, so expect to see some familiar faces." Dutch chuckled and glanced at the cars that were now only moments away.

From his time in the Brigade, Smythe knew the men he'd served with had a similar taste in transport as he did. Hell, it could be argued that he'd acquired his taste from them. If they had brought in familiar faces and they all drove these sensible vehicles, it meant they were flown in from outside the country as well and so had not been given an option in what they would drive.

Sure enough, as both cars came to a halt in the abandoned parking lot, he did recognize the two men who emerged. The tall, bearded redhead in the electric BMW was Sean Campbell, a loud-mouthed hand-to-hand expert from the North of Scotland, and the smaller, quieter brown-haired man he greeted was an explosives expert from Liverpool named Alan Murphy.

The four men took a moment to exchange greetings. It had been a good while since they'd all been in the same part of the world. Of course, the part of the world in question had been Eastern Iraq, where they'd dealt with insurgents in the area. It had been a tough and dirty campaign, which had led to most commanders being court-martialed, while the NCOs and grunts involved were given commendations, medals, and quiet retirement policies.

None of the men felt any particular need to complain. They hadn't been involved in the planning of the mission that had gone tits-up. All they had done was follow orders. Their reward for that had been a fat pension and glowing recommendations for any job in the private sector they chose. It almost made it worth it.

There were those who wanted to serve their country and had been annoyed by the decision, and they'd been given the option to sign up again. The rest, like Smythe, Dutch, Campbell, and Murphy had all chosen more money and fewer morals.

Not no morals, of course. Merely less.

"Sean," Smythe said and gave one of the few men he'd remained in contact with a firm hug. The tall man—nicknamed the Giant Leprechaun behind his back—had been one he could honestly say had impressed him. So much so that had made sure to remind whichever dumbass had called the man by his derogatory name in his presence that leprechauns were Irish—usually with sufficient foul language to make his point. Sean had appreciated him standing up for him like that as well as the language.

"Are we still waiting for the arse who put this thing together?" Campbell asked and glanced speculatively at their surroundings. "For the money they are offering, I can't imagine it'll be a milk run."

Dutch directed their attention toward the building from which a man in a light-blue suit stepped out and walked toward them. "Speak of the devil, big man. We'll see what these arseholes don't want us to know before they fly four people all the way to fucking Germany."

The newcomer buttoned his coat as he approached and adopted a plastic smile as he offered his hand to the four new arrivals. "Hello there, gentlemen, my name is Raymond Young." He spoke in a distinctively American accent. "I'm here to represent the Phoenix Industrial Group, and you have all been brought together to further investments by the Group."

"Phoenix Industrial Group?" Smythe asked with a hasty glance at his companions.

"PIG?" Campbell chuckled and shook his head. "Did nobody think to vet the acronym, or was that something you intended from the get-go? You'd think someone wouldn't want to be associated with the police."

Raymond's fake smile grew. "How classy."

"Bite me," the Scot snapped in response as he leaned

forward and made the smaller, slimmer man take an instinctive step back. "I assume the kind of money PIG is paying us more than makes up for any snide comments we might make. Can you say the same about your job?"

Young's smile disappeared for a second and he sucked in a deep breath. "If you gentlemen will please follow me, I'll show you the reason you have all been brought here."

"That's what I thought." The large man smirked, his expression smug. Smythe didn't particularly approve of bullying like that but even he had to admit that Raymond Young simply rubbed at his nerves. It wasn't so much his actions as much as his demeanor. Everything from his suit to his shoes to his black, slicked-back hair and scarecrow-like build screamed fake. It grated on him like a bad song that he couldn't get out of his head.

The man retreated quickly to the warehouse he'd exited scant minutes before, which gave the other four men a moment to collect themselves before they followed without argument.

"You gentlemen will have to forgive the digs." Raymond chuckled nervously as they entered the mostly dilapidated warehouse. All the processing plant machines had been uprooted and sold for what Smythe assumed was a very low going-out-of-business price.

The eastern corner of the building, however, could not have made a sharper contrast to the overall decay and neglect. The area had been cleaned and polished to a literal sheen. Fluorescent lights provided bright illumination, and a group of men in lab coats definitely appeared to know what they were doing with the quartet of pods in the center of the room in which they stood.

"What's this about?" Smythe asked as he studied the scene. He wasn't all that savvy with the technological advancements of the age, but these already seemed a little too advanced for him or any of the other military men to use.

"The four of you were hired due to your skills and 'get it done, no matter the cost' attitudes. These are consistent, while in the Royal Marines and out," Raymond explained.

Smythe glanced at his three companions and noted that Dutch had taken a step forward. He was the natural leader among the four of them and as the only NCO, he also had the benefit of a little more command leadership.

"Just so you know, we won't do anything that might be considered…immoral, no matter what kind of cash your people throw at us. Legal can be bent here and there, but there are certain standards we won't compromise on. Given that, be prepared to watch us walk away if the reason you won't share your plans is because you're afraid we'll disapprove."

"Of course," Raymond said and immediately pasted his smooth smile in place. "We wouldn't want to suggest that we are that kind of company, after all. We merely want to make sure that we have a team that doesn't give up easily. You know the type, yes?"

Dutch nodded and shrugged at the rest of their team. It was like he'd said, Smythe mused. They had all been paid a hefty signing bonus, so if at any point they decided they didn't like what they were doing, they could simply walk away. It was up to PIG to make sure no lines were crossed.

Smythe couldn't help a chuckle. PIG. How in hell had

that escaped the geniuses who decided things in their corporate office?

Raymond maintained his oily smile as he moved into the room with the four pods. "This, gentlemen, is the future in training technology. Inside these, you will learn how to fight in new and improved ways, all at a minimal cost both to our company and your own collective health."

Dutch tilted his head speculatively and stepped forward to give the nearest device a light tap. "They don't look that impressive to me. Besides, we already know how to fight, so the cost is already paid for, between you and me."

Andy eased in closer to another pod and immediately noted an erased insignia on the side. He couldn't tell what it had been, but the defacement appeared to be very much a rushed job since he could still make out what looked like a winged horse on the side. Maybe they'd been donated the equipment from another company—a parent company, perhaps.

It wasn't at all comforting to consider the possibility that they would use second-hand products. Then again, if they did end up at the line that couldn't be crossed, he could call it a day and head home. If nothing else, it would be an opportunity for a road trip to Vegas since he had already signed off work with the security company for another week.

He did know what they were, of course, or at least something about it. They'd used basic versions of combat simulators for years. These appeared to be newer versions of those they used regularly at the contractor conventions.

Raymond studied his challenger for a moment and his smile took on a genuine edge for the first time since they'd met him. "You don't know how to fight. Not like this, anyway. I'll need you four to step into these pods whenever you're ready, and we can get started."

The team exchanged another look, and each tried to discern what the others thought. It was a futile interaction, but old habits died hard. In the end, they would all go in without argument. The reality was that they didn't like the way Raymond had challenged them, and if nothing else, these men were predictable. Smythe was too, but that didn't mean he couldn't see the truth. And that was the worst part—knowing how stupid you were but doing it anyway.

His honest appraisal was confirmed when they all complied and entered the pods. He looked around the interior and watched the electrical currents rush from the device into the user interface. His skin tingled and he knew within moments that it was different from anything he'd used in the past. This was an immersive experience, he realized as the screen lit up and immediately transported him into a foreign location. His gaze settled on the ground with real curiosity as his heavy, mechanized boots sank a little into a slightly shifting foundation of sand.

He'd worn combat armor suits before. Not often, but there had been a couple of missions in the Middle East that had required the boots on the ground to wear the mechanized gear. They'd been heavy and slow, but they basically worked like tanks, which was more than Smythe had come to expect from your average government acquisition. They'd used the suits afterward to play a game of rugby in the desert when word came that the mission was over and the suits would not be returned. He'd come to associate that with illegal weapons testing, which was one of the reasons why a group of the brass had been very publicly smeared.

There were other reasons, of course. Ordering the execution of civilians, torture, and a whole swathe of unseemly actions had made them unfit. Of course, anyone who knew anything about the job they did could tell that the public noise the government had caused only meant they were covering for something much, much worse. That was how the government did things. He didn't even need to know what they did, having learned the signs a long time before.

As all four team members were brought onto the server, Smythe drew the heavy assault rifle and allowed himself a moment to enjoy the smooth movements of the mechanism. Maybe this wouldn't be so bad, after all, if… The thought faded as his gaze settled on the dense jungle that appeared to be their destination.

"Where on earth do you find a place that has desert leading directly into the jungle, anyway?" Campbell asked and locked his rifle in place.

"These people are all nuts, so it's best to not question them too hard," Dutch replied. "Let's get this done, get the fuck out, and get paid. What say you, lads?"

"Fuck, yeah," Smythe answered and wondered if the lab rats could hear the shared comm channel set up for all four suits.

CHAPTER TWO

Sal leaned back in his seat on the couch and watched Courtney as she worked on the paperwork that had been forwarded to her from Philadelphia. Of course, it was paperwork in all but name. Everything that could be was done online these days, which highlighted the inevitable march of progress. Anyone who disagreed would be left behind. It was a brave new world and certainly brought some impressive benefits. Of course, she could complain that he was distracting her from her work, but that didn't concern him overmuch. She was the kind of person to tell him to shut up for a while when she actually needed to focus.

Otherwise, she'd told him that he was a welcome distraction to the monotony of work that would always follow her around the world, whether she wanted it to or not. And, as always, he was more than willing to provide her with the necessary diversions when they were required.

"So, you vetted Anderson bringing this merc in?" he

asked when the silence threatened to drag on longer than expected. He couldn't really understand why she'd allowed him to go off on his own, given that the man was barely out the door of working for Pegasus in the first place. "I saw the film you guys used to justify having him on the team, and yes, he's good. But how do you know he's trustworthy? Why couldn't Madigan have vetted someone for him?"

"He'll run most of that particular show," Courtney replied, her gaze still on her computer screen. "I talked to him and I trust him to choose the right people for the job. We merely have to hope that Savage meets the expectations."

"I still feel like we should have had more say in that." Sal shook his head, even though she likely wouldn't notice. "We could have at least headed back there to make sure he has things under control. Or maybe have Madigan put the fear of God into this guy. Give him one of her speeches."

"It sounds to me like you simply want time off in civilization." She chuckled and finally looked away from what had held her focus. "Although, between you and me, it's not that civilized these days. At least out in the Zoo, you know the shit will hit the fan. You expect better from city life, somehow, and you never fail to be disappointed."

"Why would I want to go back?" he asked honestly. "I basically have everything I want here. Action galore, shit to do, and more than enough things to keep my mind occupied. Why on earth would I want to head back to where people want us all dead?"

"Maybe because your postgraduate committee won't

make a visit to the Zoo anytime soon?" She tilted her head in a definite challenge.

Sal opened his mouth to retort but realized that he didn't have anything to counter that particular suggestion. "You're right. I've gathered more than enough data to create a dissertation that would more than satisfy any committee, but who in the hell will believe a word of it? We're literally breaking ground in biology and physics all at the same time."

"Get video evidence," Courtney suggested with a smile. "If you have videos of what you went through to get all this data to their ivory tower of academia, they won't have anything to contest it with. Even better—given that we're writing the books on what goes on in there—you can drop said book onto their lap and flip them off while you do it. If they don't agree with any of your assertions, and if they don't think your work makes you worthy of your PhD, you can tell them to take their toys and get the fuck out of your sand pile since they don't know shit about the Zoo. Let them conduct their own research in here and until then, hand that doctorate over, peace out, mic drop."

"While I agree with the general sentiment, I do know for a fact that many of the committees aren't above denying applications because they simply don't like the person presenting," he said. "I'll still need to be diplomatic. Or, at least, not fully hostile, anyway."

She chuckled as Madigan made her way in.

"Not fully hostile about what?" she asked and glanced at the others while she poured herself a mug of coffee.

"I'm trying to convince Sal to go back to the States to

finish his doctorate," Courtney explained before he could say anything. "And to be flashy about it."

"Hell yeah," Madigan agreed. "Hell, show off and be arrogant all you please. If they don't like it, we can start our own doctorate program—with blackjack and hookers. Tell those motherfuckers that the Zoo gave you that doctorate and they're only there as a matter of tradition."

Sal grinned. "I can't argue with that."

"Damn right." She grinned and leaned closer to bump her fist against his. "Now, Courtney, I need your help with something. Let Sal daydream about finally putting those three pretty letters at the end of his name."

The other woman pushed from her seat and they hugged briefly before they wandered out to where Amanda could be heard arguing loudly with Connie. The armorer had obviously moved past the point of rational discussion and now resorted to cussing volubly in Spanish. Since Connie wasn't programmed to respond to any language but English, it seemed a futile rebellion.

Sal looked at his phone, his thoughts mulling over the issue of his doctorate. Neither Courtney nor Madigan had been wrong. He wanted it. Not more than anything but it was certainly high on his list of priorities. He might as well get it out the way now, right?

Besides, it would be nice to not have to correct people about it continually. They had hit the nail on the head too. He was a doctor in everything but name, and it was about time that he simply wrapped it up and put it to bed so he could move on with his life. He had more important things to deal with at the moment, of course, but nothing that couldn't be managed. With the work that came in from

Amanda, Madigan, Courtney, and even Anja, the business was sustainable without him for a short while.

That was what successful managers did, right? Delegate?

Sal made a face and shoved out of his seat. He had never wanted to be considered upper-management. That was reserved for the assholes—whom he'd always hated—and he had had no intention of being someone the others loathed and simply pandered to for expediency's sake.

He was no longer built to endure this kind of shit.

There had been a day when Professor Peter Tellisman, PhD, could run with the rest of them. He'd never had any military experience, of course, but he'd always been one to break the familiar stereotype of the stuffy, college-educated academic who never left the university and hid from life as a perpetual student. He'd played as a quarterback in high school football and had even attended the University of Minnesota on a football scholarship. And he'd been an all-rounder, too, with time on the chess and debate teams while he enrolled as a biology major for his BA. He'd declined the offer to continue with the team for his sophomore year, though, and chose to focus on his studies instead.

He'd gone to Myanmar for his dissertation and survived in a country in the middle of a civil war while studying the evolution of the local fauna. Those were the most exciting years of his life, even if he wouldn't ever wish to repeat them.

In all honesty, the Zoo had happened perhaps ten or fifteen years too late for him. By the time he was called in as a specialist, there was a horde of problems that confronted his body. He was still only fifty-two and in great shape for someone his age, or so he was told.

And yet there was something about the jungle that drained a man like him. He'd taken a couple of trips inside early on, and that had been all he could manage. When they offered him a job in one of the research buildings in the US base, he'd jumped at it and hadn't been ashamed about it either. He was too old to rush around inside a hell-hole like that. It was a young man's game.

He could have questioned why he had taken this particular job. There were more than a few dangers lurking. The reminder of that lay in the fact that his suit had been fitted with extra weaponry he had absolutely no idea how to use. The gear itself was heavy and lacked proper ventilation, which meant the heat had begun to reach unbearable levels.

And yet, as he stood there and looked at all the brand-spanking-new plants and animals around him—so dense that they literally blocked the sunlight out—he couldn't help but wonder why he hadn't returned before now.

"We'll head out in three minutes, boss," one of the gunners nearby said. The man's name was Miles, a relatively easy one to recall for some reason. There were too many for him to remember—twelve, all told—and the scientist had never been much good with names at the best of times. Miles seemed to fit, though, and if he'd somehow got it wrong, the man didn't seem to mind being called that.

"I'm almost finished here," Tellisman replied and leaned closer to the plant he examined. No plants with these particular star-shaped leaves had been registered before. While he knew better than to pluck any of the plants out of the ground, it was necessary to take a couple of samples, at least—even a small piece or two of the leaves would suffice. He noted curiously that it grew in a similar fashion to the cannabis plant.

The observation brought a quick smile. He'd only tried it in his early days in college and had honestly never acquired a taste for it. But, given the benefits the plant offered people who suffered from the side effects of chemotherapy, he could only wonder at what kind of powerhouse it would be when combined with the unimaginable abilities of the jungle.

Then again, it also raised the inevitable question as to how the Zoo—notorious for molding its flora and fauna after creatures and plants already on earth—had been exposed to cannabis in the first place. He could only imagine that someone had brought a personal stash in. With the number of illegal entries, that didn't sound unlikely at all.

If his suspicions proved correct, they had to consider that there would be a massive market for what would effectively be alien marijuana.

"I'm good to go," Tellisman called, and Miles nodded to indicate that they should begin to move out. They were only a couple of miles into the jungle at this point. Things were far more hairy deeper inside, and the expeditions that went in that deep called for larger groups and were sometimes accompanied by armored vehicles. Even then, there were stories that some of the French teams hadn't returned.

He was happy enough to simply hang back and allow his teammates to do most of the hard hitting. A couple of them had gone out of their way to eliminate some panthers that had given them trouble while they remained in one place, which explained why they were in a rush to move again. The animals around there were known to converge on loud noises, and they needed to stay in motion to avoid being caught in the middle of a massive firefight.

Tellisman was definitely not in the mood for that. He happily resumed his position in the group without argument

They pushed ahead once more, and the group of twelve men seemed to collectively become a little more nervous as their route led them deeper into the jungle. Darkness descended rapidly, although it was still the middle of the day. Even so, he was fascinated by the pale glow the plants assumed as the shadows intensified. He honestly had no idea how to explain that. They'd told him it had to do with the goop inside, but he'd never heard of any plant with visible sap. Then again, there weren't too many that had glowing sap either.

"What the hell is that?" one of the gunners asked and his startled curiosity drew Tellisman to the front of the group when they came to a halt. Weapons were aimed directly ahead, but as he reached the vanguard, he wasn't sure why. Admittedly, about a decade before, the sight of an eight-inch insect would have raised most eyebrows. These days, however—given that there were locusts the size of large dogs with scorpion tails—a new and slightly larger than usual insect barely made a blip on the radar.

Not for him, though. Ever the scientist, he moved closer and filmed the long creature with his HUD as he did so. The hard drive on his suit told him that there was no such insect registered, and it always paid—literally—to add new creatures to the register.

"So..." Tellisman grumbled as he dropped to a crouch and winced when his knee popped uncomfortably. "It looks like we have a six-legged insect here. Infrared tells me that there are toxins on the skin, which explains the bright red markings on the back. A new addition to the Zoo family."

The creature moved in closer to him as he continued to make notes about its appearance. Suddenly, it lurched forward and latched onto his shin. Tellisman took a step back, but the creature clung to him with jaws the size of fingers working as a pincer. It pinched at first, which made him laugh as he tried to shake it off. The amusement turned to irritation, though, when it maintained its stubborn hold and worse, the vicious pincers sawed into his suit.

"What the fuck?" he shouted and jerked back to shake his leg more vehemently until the creature finally fell free.

"What's the matter?" Miles asked as he pushed forward. "What happened?"

"The motherfucker bit through my suit," he shouted and leaned down to inspect the damage. "I thought these things were supposed to be impenetrable. Or at least resistant to the bite of a fucking insect."

He knew something was wrong as he spoke the last few

words. The syllables slurred, and his head felt alarmingly light. The suit prevented him from losing his balance, but only barely. His mouth worked and noises issued from it, but he couldn't tell if any of it made sense. From the looks of confusion and alarm on the faces of the other men, he could only assume it didn't.

His suit's gyro's failed and he sagged into the pull of gravity as the team rushed forward. Their shouts echoed from what seemed a long way away. No, that wasn't possible. They were close enough for him to see their lips moving, but he still couldn't make out what they said.

This didn't bode well. Tellisman knew the frightening truth in the moment when he began to lose control over his bodily functions. The creature's venom was obviously potent. He needed to get samples. Later, when he felt more himself.

CHAPTER THREE

Smythe took control of his new suit and allowed himself the time needed to adjust to the feel of it. He'd obviously taken a few minutes to read the specs, but that could never replace the real thing. Technically, this wasn't the real thing, but it was as close as people would get without actually charging into the Zoo themselves.

While he still had trouble with the notion of a jungle in the middle of the Sahara, after their first dismal run in the pods, Young had decided a little information might be beneficial to their training. He'd cheerfully—and with what might have been a smug smirk—provided them with reading material that he assured them would change their way of thinking. While the details themselves had stretched the limits of what might be even remotely believable, it had definitely made them take the scenarios they encountered far more seriously in later sims.

He glided through the first few motions required to test his mobility. The specs on this piece were for a new hybrid-style suit. It lacked the firepower and the armor of the gunner suits but was said to be harder-hitting than the usual specialist suits. The Jack of all trades of the suit world, he decided. This one was new, of course, given that it was the first hybrid suit that made use of nuclear powering to be sustainable for years without needing to recharge.

They'd never had much in the line of power complaints, though. Even the hybrid suits didn't need that much to run, so the battery packs they already had were more than enough to last longer than he would ever want to be in a combat situation at any given time. A couple of months, the statements told him. He reminded himself that he couldn't ever trust blurb provided by the companies that actually made suits, but Campbell had gone through it carefully. They had added power redundancies to the joints to gather power from his own movements in addition to solar panels along the back section of the armor during their time in the Middle East.

Yes, he was lucky to have the likes of Campbell on his team. In fact, he was lucky to have virtually everyone who was on his team—Campbell, Dutch, Murphy, and himself. They wouldn't fit in anywhere else, but in this little squad, they somehow did. He liked that they had their own kind of identity like that. Their worth was far more than the sum of the parts.

Dutch looked at him from where he wore the tank they called a suit these days. Hell, the right arm looked like it had been formed into a makeshift shield. He was testing it and rushed it forward a step or two before he raised an eyebrow in query.

"Are you good to go, Smythe?" he asked and shifted into

his business tone as he drew the massive assault rifle that would be too big on most helicopters.

"Lead the way, Dutch," he replied and stepped behind the man. Campbell took the right flank in a smaller and lighter gunner suit which allowed faster movement and better cover. Murphy assumed the role of the specialist. From the little they'd learned from Young, these were the scientists who accompanied teams into the Zoo for research purposes. He wore the lightest of the suits which required very little power. There were weapons involved and some mechanics to make hiking through the jungle easier, but his was the least defended, meaning he would hold position at the very center of their little band. Smythe assumed the rear and they penetrated beyond the tree line.

The change that came over the scenery barely five steps in was amazing. It went from desert to jungle, and the light became a thing of memory. For anyone who hadn't set foot in there, it had to feel unrealistic—like there was no place on earth that could even remotely feel this way—and Smythe wanted to believe they were right about that. He had to constantly remind himself that this was based on reality because it seemed about as far removed from normal as a weird, space-age video game designed to be as crazily unbelievable as possible.

It was a brave new world out there now, he thought with a grin as he raised his weapon and remained alert for anything that might attack them from the trees.

They moved quickly and glided through the area as smoothly as they could. Everything about their location was new, but the rules of the games remained the same. There was a location set on their maps they needed to reach. They needed to extract the items there and fulfill the mission while under duress. It was always difficult—sometimes more difficult than it needed to be. This was a training exercise, after all. It was intended to prepare people for the worst of worst-case scenarios, and they simply had to hope for the best when they actually entered the damn jungle.

Dutch raised his hand to bring their group to a halt while he scanned the trees. It took a moment of observation before Smythe realized there was no obvious threat. The team leader had responded to a deep sensory prompting and most likely didn't even consciously know what had rubbed him the wrong way. Instincts were fickle things out there. While they had only been on a couple of milk runs to prepare for the environment before, Smythe had a feeling that the tempo would increase rather rapidly from then on.

Besides, he had learned to trust the same wariness within himself. It had saved his ass more times than he could count, both in these simulations and out.

He brought his mind to the task at hand. "In the trees," he stated quietly and aimed his rifle into the branches above them. More than a little movement could now be seen and indicated the presence of a handful of the creatures they already knew all too well. The darkness made it impossible to make them out in detail, but the movement patterns as well as the six legs plus the elongated tail with a stinger at the end were indisputable.

"What are they doing up there?" Murphy asked. "Don't they prefer to be on the ground?"

"You're mostly right," Smythe replied and recalled their initial sims.

"Oh, shit," Campbell grunted and looked around hastily.

"Right," Dutch grumbled. "They only try to reach high ground when there's something big in the area—like they don't want to get in the way of what might happen but want to have a decent view."

"That still sounds like too much conjecture," Murphy pointed out. Of all of them, he remained the most skeptical.

"Well, given that was how the event was described in the reading materials they gave us—almost word for word, I might add—you can see they would inevitably add it to one of these sims." Smythe squinted into the shadowed foliage. He didn't like how quiet the jungle was. It was supposed to be alive with noise and intense signs of life. For the most part, that was true enough, but there was an ominous quality to the muted soundtrack that, to his mind, definitely spelled trouble.

The motion sensors went wild, but the activity was focused on one section of their view.

"Dutch," Smythe called and pointed to the source of the vibrations that moved toward them. The leader nodded to confirm that he'd seen the potential threat and directed the four of them to take defensive positions. Murphy had his weapon ready but remained toward the back. The other three hurriedly formed a triangle with him at the center, their weapons trained deeper into the Zoo.

"What the fuck?" Dutch asked no one in particular as the vibrations grew more and more intense to the point where sensors were no longer needed to detect them. The ground shuddered beneath their feet aa a massive but as yet undetermined beast pounded toward them with alarming speed.

Smythe tensed and strained to see what it was in the seconds before it cleared the underbrush in a single mighty leap that swallowed ten meters with ease. Dutch opened fire first when the colossus made no effort to stop.

It resembled a massive simian, complete with forearms that seemed to have opposable thumbs. Everything about it screamed enhanced ability and capability. The creature was definitely gorilla-like in build, down to the high forehead and the knuckle-walking, but stood two and a half, maybe three times larger than even the largest silverback Smythe had ever heard of. In the darkness, colors weren't visible but were restricted to a ghostly gray view courtesy of his HUD.

Damned if it wasn't one of the most beautiful things he'd ever seen. Despite the obvious danger it presented, he really hoped it wasn't merely the invention of the people who ran the sims and was based on reality. A titan gorilla mutant seemed like something worth seeing in person.

The entire team responded with a barrage of shots, and although bullets clearly punched into the monster—with splashes of blood visible in the motion sensors—it had little effect other than irritating it further. An ear-splitting roar issued to challenge the gunfire and it focused its attack on Dutch, who stepped forward to try to tank his way past it.

His tactic didn't end well. Smythe grimaced when it dismissed the man's attempt at a retaliatory charge with a backhand that catapulted his supposedly three or four-ton suit between a couple of trees before he rolled to a halt and huddled on the ground.

Murphy tried to step in and pick up the slack, but the monster simply pounded its right forelimb into its new adversary with a crunch that effectively ended the encounter. It moved too quickly for something that size. Smythe scowled as he ducked and tried to circle the beast that had moved opposite Campbell. Dutch was already out, and so was Murphy. The mission now relied entirely on the two remaining teammates.

The enemy turned to him first, for some reason, and Smythe gulped instinctively when the belligerent eyes focused grimly for a half-second before the massive fists descended on him. The meaty hammerheads crushed his armor but fell short of the obliteration that should logically have followed. His assailant seemed satisfied that he was disabled sufficiently to keep him out of the battle for now. Despite knowing the circumstances, he waited to feel the pain when every bone in his body shattered, but the sim cut the sensations off long before then. It wasn't a torture machine, after all.

He watched numbly as the creature spun with effortless grace for something so large and used its hind legs to kick Campbell away. The man had almost succeeded in his attempt to flank it, but his life signs flat-lined at the same time that he hammered into a nearby tree.

Which made Smythe the last man standing. He groaned inwardly and tried to move. Nothing responded, though, so even the simple act of standing seemed all but impossible. Of course, it didn't really matter either way. He wouldn't be around for much longer.

"Not to be all Steve Irwin about this," he grunted as the monster circled to finish him off. "But you are a fucking beauty."

It merely growled with brutal disinterest as it pounded him into a paste.

The sim deactivated and Smythe waited, absolutely still for a few moments as the software shut down, before he pushed himself out of the pod that had pinned him in place.

"What the fuck was that?" Dutch was already berating the technicians while they reviewed the technical aspects of the simulation. "You'd better fucking tell me the monster there is verifiable as something that exists in the Zoo and that its usual stomping grounds is five minutes into that place. If not, I'll call it a day from here on out."

"The gorilla monster is actually one of the more vanilla creatures of larger size found there," one of the technicians said, his attention still largely focused on the pad he worked on. "You should see the huge armored centipede they added to the databases last month."

Murphy shuddered and pushed himself out of the pod, and Andy remembered that the man didn't much like insects.

They had all been warned there could be a kind of phantom pain while their psyche tried to process that what it had experienced wasn't real. Sure enough, an ache rippled across Smythe's entire body as he rolled his shoulders again.

"That doesn't fucking matter," he said and shook his head. "Learning is what we're here for—to make sure we don't make the same mistakes again."

"What mistakes?" Dutch asked with a dark chuckle. "There was nothing we could do against something that size that could simply shrug bullets off."

"Well, for one thing, when something that big comes for us, maybe next time, it would be best for us to bug out and try to find cover," he replied. "There are things in the Zoo that aren't worth engaging as far as I'm concerned."

The technician gave no indication that this was the lesson to be learned or even whether there was any lesson to be learned at all. He honestly didn't give a shit. These people had acted cold and distant from the beginning to the point where the other team members suggested they get their asses in the pods instead.

This was, after all, what they were being paid for, and honestly, if that meant seven figures to play video games like this, he would call it a steal.

As appealing as that thought was, he was sure there would be other factors involved in their mission. This was merely the preparation, and it was very likely that these people made things difficult because they didn't think the foursome was worth the money they were being paid. And they were fucking right. The Royal Marine Commandos needed to up their game. So far, it was tough going.

"Let's get coffee," Smythe said and stretched to ease the odd stiffness that had scooted in behind the phantom pain. "We'll be ready to go back in...ten minutes? Maybe fifteen. If we have to wait any longer for you assholes to get your shit together, we'll go back to the hotel, got it?"

The technicians watched their exit with undisguised annoyance, which was understandable. They probably weren't paid seven figures, after all. Jealousy was a bitch.

Dutch looked at Smythe and grinned as the group sauntered out to the coffee room they'd seen on their arrival. They all knew the lab rats would take at least another half-hour to get their ducks in a row. By pulling the impossibility card, Smythe had earned them the rest of the day off while looking like he was the reasonable one.

It was a shitty thing to do but the way he saw it, they had flung the shit first. This was merely him taking advantage of it.

CHAPTER FOUR

S al couldn't help a sigh of annoyance as he sifted through the documents he still had on his laptop.

These comprised all the data he'd gathered during his time in the Zoo. Literal blood, sweat, and tears had been expended on everything on his hard drive. There were also whitepapers that had been handed over for him to edit by others who wanted his input on their research, and he'd had much to add.

Given that most of the money he put into Heavy Metal came from his work, it meant the time he'd given to research had largely been focused on raising the money that had gone into the business. As it turned out, though, most of the people were more than happy to pay for his work but they weren't quite as enthusiastic about allowing him to use the same papers in his presentation for a disser-tation committee. Courtney had run over the legal prob-lems and copyright and ethics issues with him, but the basics were that if he had submitted anything to the base's database, he couldn't use it for a dissertation. Which sucked massive balls, no doubt about it.

"Fucking hell," Sal grumbled. He could have sworn he had things saved for himself, but the more he studied his notes, the more he realized exactly how many mistakes he'd made in turning his work in for a quick payday. In fairness, they had been good paydays, but if he hadn't jumped the gun, he might have something valuable to draw on for his dissertation.

Even more annoying, it wasn't something he'd even thought to do. With all that talk about not being a doctor in his early days, he'd allowed himself to focus on the money. It had been a business decision, of course. He'd wanted Heavy Metal to work, after all, and for a while, that had been his sole focus. Now that the company was succeeding and was capable of doing so without him being around, he realized he probably should have kept a couple of things for himself.

He turned when the bathroom door opened and Madigan emerged in a cloud of steam.

"Did you have a good shower?" he asked and smiled as she stepped out, wrapped in her towel while she used his to dry her hair.

"Not too bad. I heard you cussing, though. What's up? Do you need me to punch someone? Intimidate them, maybe?"

"Haven't you heard?" Sal dropped into his office chair. "We have professional muscle on the payroll these days. You can outsource all your punching and intimidating to the US, now."

She grinned and nudged him in the shoulder. "Nah, you

know me. I like to do my own dirty work. Besides, that dude is on Courtney's payroll. I wouldn't want to put her out for you. No offense."

"None taken."

"So what has you cussing over there?" Madigan asked and sat on the bed while she rubbed her hair.

"I've been here for a while, right?" He spun his chair to face her. "And now that I have the dissertation on my mind, I've looked at the shit I've gathered. It's all been copyrighted and locked into someone else's research, and I'm left with nothing."

"Well, you have a successful startup and an alliance with not one, but two, Fortune Five-Hundred companies, thanks to Courtney," Madigan pointed out and made a face. "I wouldn't call that nothing. But yeah, I get what you're trying to say."

He shrugged. "I've worked on getting stuff done out here, and while the money's great, my interests have always been academic. Which makes me wonder why I haven't saved anything for my academic career. Is it because I don't want to go further than I already have and I simply don't want to admit it?"

"That's bullshit," she grunted matter of factly. "Come on. The stuff out there changes all the time. Say the word, and we'll go out for a couple of days and get you enough to drop any committee dead. Boom, done, have a couple of drinks to celebrate, and make a quick trip to the States to make it official. Hell, with Courtney's connections, we could probably put up someplace classy and make a vacation of it. I need a fucking vacation."

Sal nodded. "I think we all need a vacation. Of course,

having to defend my findings to a group of old dudes who haven't been out in the field since the eighties isn't my idea of a vacation. It would have to be marginally more relaxing than your average run into the Zoo, I suppose, but not by much."

"Don't be a drama queen." She laughed and pushed from his bed, took a quick step, and punched his shoulder again. "We'll find something, we'll get it done, and you'll stop moping about not being a doctor so we can get around to doing what's more important."

"Like what?"

"I don't know, but we'll figure it out once it's done." Her grin was encouraging. "I need to get dressed."

"Do you really?" He leaned back in his chair and tilted his head to watch her leave with a small smile. "I really like the whole towel thing you have going there."

"Maybe I should start heading out into the Zoo wearing nothing but a towel," she agreed with a chuckle.

"Hey now, let's not get crazy. I attract far too much attention and the problems that come with it as it is. Can you imagine the kind of trouble we'd attract if you wandered around like that? I think the sole reason they're developing these bigger and bulkier gunner suits is because they need to hide the secrets of what's inside away from the animals."

"Okay, I know that was an attempt to compliment me, but it's as creepy as fuck." She darted back to press a light kiss to his lips. "But thanks anyway."

Sal couldn't help a smile as he watched her leave, sadly intent on getting clothes on. He chuckled softly and rocked his chair for a moment as he refocused his attention on his computer screen. She was right. If he couldn't find anything in his existing files to use for his dissertation, they would find something to use in the Zoo. The place literally pumped scientific discoveries out every day. It wouldn't be a walk in the park, obviously, but if there was ever a time or a place to get it done, it would have to be there and now.

He leaned in to create a list of what they would need for a quick trip into the jungle when he heard a light tap at the door. Madigan had left it open and he looked up to where Amanda stood and peeked in.

"Hey, Sal, are you busy?" she asked and slipped inside when he indicated for her to do so.

"Not particularly," he answered half truthfully and turned his seat to face her. "What can I do for you?"

"I have something personal I want to talk to you about, actually," the mechanic said and shrugged almost apologetically.

"Well, take a seat and tell me all about it." He smiled and gestured at the empty chair.

It had been all well and good to have the rest of that first day off, Smythe supposed, but the result was another two hellish days spent catching up on what they had missed out on. There had been a considerable amount of it.

"Smythe, I need you in position," Dutch called and spun into his range of vision. The shield on his suit protected him enough to be able to dispose of a number of the black panthers by crushing those that were close enough and shooting those that weren't. His attacks similarly dashed any excuse Smythe might have had for not joining Murphy and Campbell on the left flank and he pushed his suit into motion. The powered joints kicked in and propelled him rapidly to where the two men had their hands full with a swarm of the stinger-tailed locusts.

He decided to take a page from Dutch's book and barreled into the group that appeared to retreat, most likely to regroup for another assault. Of course, his armor lacked the power and physicality that their leader's had but there was something to be said for a blindside charge.

Too much time in the US had him thinking in American Football terms. His Hotspur fan of a father would be so disappointed.

Smythe used his free hand to break the neck of the closest creature, crushed the next with his boot, and opened fire at the rest. A couple of the oversized hyenas bounded forward in an attempt to stop his attack, but his teammates realized what was happening and pressed an assault of their own.

He grinned and tried to wipe the blueish blood that had splattered onto his helmet. As it turned out, the armored hands weren't designed for cleaning. He stopped when it simply smudged and drew a long breath as the animals eased away from the massacre that had befallen them.

"I think we're getting the hang of this bullshit," Murphy said with a chuckle. "Do you even remember what these critters are called?"

"You mean the locust creatures?" Smythe asked. "Do they actually have names at this point?"

"They have a scientific name," Murphy pointed out and

reloaded his weapon. "*Locusta Pandinus imperator*, as I recall. But no proper names yet, no."

"I won't call that critter an emperor," Dutch stated, his tone almost a growl. "I don't care. They look like the aliens out of *Starship Troopers*, only smaller. And angrier, somehow."

"I think they called it that because they found DNA of the emperor scorpion when they brought samples out," Murphy said. "It was mixed in with various other DNA, but they assume that's where the tail comes from." He paused when he realized that his companions stared at him like he was a complete stranger. "What? I like arachnids. I pay attention to this kind of stuff."

"Right," Smythe said, his attention immediately diverted when the ground rumbled again to indicate that the animals had regrouped and launched another strike. They really shouldn't have wasted all that time talking when they had a mission to complete in the sim. The monsters would simply continue their aggressive behavior in larger numbers until one side or another won the field.

He had to admit this was hard work. He could only imagine how much harder it was for the people who went into the real Zoo. They had to face the same dangers, plus the added and very real possibility that they would be killed by the monsters. The sim was tough, no doubt about it, but they always knew that if they made a mistake, they could simply be pulled out to have a cup of coffee and be sent in again to ensure the mistake wasn't repeated. The people in the actual jungle had no such luxury.

Of course, as uncomfortable as it was, he'd long since realized that they would probably head into the Zoo themselves. This was all merely training, preparation for the main event. If asked, he would say he looked forward to the challenge, but honestly, he really hoped all this was simply to prep the sim for a release to the open market—like a video game or something. He was no coward and he would enter the jungle if they paid him to do so. Still, he didn't think he was unreasonable in saying it was one of the places in the world he would never willingly enter, not for any amount of money.

Disney World was another, but for entirely different reasons.

"What the hell is that?" Dutch asked, and Andy made a note to remind the man to buy them a round of shots. Over the past three days, they had come up with a system to make things even more interesting than they already were and pushed them around to make sure nothing became too cliché. One of the rules was that anytime anyone asked what the hell something was, they had to buy shots. Drinks were the forfeit if they asked what the fuck it was.

In fairness, Smythe had been about to make the same mistake himself. Whatever it was, the creature was long—about ten or twelve meters from one end to the other—and moved through the treetops like nothing he'd ever seen before.

The four men delivered a barrage of firepower at the monster, but nothing seemed to penetrate the seemingly armored carapace. It dropped from the branches with a suddenness that pre-empted reflexive defense and felled both Murphy and Smythe in the first blow. Andy was drawn out of the sim and watched as Dutch was immediately swallowed by the creature, armor and all, and Campbell was suddenly impaled by one of the ridiculously spindly, centipede-like legs.

"Holy shit," he gasped and hauled himself clear of the pod. "What the—"

He stopped the instinctive response in time, thank goodness. No way did he want to buy another round of shots for the crew. He'd paid for five or six the night before, and he still owed for three. Yesterday had been a productive day.

"That was the *Lithobius gigantea*." One of the technicians answered his unfinished question in a bored tone. "It's a new species but already has one hell of a body count attached to it. From what I've heard, though, it's more a problem for the Russians. These centipede-like mutants keep more to the eastern side of the jungle and leave the western and central areas for the larger creatures that could threaten their survival. The food chain arrangement in the Zoo is quite fascinating."

"It's less fascinating when you realize you're at the very bottom of said food chain," Smythe snarked in response and shook his head in an effort to clear the startled haze that still governed his brain. Honestly, he wasn't even sure how the monster had killed him. He watched the replays carefully and realized that the legs—which still seemed, in his mind, too frail to have any relevance—had simply stabbed through his armor like it was paper. The impossibility of it meant he had to work out how it had happened.

"That's some bullshit right there," Dutch muttered as he stepped out of his pod.

"I can assure you, all creatures you encounter in the

simulation have been documented, studied, and cataloged by the crews on the ground," one of the techs said and looked up from his work. "So far, you have actually confronted only about six percent of all the mutants cataloged. Of course, some aren't hostile, and others haven't been seen in months so are presumed to be extinct."

"Who the hell catalogs all these fucking killers?" Dutch asked.

"Well, there are many involved in the research and study but one name that does pop up more frequently than most is Salinger Jacobs. MS, not PhD," Murphy pointed out.

"Who?" Smythe grinned as he focused on his teammate. "What the hell kind of name is that?"

The man shrugged. "It's the name on a disproportionate amount of the papers on these creatures. I suppose it could be a pen name, but who would want to use one on their scientific work? It's not like they don't want recognition for it or something."

Andy shook his head. "It doesn't matter. We only need to know how to kill it."

"Concussive rounds are listed here," Murphy replied. "The carapace armor on it is too dense for regular bullets, but that simply means any concussive blasts will turn the insides to mush."

"Well, that sounds about right," Dutch grumbled and stiffened his posture. "Let's go back in and teach that piece of shit a thing or two."

CHAPTER FIVE

"So, what's up, Amanda?" Sal asked as the silence threatened to drag on interminably. She had come into his room, asked to talk to him about something personal, and seemed to be gathering the courage to do that. Which was fine. He understood that some things needed to be pondered before they were discussed. With all his social anxiety issues, he understood that more than most.

At the same time, though, he had stuff to do, places to be, and people to see. While he gathered that whatever she wanted to say was important enough to warrant this kind of hesitation, his patience wore thin. He wondered if there was anything he could say or do to speed things up a little.

Of course, thinking like that felt trashy. It wasn't like what he was working on was time-sensitive or anything.

"Right, sorry. I'm trying to decide on the right way to say this," Amanda said finally with a nod but kept her gaze lowered. "I guess I'll simply come out and say it. Do you know that I've been seeing this girl, Dr. Beverly Chance? She works in the research department of one of the Zoo companies and handles everything that's sent back."

"I did not know, actually," Sal responded with a small shrug. "Well, I know Dr. Chance, of course, and I do know you prefer the gals to the guys. No judgment there, you know that. I'm very pro-LGBT. All the other letters too. I'm totally…um, fine?"

"You can stop now." She chuckled.

He sighed. "Thanks. I'm not used to people sharing personal stuff with me, obviously. What…uh, were we talking about again?"

"Well, Bev has been offered a job in the French base, and she asked if I wanted to move there with her," the armorer explained. "I've already called the folks working the base there, and they said they desperately need someone with experience to coordinate their mechanical divisions. They're more than willing to pay top dollar for my work and—" She fixed him with an almost desperate look. "You know, I'm doing all the talking here and you're simply listening, so maybe you should say something."

He realized that his face had gone slack and he made an effort to recover from his apparent stupor. "Oh, sorry. I'm, uh…a little… Yeah, I think stunned is the right word. Well…this sucks. For us, obviously, but I couldn't be happier for you. Both for the job and for you following your heart like this. It's fantastic. Was it Connie? Is she the reason you're leaving? I will kill that damned AI."

Amanda chuckled. "I'm actually as conflicted by this as you are, but I think it's the right decision. And while

Connie is a complete bitch, I think I'll miss the stupid cow. Please don't kill her."

"Well, doors around here are always open for you," he said after a brief pause while he gathered his thoughts. "In the meantime—and on a completely unrelated note—do you think you might know anyone who has similar qualifications to you and wouldn't mind moving to the compound? Completely unrelated, of course. I'm trying to branch out. Or something."

Her laugh lit her features appealingly. "Huh. Completely unrelated to my leaving, you want me to find someone to fill the job I will be vacating? Interesting. Well, on the off-chance that you weren't looking for someone to replace me already, I do have a couple of names I think you should look at. On top of that, I discussed this with Anja earlier, and she mentioned there might be room for some —how do I put this delicately?—she wants a little more sausage in this here estrogen salad, if you know what I mean."

Sal chuckled. "I…right, yeah, that is a good point. Either way, though, as long as I find the best person for the job, they can have a size-two pencil-sized dick for all I care."

"I'm the best person for the job," she pointed out. "I'm simply trying to find you the second-best, understood? But the way you describe it, you make it sound like all really well-hung and excellent mechanics need not apply."

"Of course," he quipped. "Besides, I doubt you'll find any well-hung stud who can turn a wrench properly."

"Well, I know I won't check the pants of the men and women whom I think are qualified for the job." She

43

grinned. "Anyway, I'll let you know. I'll talk to people and I'll get back to you, okay?"

"I appreciate it. Sorry if I was weird about it or something."

"Don't worry, I've come to anticipate weird from you," Amanda replied as she stood quickly and squeezed his shoulder. "In the best of ways, obviously. It's been awesome working with and for you, Sal."

"Right back at you." He stood and laughed as she wrapped him in a hug.

"*Cuídate*, Jacobs," she whispered in his ear and pressed a light kiss to his cheek before she wandered out the door and left him pleasantly surprised by the display of affection.

He knew he would miss Amanda. While he doubted they would find someone as skilled with machines as she was on such short notice, he had also thought of her as a friend during her time with them. They would need someone, that much was obvious, and if there was anyone who could find a good replacement, it was her, right?

Also, despite their teasing banter, he didn't mind having another guy in Heavy Metal with them. Technically, they had Anderson working on their side now too, even if he didn't fall directly under Heavy Metal. It wouldn't be a problem.

That said, he hoped Amanda's referral didn't come in the form of a bulky Dwayne "The Rock" Johnson type of manly man. He wouldn't complain about it, of course, and if the candidate was qualified, there would be no problems. Still, he was at least honest enough to unashamedly admit to himself that his ego would take a hit. He had put muscle mass on during his time in the Zoo, but there were still niggling insecurities he disliked about himself.

Whatever. He would get over it. Life had taught him he was stronger than he'd ever thought he could be. If problems arose, he knew how to handle them—or he would learn what he had to.

He chuckled and eased into his seat as he made a mental note to give either Madigan or Courtney a call to enlist their help. They'd need a going-away party planned for Amanda before she left, and a day off felt like the right time and place. Madigan's suggestion would involve copious amounts of alcohol, of course, while Courtney would bring something classier to the mix. As always, they would have to compromise somewhere and send their armorer off with a bang—figuratively speaking, hopefully.

Smythe stepped out of the aircraft first and paused on the steps to study the area around them. He'd never been to Northern Africa before. The Middle East was the closest he'd ever come, and for some reason, he had imagined that all the deserts in the world would look the same. He was annoyingly wrong about that.

There were few views on Earth quite like the Sahara Desert, the largest, most expansive section of unlivable wasteland on the planet. The massive area itself spread as far as the eye could see to become a tapestry of dunes that undulated onward without end, gorgeous and monotonous at the same time.

Even the atmosphere felt different. For one thing, there

was the wall they were erecting as rapidly as they could. It was a feat of engineering to build anything when the foundation was nothing but sand—and had been nothing but sand for thousands of years. The size and scope of the project, however, were somewhat overshadowed by the second landmark that dominated the horizon.

The construction had pushed to take the wall section at the base itself to a significant height. On either side, the level was much lower and the section near the airstrip afforded a distant view of the dark, sprawling reality that was chilling. A massive, constantly growing smear of green curled over the hundred-foot-tall dunes and transformed them into something full of life and rife with danger. The Kudzu, the locals called it. For the life of him, Smythe couldn't remember why or what the translation was. But everyone else simply called it the Zoo, a fitting name if there ever was one.

The other three men on his team pushed through beside him and regarded their destination with similar expressions. Andy recognized the respect in their eyes but saw no trace of fear. They looked fear in the eye every day, and while they felt it, they knew how to use it to their advantage. His driving purpose for the duration of their stay was to keep them alive. He had no desire to walk any coffins back to England. At this point, he didn't even care about the money.

"Come on, lads." Dutch was the first to shake off the sinister enchantment of the jungle. "We need to settle in."

Smythe nodded and followed the man as they descended from the massive aircraft that had brought them from Germany. They'd been briefed on the way. The

Americans had set up the first base outside the Zoo and had called it simply the Staging Area. They'd probably expected that everyone would simply use it for any future operations, but they had been wrong. The Russians hadn't wanted to run any missions off an American-owned base and had set up their own on the eastern side of the jungle. Various UN countries had followed their lead and set up smaller, more defensible locations around the perimeter. Their team would work out of the French Sector.

They moved out onto the open tarmac and turned their attention to their temporary home a fair distance away. Most of the base was already built, although it was surprisingly lacking in activity for a facility this size. They must have wildly overestimated the number of people who would volunteer, he assumed. That said, there was far more activity than he'd thought there would be.

A JLTV broke away from the roads that spiderwebbed across the settlement and pulled onto the tarmac in their general direction. Hopefully, it was their ride. Even in the late afternoon, the heat beating down from the too-bright sun was unbearable—one more reason why no one would choose to live there.

The vehicle was, in fact, for them and the driver eased to a halt and nodded a greeting.

"Good afternoon," he said with an accent Smythe couldn't place. It sounded vaguely Italian, but he couldn't be sure if the man was from there or if it was something else entirely. While he could place anyone within about three miles of their hometown in England, Wales, Scotland, and both Irelands, outside of those areas, he was weak.

"My name is Jean Kontant," he said with a smile and shook hands with Dutch first, then the others. Each man introduced himself in turn.

"I've been sent to show you where your team is set up and to provide any assistance you might need to accommodate yourselves."

"I'm guessing and...hoping, maybe, that includes giving us a ride?" Smythe asked and glanced into the back seat of the JLTV.

"Of course." Kontant chuckled. "Hop in and I'll take you lads where you need to go."

"Fantastic." Andy grinned as he flung his bag on the back seat and scrambled in after it. His teammates needed no second invitation, and the vehicle accelerated and circled to head to the mostly empty streets of the base. The short trip proceeded mostly in silence, but he didn't much mind it. There honestly wasn't much to talk about. Kontant clearly wasn't here for their amusement, and despite his friendly nature, he didn't seem at all curious about what they were doing there.

He dropped them off at one of the squat prefab buildings. As he drove away, they were met by two men and a woman in lab coats who stepped out of what looked like an air-conditioned room to greet them.

"Gentlemen, I'm so pleased you made it," one of the men said. "I'm Dr. Morel, and these are my assistants, Drs. Laurent and Martins."

"Nice to meet you." Dutch took point again and shook everyone's hands. "We were told we'll head into the Zoo tomorrow morning. Is there anything we might need to prepare for beforehand?"

"I was told you four were given combat training for the Zoo before being shipped here?" Laurent asked and looked satisfied when they all nodded agreement. *"Parfait,* that should be enough—before the prelaunch briefing, anyway. Most of the technical aspects of the mission will be handled by *moi* and all you four have to do is get me in and out alive for our test run tomorrow. With that out the way, we were closing up shop for the evening and will head out to get some food. Would you care to join us?"

"Of course." Dutch looked at the other three men to confirm that they were, in fact, interested in getting something to eat with their three new teammates.

A few minutes later, they sat around a table in a small bar that, interestingly, showed far more action than the rest of the base combined. Smythe smirked as he assessed the venue while they ordered food and drinks. The menu consisted mostly of pub food, which didn't pose a problem at all. The team ordered selections that were deep-fried and probably not that healthy, but the way they saw it, they were already risking their lives. What the hell was high cholesterol compared to the monsters they would go toe-to-toe with the next day?

Or cirrhosis for that matter, Andy added silently when Laurent ordered a round of vodka shots for the table.

"The Russians started selling some of their stuff to the other bases, and while I'm not usually much of a vodka man, I have to admit their stuff is fucking good," the man explained as he handed the shots around the table. "Here's to coming back for another round of shots in a couple of days, eh, men?"

"I'll drink to that." Smythe grinned, leaned in, and took

his shot. Damned if the Frenchman wasn't right about it being the good stuff. He smacked the empty glass onto the table with a hoarse wheeze as the liquid burned all the way down his throat.

"Hear, hear," the others responded and followed his example with real enthusiasm.

CHAPTER SIX

S al didn't like being up this early. He wasn't a morning
person, and despite the fact that the whole world
seemed to hate the necessity of being awake at this ungodly
hour, people still insisted on running their clocks on the
worst possible times. Maybe it was so everyone could be
miserable together.

He sipped the mug of coffee in his hand, surprised at
how it was almost empty already. For fuck's sake, it was his
second one of the morning. Courtney wanted him and
Madigan involved in what she was doing in Philadelphia
with Pegasus, and he was interested in keeping tabs on the
people who had tried to kill them and now worked for
Courtney. Nominally, anyway, because having the power
didn't always mean holding onto the power.

Call him crazy, but he didn't trust these people to not
try again, no matter what their professional relationship
with Heavy Metal was.

"I'll have to do a conference call with the board later
today," Courtney explained to Madigan, whose eyes were

as bleary as his were. "They've given Anderson a hard time lately, and while I didn't expect him to make friends left and right, I did hope that he would manage all this with somewhat more tact."

"Tact like…you showed?" Sal asked and leaned forward. "As I recall, you left a damn cow's head on someone's bed—or did I not hear that part right?"

"I was pissed," she replied with a careless shrug. "She tried to have me killed in my father's home, and from the sound of things, she did kill my father. Giving her a warning straight out of the *Godfather* felt like a good move at the time."

"And does it still feel like a good move?" Madigan asked, ever the devil's advocate. "Given that things escalated to the point where we had to draw her into the Zoo to have the animals in there finish her off?"

Courtney glanced quickly at each of them before she answered. "I stand by my actions. I had to stake my claims and let these people know I wouldn't let them simply walk over me."

"Well, from the sounds of what's happening in Philadelphia, I'd say your complaining about Anderson's tact is a mite hypocritical." He grinned. "Hypocritical is the right word, yes?"

Madigan nodded and Courtney chuckled, unruffled.

"Well, I still have to give the boys and girls in the corner offices some explanation about what he's doing there, so pray I'll have a suitable cover story by the time I have to make the call." She sighed and sipped her coffee. "So, what are the two of you up to this morning?"

He looked at the other woman, who shook her head. Unperturbed, he shrugged in response and grinned.

"Well, way to sound unimportant compared to what you have going on," he pointed out and scowled at his empty coffee mug. "But we were actually planning a party —a bash to send Amanda off with happy memories. She's moving out to take a job at the French base, and we wanted to make sure she knows that her contributions to Heavy Metal were very deeply appreciated."

Courtney raised her eyebrows. "That sounds like fun. What did you guys have in mind?"

"Beyond copious amounts of booze?" Madigan asked. "Nothing much. What kind of party do you throw for a lesbian-slash-genius mechanic?"

"One with all her friends?" she suggested. "Which means we need time to get everyone to attend. When is she leaving?"

"Later today," Sal replied.

"Well, that won't do. Maybe it would be better to hold something there—something big and grand. She's going to the French base, right, which is a good few hours of driving from here? We could go there, make a couple of days of it, and celebrate her new job in style."

"I'd suggest not inviting Connie to this bash," he said with a nod of agreement. "In the meantime, even Anja and your assistant—what was his name again?—will be in attendance. Aside from that, I don't know any of her other friends. I assume she still has a couple whom she's on speaking terms with at the US base garage, so we could ask around to see if any of them can make it."

"Get Anja to work on it," Courtney suggested. "She

should be able to track Amanda's Internet traffic and see if she's still in friendly contact with any of her friends there. That's always a good way to get a guest list, right?"

"If Anja will be anywhere that isn't an IT convention, she needs a massive makeover, and stat," Madigan pointed out hastily. "Don't get me wrong, I dig the girl's style like nobody's business. But the whole Russian Hacker Chic is so last decade or so."

He flashed her an odd look.

"What?" she asked and shrugged. "Just because I can break you fifteen ways from Sunday doesn't mean I can't look fabulous while doing it. And that girl needs a makeover."

"Agreed." Courtney grinned, and the women bounded to their feet and headed to the server room, where both assumed Anja would be. Given that the woman spent more time in there than in her quarters, he thought it was a good assumption and trailed after them.

Sure enough, the Russian hacker was inside with most of the lights dimmed, talking into her headset.

"Rest well, Jer," she said. "Long day tomorrow."

The call ended, apparently, as the girl removed her headset and turned to look at the trio who had entered her domain.

"What's going on, guys?" she asked and looked suspiciously at her visitors.

"These ladies seem to think you need something of a makeover before Amanda's going-away party," Sal said and fought a grin.

"I won't like this, will I?" she asked.

"No, probably not," he replied as honestly as he could.

"Do I have a say in the matter?" Anja directed her question to the two women who swooped down on her.

"Nope." Courtney smiled wickedly and hauled the hacker off her seat and away from the comforting light of her screens. "But I think you'll like the results."

"Save me," the Russian whispered to Sal as she passed him.

"If you think I'll get between you and the two women who want you looking presentable, you're crazy."

If there was one thing the sim hadn't properly prepared them for, it was the heat. The sun in the Sahara Desert was well-nigh unbearable, and the canopy of trees above them did little to diminish it. In fact, all the foliage seemed to do was trap the heat on the ground, which ensured that not only was the temperature well above what he would have considered comfortable but also heavy and stuffy.

The developers had simply not duplicated that in the sim. While the suits were supposed to help to decrease the effect of heat on those who wore them, they could only do so much. Sweat tricked ceaselessly down his body. They needed to install some kind of water collection device on these suits—something like they had in *Dune*—to make sure all this extra water didn't go to waste. The idea was a little gross, but when things were this bad, one couldn't afford to be picky about where one's hydration came from.

That said, they didn't have much time to focus on the temperature anyway. There were more pressing concerns to deal with, the most prominent of which was the wide selection of monsters that wanted them dead. Whether it was because they wanted to feed or merely didn't like people to intrude on their territory, Smythe wasn't sure. What he was sure of was the fact that the way these animals fought hadn't been accurately depicted in the sim either.

The movements and actions of their adversaries had been caught fairly accurately. The team knew what to expect in that regard, but the way these creatures all banded together and fought in unison like they were somehow coordinated was an entirely unexpected phenomenon. Honestly, he doubted they would have believed it or taken it seriously if they hadn't seen it in the flesh.

And there was altogether too much flesh to go around.

Smythe stepped beside Dutch and grasped his assault rifle in one hand and knife in the other. The panthers began a slow retreat into the trees from where they hissed at the intruders. He ignored these as best he could and kept his eyes focused on those creatures that still clustered threateningly around them. After a few moments in which the group of five concentrated their fire on their attackers, these showed signs of withdrawal as well.

One of the locusts, now lacking a tail, twitched in front of him. At any other time, he would have felt some sympathy for the poor beastie. In this case, though, the stress of the situation had begun to seep into his body, which created an interesting lack of any moral quandary. He dropped to one knee with his rifle still held at the ready —one couldn't be too careful—and plunged his blade into the creature's carapace a few times to be sure it was dead before he straightened.

The other thing, he realized a few minutes later, was that the sims hadn't considered how long it took for these weapons to reload. Or perhaps there was simply so much more adrenaline coursing through his body that it seemed like his rifle's response was slow. While irritating, it was possibly for the best under the circumstances. He found it incredibly hard to resist the desire to gun down everything in sight. That wasn't a great idea when they needed to conserve ammo.

He glanced at the rest of the team as they resumed their trek, still focused on maintaining their defensive readiness. Laurent, for his part, had held his own rather admirably since he only carried a sidearm and a combat knife. They couldn't rely on him to cover any flanks, but the man certainly wasn't helpless around there.

"You gents seem to know your way around these suits," the scientist pointed out and reloaded his weapon crisply. "And around the Zoo too. Not bad for first-timers. Hell, it's not bad even for veterans of this jungle."

Smythe nodded and accepted that as the highest of praise. He'd read Laurent's files the night before. It had taken a little digging, but what he'd discovered was impressive. The man was actually born Algerian, but after spending a few years with the French Foreign Legion, he'd gone to the University of Paris to finish his studies in biology and physics and obtained a couple of doctorates before he volunteered for the Zoo. That made him one of the few volunteers, Smythe had discovered. Most of the others had been transferred, posted, or otherwise persuaded, by all accounts.

The man was all-round hard-core, and still only in his forties. Andy wondered why he didn't wear a combat suit himself. He knew a thing or two about the Foreign Legion and had also learned that they had been one of the first official militaries to be involved in containing the Zoo animals soon after the Americans had sent their troops in. The soldiers were tough and formidable, which wasn't something you would usually attribute to French people.

He wasn't ashamed of that particular stereotype. The Brits and the French had a rivalry that spanned a thousand years, and it wouldn't go away anytime soon.

"It's one thing to be in the sim, though," Dutch responded darkly and shook his head while he cleaned monster blood from his armor. "But it's a whole other thing to shoot their asses while they screech and howl and attack you for real."

He paused and drew his sidearm to fire a couple of shots into one of the panthers they'd already eliminated from the branches early on in the fighting.

"Don't do that," Smythe snapped. "We need to conserve ammo. There's no telling how many of these attacks we'll have to deal with, and I think we can agree that we'll fare better against them with actual bullets in our guns."

"It was still twitching," the man protested defensively.

"No, it wasn't," he replied and shook his head. "Get your shit together. We have this in the bag. Stay focused and stop wasting ammo, okay?"

Dutch nodded but looked a little resentful. The man was the ranking officer and was considered the de facto leader of their little group, despite the fact that they weren't in the military anymore. But he showed some bad colors at the moment. He was usually cooler than this oddly unfamiliar person his teammate didn't quite recognize. Still, he did trust him, and once he worked through whatever issues he confronted, he would be in shape to lead them. Andy wouldn't undermine him, but his friend did trust him and any of the other members of their team to call him out on any bullshit he might pull.

He nodded once more—this time a little less tensely—at Smythe, who nodded in return. They were all a little shaken by the reality of the Zoo around them and everyone needed to calm themselves. Dutch tapped his friend lightly on the shoulder in passing to acknowledge both the rebuke and the sentiment behind it.

"All right, lads, give me an update on your weapons and ammo statuses. We're on the move in thirty seconds," Dutch ordered the team. "I don't want to see what happens to us if we wait around to discover what the Zoo has in store instead of being ready."

They ran a quick weapons check and sent the results to his HUD before they forged on.

CHAPTER SEVEN

I t was meant to be a short trip, a trial run to make sure they were compatible as a team before getting into the meat of their mission—which had yet to be revealed to them. Even so, it had provided more than a few surprises, most of which were unwelcome, but there were a few that brought some compensation.

The sim had failed to capture the pure alien nature of the jungle they now walked through. For one thing, the trees didn't seem to fit. Nothing stood out in particular as wrong about them but something definitely felt off. The blue glow from directly under the bark was visible when things got darker too. Then again, it wasn't only the trees. Everything seemed to make everyone involved uncomfortable. Even Dr. Laurent, the veteran among them, looked like he teetered constantly on the verge of nausea.

They had caught sight of a cluster of Pita plants on their way back. Of course, they hadn't needed to refer to the reading material they'd been told to absorb during their time out. The famous—and infamous, according to some sources—plant was known well enough throughout the world that someone might be able to identify it by its signature blue blossoms alone. That said, the motion sensors also identified a significant number of animals huddled in the area.

If he'd thought the animals were capable of laying a trap for them, he would have immediately made that assumption. Their adversaries seemed a little too coordinated—even across species—for his liking, but planning and effecting traps for groups of humans? That was a little far-fetched.

Right?

Either way, none of their small group felt comfortable enough to push in closer despite the standing cash bounty on the blossoms. Even though one of the plants was reported to have been extracted from the Zoo, there was still a massive demand for the flowers.

There simply wasn't enough money in the world, though, to risk their necks unnecessarily. It seemed the team had all come to the same conclusion and simply continued to where they'd left their Hammerheads.

Overall, it had been a productive visit, Smythe thought as they loaded up and drove away. Laurent had collected a sizeable amount of data, and the team had proven that they were all capable of working well together, even under the demanding circumstances.

Besides, if reports from the various people he'd talked to about the jungle could be believed, getting in and out alive was more than what many people had managed. It was considered to be one of the most dangerous places to be in the world, Smythe remembered, and people seemed to forget how much blood and effort went into obtaining the source of their stay-young creams.

Dutch dropped them off at the front of the base, and Andy was the first to disembark. The drive had essentially been a silent one, and this continued as they stripped out of their suits.

"I've seen that look in people's eyes before," Laurent stated matter of factly and put a welcome end to the quiet. "It's a little haunting but still better than having no look at all, I suppose."

"What look?" Smythe asked, desperate to keep the conversation going.

"Like you've only now realized what's in that fucking jungle and you're reevaluating all the life choices that led you to set foot in that place." The scientist spoke the thoughts that were in each of their minds in an annoyingly unemotional tone. "It'll take you a day or two to come to a decision as to whether you'd like to continue working here, and for that, I'd say there isn't any better remedy than a pint and a meal at the bar. What say you, gentlemen?"

"I'll go for that drink, yes," Dutch responded with alacrity. "I think Murphy owes us a round of shots. You really should know better than that, Murph."

The other man scowled at him but turned his unhappy attention to the armor he now tried to strip off. They'd never actually reached a section in the sim where they had to remove it, which was rather depressing when you thought about it. They hadn't completed any of the missions set up in the simulations, so while they were better prepared to enter the Zoo for the first time than most, it was still annoying to have to deal with these practical difficulties.

"You don't generally think of the kind of damage your suit takes when you manage to get out," Campbell complained. He removed a chunk from his arm that revealed a pair of jagged claw marks from a panther that had made it a little too close.

Smythe hadn't had any close encounters, but there was a selection of pockmarks across the steel of his suit that hadn't been there before. He wasn't sure where they'd come from, but he was sure it was something they needed to identify on their next trip in. He examined the armor and tested the joints with a growing scowl. There was way too much sand stuck in there for him to be comfortable.

Everything in the jungle tried to kill them, he thought as he pulled the rest of his suit off. Even the sand and the air somehow did their best to join the party.

Fuck this place. Fuck it right in the ass.

"Come on, let's get an early start on dinner," Laurent said with a chuckle. "Yes, it's still mid-afternoon, but this way, we at least miss out on the dinner rush, right? Come on, the first drinks are on me. You were terrific out there, so I want to make sure we have you around for a good while to come."

Smythe smiled as he pulled his clothes on and joined the others, all of whom were ready to kick back a little and relax. The bar was as empty as Laurent had said. Their drinks arrived quickly, and they waited to order food until the kitchen was once again open for business. They'd had to settle for pretzels in the meantime.

Waiting involved more vodka, Smythe realized and

raised the glass of clear liquid. While it was one hell of a stereotype to confirm, damned if those Russians didn't know a thing or two about making vodka. He smiled and shook his head. Dutch was making a toast and seemed determined to make it long-winded and full of a mixture of profanities and Poe quotes. The man was a sucker for Poe. It was a weird thing to be a sucker for but not the weirdest guilty pleasure of the group.

No, absolutely not the weirdest. They had some definite oddballs among the four of them.

He waited for his friend to finish his speech before he knocked the shot back and sucked in a deep breath, trying to either feed or extinguish the burn that traced his throat all the way down his gullet.

"Fuck me," he gasped and shook his head before he breathed again.

"So, you four must have something to say about your first trip into the Zoo," Laurent challenged. He seemed a little red in the face once they had made short work of the shots Murphy owed them. "Something about how your life changed, your life flashed before your eyes…there has to be something. It wasn't the toughest trip I've ever been on, but there are no safe trips into that place. What did you guys think?"

"Honestly?" Campbell tilted his head in a vaguely questioning gesture. "I really can't believe you nuts come out here on purpose. It's crazy that you decide to go out there into a place where everything around you wants you dead, and you still want to study it."

"It's interesting," the scientist admitted with a shrug. "Even if everything in there wants to kill you—which there are arguments for and against, to be honest—I find that having a place as alien as this on the planet waiting for us to explore and dig into it is one of the best things that's happened to modern science. I enjoy it, that's all."

"I assume you have some good stories from when you were in there?" Dutch asked and leaned forward in his seat. "I mean the good stuff. The learning experiences."

"Nothing that you haven't learned already," Laurent demurred. "I've submitted most of my findings to the public databases."

"Come on, you must have something." Smythe laughed. "We have some wild stories from our time with the Royal Marines, but that was nothing compared to what we have out here. I assume, anyway, based on what I've seen so far."

"Well, I suppose you boys know we have what look like living dinosaurs walking around in there, right?" Laurent asked after a slight and very expectant pause from his audience.

"Yep," Campbell replied. "It took a ton of firepower, but we finally managed to annihilate one of the suckers."

"Well, what you might not know is that the larger monsters all have these sacs of the blue goop near the skull, right?" the scientist continued while the waitress set a round of beers on the table. "Well, there was this one time when we were in the middle of a huge gunfight. Thirty of us had headed into the jungle when a whole group of enraged beasts attacked us out of nowhere. Then, one of the big ones charged in and scattered all the others. They drew back and let us work it over on our own."

Smythe leaned expectantly on his elbows and listened intently. He was a sucker for a good combat story.

"Anyway, the bastard falls and shakes the whole ground around us when he does so," Laurent continued after a sip of the beer. "My team tells me to jump in and get the sacs out. That's a seriously gross process, but those things are worth almost twenty-five thousand euros a pop. They get me up on the top of the beastie, and I start cutting. The animals attack us in earnest now since they go plain crazy when one of the big critters is killed—or when you pick one of the Pita plants.

"Anyway, there I am with my scalpel in one hand and a sidearm in the other, trying to cut through the inch-thick skin while I help them to keep the animals away. Eventually, I run out of ammo and I need to focus on getting our prize out. I do, but one of the panthers jumps from the trees and tries to take the sacs from me. I am covered in monster blood and with only my scalpel in my hand.

"When the panther tried to attack, I did the only thing I could—I rushed over the body of the dead T-Rex and slashed at the bastard with the scalpel while I tried to keep the sacs safe and intact at the same time. I lost one of them, but the other one was fine. That was a profitable trip, although we did lose a number of people. Five out of the thirty were dead and another ten had to be sent to France for treatment and recovery."

"Fuck me," Campbell grumbled. "I imagine that many of them didn't want to go back in after a trip like that."

"And you would be right about that." Laurent chuckled and Campbell had to order another round of drinks to reward the man for the story. "The rest, though...they get addicted to the action. There's no place in the world that provides an adrenaline rush quite like the one people get while in there. You can't replicate it anywhere, and they become like junkies. Yes, that's apt. They come back for another hit even though they know the next one might kill them."

Smythe nodded. There were people like that in almost any profession that involved real danger. When soldiers assumed that reckless or daredevil attitude, they were usually sent home for an evaluation. And with the kind of hit this place provided, he could only imagine that the people who came back for more all had a little extra crazy on top.

"Well, here's to the bastards who died," Murphy said and raised his glass. "And to the unlucky bastards who survive. May we always be among the latter, drinking to the former."

"Hear, hear." Andy chuckled and reaffirmed that sentiment in his head as he took a long sip of the cool lager.

There weren't too many choices available when shopping for clothes out in the middle of the Sahara. The closest cities with decent clothing lines were about five hundred kilometers away, and there simply wasn't time to get all the way there and back without seriously compromising the timing of their celebration.

Desperate times called for all kinds of desperate measures, and Courtney was all for that too. She had a fairly impressive collection of new and improved clothes she had managed to ship from the States. About a year before, all her garments had been either functional or comfortable and suited the purposes of either being at work or at her little apartment.

How times changed, she thought was a grin. She had to carry a whole wardrobe with her around the globe these days, and not only because she needed to look presentable at the head of not one, but two, major companies, but also because... Well, she would never admit this aloud to anyone, but she had a reason to want to look good every day these days. Not that she didn't have one before, but this one was much closer and more personal than any other reason she might have had before.

No, she definitely wouldn't admit it to anyone.

With that left unsaid, she had a wide selection with her that was more or less Anja's size and enough cosmetic products to beautify the whole Zoo if she chose to do so. Allen had joined them. Having a gay assistant was always a plus since he would be able to let them know—objectively of course—exactly what Anja was looking for. The two of them had gotten along rather well since he'd decided to stay at their little base semi-full-time.

The hacker stepped out of the bathroom and a deep scowl marred her features.

"I look fucking ridiculous," she snapped and tugged at the plunging V neckline of her dress. Courtney narrowed her eyes. There was a fair amount to unpack, obviously. For one thing, Anja was absolutely gorgeous. The fact that she had hidden it with a goth Russian hacker look felt more and more like it was an intentional move on her part. It had to be.

Secondly... Was there a secondly? No, Courtney

thought as she joined Allen to inspect the dress from even closer.

"I would guess that's as low a neckline as you're willing to go with for a tank top?" he asked and tilted his head in fixed scrutiny. "You still look amazing but come on, girl. You have it so why not flaunt it?"

"Because I want people to think about my brain more than my...uh, flaunt," she snarled in response and shoved him back a couple of steps.

"Well, I think you look amazing," Courtney confirmed and bravely stepped in closer. There was a hint of a wild woman about the Russian, and with the casual look and the suggestive neckline, she had to admit that Anja had selected her normal attire very much out of personal choice. "Don't you agree, Madie?"

The woman didn't look up from her phone. "Fucking amazing," she called out. "Top scores all around. Bow for the judges, et cetera."

"You're not even paying attention," her friend complained, and Allen looked equally disappointed with her lack of interest. Anja seemed a little relieved.

Madigan looked up from what she was working on. "Look, this is a going-away party. People aren't supposed to be there on their best behavior. This isn't a cocktail bash with a group of senators and ambassadors. No one will want to make good first impressions. We're there to make one hell of a closing impression, and people only do that once they're comfortable enough to do so. So the question, Anja, is if you're comfortable with what you're wearing."

Anja looked at her clothes. "Sure. It's not uncomfortable, not practically. But I don't like to expose this much of myself to people I don't know."

"Back to the drawing board?" Allen asked.

"Nah, I think I can make it work with this one," Anja said and studied her reflection in the mirror. "I do look amazing. And besides, if anyone I don't know gets handsy, Madigan has taught me a few ways to discourage that kind of behavior with maximum prejudice. Give me a minute."

Madigan nodded and looked proud of her protégé's progress. Courtney smiled because she knew the kind of instruction their friend had passed along would end with broken fingers and aching balls for any unfortunate man who tried to pressure her for attention. Again, there was that wild aspect to Anja she thought was more than enough to keep those who were ill-intentioned away, even without the added training.

"It's complicated," Anja said with a shrug. "But I think we all need to get some sleep now. I'll see you tomorrow once I've decided what to wear."

"Take your time," Courtney said with a smile. "We'll see you later. Come on."

Allen paused a second before he stepped closer and gave the hacker a quick yet firm hug. He headed out of the room with Courtney and Madigan and left her there to continue her inspection.

CHAPTER EIGHT

"Don't do it, Doc," Smythe warned quietly.

Laurent looked at him with a quizzical expression. "Come on. Live a little, Smythe. We're all in here for the money, and the prize for one of these sons of bitches is enough to pay for all of us to get out of here. The standing bounty is into the eight figures by now. Split five ways, that's retiring money."

The four mercs exchanged glances and wondered how much the man knew about their pay structures. They had been brought into the work with a significant amount of money already promised—paydays they wouldn't see if they didn't make it out of these little missions alive. Smythe very much intended to get out of this mission alive, if only because he really didn't want to know what would happen to his small yet growing car collection if it was prematurely passed on to another less enthusiastic owner.

"Just leave it, Doc," Campbell concurred, his expression grim. "It's not worth it. Go for the smaller payday and we all get out of here alive. We don't have enough people to handle the rush of bad when these monsters come to get their plants back."

They'd never seen one of these attacks in the flesh, of course, since this was only their second time in the jungle, but there was video footage of it. The entire Zoo seemed to react to the actions of a couple of men as hundreds if not thousands of frenzied beasts converged.

The specialists still weren't sure what exactly prompted that kind of reaction from the creatures. There was considerable speculation about how the plants released pheromones into the air that agitated the animals, but nothing quite explained the furious response they always met with. Nor did it explain the range of the actions, as animals seemed to pour in from all sides and from miles away to annihilate the transgressors and retrieve the plant —far beyond the expected range of any pheromone that might be released. But this was the Zoo, after all, so maybe normal ranges were extended or hell, it could be that the animals passed the message on themselves.

Everyone did seem to agree, though, that the entire Zoo reacted, while no one could really provide any practical explanation. It was a somewhat frustrating lack of knowledge given the crap that resulted and he wished someone had been able to find out a little more of the how rather than only the what. Of course, he had to admit that studying a scenario while a whole jungle of angry monsters attacked in force was a little difficult.

They moved in closer to the plant as the scientist withdrew a device from his pack. It resembled a lamp in which one might enclose a couple of candles to protect them safe from the wind but with a scooping contraption on the bottom.

"I'll be honest, I stole this design," Laurent admitted and shuffled closer to the plant. "But if it works, we'll all be richer than we could possibly imagine."

"I don't know... I have a good imagination," Dutch responded darkly "and what it sees is definitely not good. I'm afraid I'll have to insist that you step away from that plant right now, Doc."

"I can do this," the doctor snapped. He obviously felt he didn't need permission and simply lowered the device over the plant very slowly and carefully. Unfortunately, he had failed to judge the full height of the plant, and the enclosure didn't extend to the ground. That left him stuck with no way to close the contraption completely.

With a muttered oath, he raised it again as carefully as possible. Smythe winced at a soft click followed immediately by a clipping sound. The man had depressed the button that activated the tiny shovel parts at the bottom. These closed rapidly and severed the plant's stem completely.

"Oh...fuck me," Laurent gasped, his expression panicked as he looked around.

Andy recognized the vague hope in the man's eyes. One might argue that clipping the plant even as low as the stem couldn't be as bad as actually taking it out. Hell, it had to be on par with something like plucking the flowers, right?

But no, the change was there, as instant as it was dramatic. The air was suddenly laced with a pungent and sour smell—like bad tomatoes that had been set aside to make a Bolognese sauce but left for a little too long. Everything seemed to shift and writhe around the group. Even the trees seemed to have fallen into an utter absence of normal motion, and a hoarse cry of desperate anger issued from the animals that had already begun to converge.

"Damn it, Doc," Dutch snapped and looked for a moment like he could happily kill the man himself. "Now you've landed us in a massive pile of shit, do you know that? How the fuck are we supposed to get you out of this one? And the rest of us, of course."

Laurent looked paler than Smythe had ever seen him, but he steeled himself visibly and straightened his back. "I can do this. With this much of the original plant, I will be able to recreate it in the lab and get it to grow. We'll still have the huge payout. You only need to get me out of here alive."

"The motion sensors are going crazy," Murphy called over the comms. "We need a plan—either for combat or for bugging out, but sooner will definitely be better than later."

Dutch nodded and immediately scanned the area around them. "We head back the way we came. That seems to be the last unobstructed pathway out of here. Come on lads, we'll get through this."

"Goddamn fucking hell." Smythe snarled with fury and shook his head vehemently as he set off in the chosen direction. Already, a pack of the giant hyenas slunk through the underbrush. Compared to the other monsters, these didn't pose much of a threat other than in their numbers. He intended to eliminate as many of those as he could before they actually began their attack and pulled the trigger of the assault rifle pinned to his right arm.

At this point, he didn't know if they were, in fact, on

their way to the Hammerheads. There was no time to consult a map before another wave of the hyenas swept forward. The few that had attacked them earlier had backed away rapidly once they realized there was resistance. They were scavengers by nature, and when the fighting was too intense, they chose to simply retreat.

Not this time, however. They launched blindly into the volleys from the five men who maintained their push through the jungle with Laurent in the middle of their group. The mercs all knew to drive forward harder and faster without the necessity to say it. They had to get out of there, but it was a fact that there were no success stories of anyone who tried to escape something like this. Even killing and harvesting the larger creatures with the sacs didn't seem to elicit the kind of reaction they had engendered in the monsters now.

"You had to try it, didn't you?" Smythe complained bitterly when his assault rifle seemed to take forever to reload again. "You absolutely had to try to be the second person to pull a Pita plant from inside when surrounded by only four guys. Bloody hell."

Campbell flashed him an odd look as if he'd heard him speak but seemed unsure of what he was saying, but they all came to a sudden halt before he could respond. Something descended from the treetops. Smythe wasn't sure what the mutants were, but they approached in the hundreds to try to encircle them like a web being woven on the spot.

"Fuck, this isn't good," Dutch muttered, his entire demeanor tense and focused. "Okay, there is no way out through there. We need to find a way to make this a defensible position. Murphy, set me up with a mine perimeter."

"Roger that," the man replied and quickly retrieved a selection of incendiary and cluster bombs that he set out. His task complete, he rejoined his teammates and took his position.

"What the fuck are you doing?" Laurent screamed. "We can't stop here. We have to keep moving and get out of here. The whole Zoo is literally closing in on us and you want to set up defensive positions? Really?"

"We can't move back and can't move forward. Defense is the only weapon we have left," Dutch retorted harshly and took command of the team. "Those tentacles coming down from the trees—do you know what they are?"

"I have a couple of theories," the scientist replied but declined to share them when the appendage-like vines surged through the tree line. He seemed poised in a place of panicked uncertainty before his nerve finally fled. Smythe saw the man make the decision a second before he acted on it, but he really couldn't believe someone so smart would be that stupid.

The moment of frantic desperation would cost them dearly, he realized when Laurent plunged into the trees again and tried wildly to navigate through the descending creepers. He made it through the first few clusters and the plants didn't seem too focused on catching him or even interfering with his flight.

The man yelled something incomprehensible before his foot caught in one of the vines and he sprawled face-first onto the jungle floor. He tried to block his fall and on instinct, released the stolen plant. The receptacle shattered and glass spun around him as he searched desperately to locate and salvage the now exposed Pita. Laurent scrambled to his feet when he located his prize.

Something moved too fast for the naked eye, but the motion detectors caught it. An enormous creature lurked in the trees, hidden among the drooping vines, and suddenly lashed out with what looked like a very long, very sharp, and incredibly fast tail. The scientist looked stunned for a moment and his body quivered in place until his head fell away, severed cleanly from the rest of his body. The corpse dropped in rapid succession and blood gushed from the suddenly exposed carotids.

Smythe fought the sudden need to puke, a challenge that got easier when the jungle appeared to go quiet. He stared, a little uncertain that he wasn't perhaps seeing things, but something definitely slithered to the Pita and snaked it up into the trees.

The four eyes of the gigantic monster flickered in the treetops before it moved silently away. While the four-man team simply stared at their surroundings, the other animals melted slowly into the shadowed underbrush. Shocked into disbelieving silence, the friends exchanged hasty glances and heaved the deep breaths of those suddenly reprieved.

"What the fuck?" Campbell asked, and no one pointed out that he would have to buy them all drinks when they got back. If they got back.

The attack had dissipated almost as quickly as it had started, and it all seemed to revolve around whether or not the Zoo reclaimed the stolen plant. That was too advanced for a fucking jungle, and yet Andy couldn't deny the evidence presented by his own eyes.

He glanced at the other men again, who all looked confused but more than a little relieved. Dead man or not, Laurent had seriously saved their bacon.

"He was too brave and then too stupid," he muttered, prompted by the sudden need to say a few parting words.

"Yeah," Campbell agreed. "It's too bad, though. I liked the man. He had some serious balls. I guess they weighed him down when he tried to make a run for it."

Dutch was the first to move on and once again, inspected their position. "I say we set up camp here for the night. We've already laid the mines out so we can add motion sensors and try to get some sleep. In the morning, we'll regroup and see what the fuck to do next."

CHAPTER NINE

"Come on, Anja." Sal laughed. "You're not built for this kind of thing."

The Russian flipped him off as she drew another shot of the clear liquor toward her. "Jacobs, please. I was born and raised in Russia, the land where they literally sell vodka in juice boxes with a tiny fucking straw. Don't you tell me what I am or am not built for."

He raised an eyebrow and grinned as he took a long sip from his beer. Sure, a little help from Madie had made sure that his alcohol tolerance was at an all-time high, but that didn't mean he enjoyed the feeling. He honestly didn't. Being drunk was low on his list of endorphin-producing vices since he preferred his wits about him. As such, as long as Madigan didn't engage him in any drinking games to show off his ability to hold his liquor, he was happy to simply drink socially.

Unlike the woman herself, who was on her second drink of the night in addition to a handful of shots and didn't look for a minute like she would stop anytime soon.

Sal shrugged when Anja pushed one of the shot glasses to him. "I'm not used to seeing you drinking like this. It's both awesome and terrifying."

She smirked and swallowed her third shot without so much as a wince at the strong liquor. "You haven't seen anything yet, boss-man. Keep watching and you'll see something really impressive—a Russian woman who can't get drunk."

He narrowed his eyes and leaned in closer. "I want to dare you to prove that, but I think you and I have to work tomorrow so I really don't want to render you incapable of performing your tasks while trying to prove a boast."

Anja merely grinned and poured a couple more shots. She handed him one of the glasses. "That sounds like a challenge to me."

"It wasn't." Still, he took the shot.

"Well, I'll pretend it was," she replied. *"Tvoye zdorov'ye."* She raised her glass to clink with his and downed it as quickly as she had the others. It seemed to indicate that the potent drink had no effect on her. She looked at the bottle and scowled when she saw it contained too little to top off another shot glass. With a small shrug, she tipped the bottle to her lips and swallowed the last few drops before she moved toward the bar for another. He wondered if that was the best idea, but she'd already made it clear that she wouldn't listen to any of his advice.

Madigan joined him a moment later, her head tilted and a cheeky smile on her face.

"What?" he asked.

"Don't you think you should teach little Anja some portion control?" she asked. "I know she has one hell of a tolerance for the stuff, but she hasn't been out drinking in a while. I haven't seen her drinking since she got here, come to think of it. Her tolerance may not be all she made it out to be."

Sal shrugged. "What the hell do I know about this? All I know is that my tolerance is interestingly increased thanks to me going against the usual scientific protocol to smoke what I sell, to put it crudely."

She grinned and moved closer. "It is a risky endeavor, but I think I speak for both of us when I say it's paid significant dividends."

"You think so, do you?" He sipped his beer and winked at her from over the rim. "Well, I'll make sure it continues to pay dividends—and, hopefully, make sure I don't end up fucked over by some as yet unknown side effect from licking Madie."

"Well, you could stand to lick Madie a little more if it were up to me," she murmured, her tone lowered enough to be sure that he was the only one who could hear her speak. "Or maybe let Madie lick you?"

"I thought you didn't like it when I called you that," he retorted blandly.

"I don't," was her cryptic reply as she pushed from the table and leaned closer to press a light, teasing kiss to his lips.

"We might want to give Anja a shot of the blue hangover cure," Sal noted. The woman now drank directly from the bottle the bartender had provided. "Given that she'll be working with Savage tomorrow and we need to her be at the top of her game."

"I'll keep that in mind." She traced her fingers lazily

over his jawline before she sauntered to the bar where the rest of the party drank noisily to celebrate Amanda's new job on the French Base.

They'd talked a few times about what they might do if they were no longer around the Zoo. The damn place would always provide healthy business, and with the way it continued to grow, it was a cash cow that would be milked for years to come. Until, of course, someone decided they were done with a jungle that had a tendency to drag creatures from the recesses of their darkest nightmares and decided to nuke the place.

Sal still wasn't at all sure that a nuke would be effective. All the tests initiated in that respect indicated that it soaked up the radiation from places around the world as far away as Japan and as disastrous as Chernobyl. The estimates for those disaster areas becoming viable again had doubled, and scientists all seemed to agree that the Zoo absorbed the fallout. Logic said the recovery number could continue to accelerate much faster each time the Zoo expanded. Then again, the heat from a nuclear explosion might incinerate it—hopefully—but given its propensity for rampant growth, there was no guarantee that it wouldn't simply bounce back.

Of course, he didn't trust the Zoo. It wasn't scientific, but he didn't want to think about what a place that absorbed DNA to make monsters on a daily basis would do with Chernobyl-amounts of radiation. Probably nothing, he reasoned quietly, but the maybe something part of that exchange had him worried.

It was the curse of someone like him to somehow constantly think about what it would throw at them next.

He liked to think it was what had kept him and Heavy Metal alive for as long as it had been, but the fact remained that it wasn't exactly something he could turn off.

He tipped the beer and finished it to the dregs before he shifted his attention to where the party was in full swing. It was time to get involved. He wasn't sure what Amanda expected him to do for the duration, but it sure as hell wasn't sulking and hanging out in the back booth.

His mind made up despite the small niggle that wanted to pursue his solitary musings, he pushed from his seat and stretched, then wandered to the large group. Amanda peeled away from the gathering before he reached them and approached the bar with another woman whom Sal recognized—Dr. Chance, he thought with a smile.

The armorer had good taste, he conceded and immediately felt sleazy for thinking it. He changed direction to join them where they waited to order their drinks.

"You know you didn't need to do this, right, Sal?" Amanda asked when she saw him and patted him lightly on the shoulder. "And you know I appreciate it too? This whole shindig as well as the opportunity to work with you guys."

"Yes, and…well, I do now," he replied to answer her questions in order. "You were an integral part of the successes that Heavy Metal enjoyed, and you saved our lives both in the field and with your work on the suits. And you're an awesome person."

Dr. Chance cleared her throat from behind Amanda, who looked around and laughed. "Where are my manners? Sal, you already know Dr. Beverly Chance, right? And Bev, you know Salinger Jacobs?"

"Of course, not-a-doctor Jacobs." Chance grinned and leaned forward to offer Sal a handshake, which he took.

"Way to rub it in, Doctor," he replied and shook her hand firmly. He noted that a group of four mercs near them at the bar all turned when they heard his name. It wasn't a completely unheard-of occurrence, of course. While he wasn't quite a celebrity, his name was well known in the various bases around the Zoo for his actions in and out of the damn place. Being the first to bring out a live animal and then the first to bring out an intact Pita plant was enough of a resume to guarantee that people who had their finger on the pulse of the area would at least recognize the name.

Most did a double-take when they saw the man behind the stories. Sal turned his back on the group and focused on his two companions as they gave their drink order to the bartender. "So, how did the two of you meet? Don't take this the wrong way, but I didn't think you ran in the same circles. I don't mean to pry, of course. I'm merely curious."

"You're not prying at all." Amanda grinned. "And you're right, we don't, but there was a small online convention on the different additions to the suits that were shipping over here this year. I wouldn't have thought it, but it was something Bev was interested in. We met to talk about it at the bar afterward, and not to sound cliché or anything, but one thing did, in fact, lead to another."

"Say no more." He grinned and raised a finger to point to the beer tap when the bartender asked him what he wanted.

The armorer grinned. "I wouldn't say any more, you

perv, but it's nice to see you trying to keep your colors to yourself, eh?"

He opened his mouth in mock shock. "Why, I never. I would never. I have never. I promise, I wouldn't."

The last statement was directed at Chance, who was already sipping what looked like a daquiri. She almost spurted some of the drink out her nose when she laughed.

"Oh, God, I did not need that." She gasped and snatched a napkin to clean herself. "No worries, Jacobs, I'll take the secret of your perviness to my grave. Or my next drink, depending on how strong that actually is." She grinned and wiggled her eyebrows at him before she placed a light peck on Amanda's cheek. "I'll head to the table, babe."

"I'll be right with you, *Guapa*." The other woman chuckled, returned the kiss, and watched her move through the rapidly filling bar to where their table was.

"Aren't you two just the cutest?" Sal smirked.

"I think we might be," she replied and tried not to blush. Or if she did blush, the dim lighting in the room hid it sufficiently.

"I'm really happy for you." He squeezed her shoulder. "You two look like you make each other happy, and I'm all for that."

She nodded and sipped her drink. "Between you and me, I think I've avoided settling down with someone. I simply went for the easy fucks with chicks who want to try out their bisexual phase or something—free and easy sex to avoid being rejected, I guess. But with Bev, it's different. With her, I want to try something more permanent, which is why I eventually chose to come here to be with her."

He nodded and sucked in a deep breath. "I respect that.

You're growing as a person and that calls for personal change too. I might even say I admire the hell out of it."

She grinned and gave him a half-embarrassed look before she punched him lightly on the shoulder. "Thanks, Sal. And not only for the opportunity you and Kennedy gave me. For you being you and not being your typical guy."

"I'm not really sure how atypical I am," he admitted after another slow sip. "Not when both my girlfriends can kill me and know where to hide the body where no one will ever find me."

"Well, we always knew you were crazy," she pointed out. "Nuttier than a squirrel's shit but still a good guy. Or you try, anyway, which is more than can be said for most folks."

Sal nodded. "I appreciate you saying that. And you should consider doing side work for Heavy Metal at full market price. I know what someone like you is worth and I know that rent isn't cheap."

"I'll think about it." She chuckled but looked pleased by the suggestion.

"You do that."

"Okay, are we done sharing our feelings now?" she asked and patted him on the shoulder. "Are we prepared to get our literal or metaphorical balls out of our metaphorical and literal purses?"

"That sounds good to me." He chuckled at her word choice. "You get back to your girlfriend. I think I need a couple more drinks in me before I'm ready to join you."

"Don't wait too long." She nudged him again before she picked her drink up and headed away to the table and the round of cheers that followed when the others saw her approach. Sal raised his glass to them before he downed the rest of his beer—just for Madigan—and set it down. He gestured to the bartender for another drink and the man nodded but looked a little confused as he poured another pint and handed it to him.

They had a tab for the party that would be paid for by the Heavy Metal card. Courtney had said she would cover some of it too since she couldn't attend. She'd been prevented from doing so by problems that resulted from her and Anderson's battle with Pegasus. He wasn't happy to hear it since most of the work of planning the party had been hers. It didn't feel right that she had to miss out. He decided he would have to make it up to her somehow.

A smirk settled on his face at the thought. He had a feeling she would have something in mind when he got back.

Sal glanced to his left and at the four mercs he'd noticed before. They now stared at him in a way that made him feel uncomfortable. He decided to give them the benefit of the doubt and turned his attention to his beer, took a long sip from the glass, and watched them out of the corner of his eye. They continued their fixed appraisal.

"What's your pro—" Sal needed a second to realize that he hadn't finished the word and inclined his head with the effort it seemed to require to mouth it to completion. Pro — what came after that again?

His brain worked with a chronic slowness that had nothing to do with how much he'd drunk. Even before he'd started self-medicating with goop, a couple of beers weren't enough for even remotely close to this.

The only conclusion was something hinky with the beer. From the way the mercs and the bartender had watched him, it could only be the intentional kind of hinky. People still called them roofies these days, right?

A hand settled heavily on his shoulder at the same moment that one of the strangers slid a couple of bills across the bar. He was pulled away from the counter and realized he had no ability to resist. Something sapped him of all his strength, but his mind still managed to work on a basic level. If there was any time to make a fuss, it was now. He needed to draw the attention of his friends who were less than ten meters away.

His captors clustered around him and blocked the group from sight as they mostly carried him through the doors. The opportunity to put up a fight had passed. The men looked like pros and weapons poked tellingly from under their clothes.

One of them noticed the direction of his gaze and patted him on the cheek as they reached a strangely fuzzy JLTV.

"Don't worry, lad, we won't kill you tonight." The tall redhead sounded anything but reassuring as they shoved him into the back seat of the vehicle. Sal tried to move his mouth. For some reason, he had a quip lined up and ready to go but it remained frozen on his tongue. His jaw no longer worked the way it should have.

His kidnappers sandwiched him between two of them as the others slid into the front seats. The vehicle started and eased away.

Well, this can't be good.

CHAPTER TEN

Madigan could hear herself groan—a grim, unnatural sound that should have concerned her. As if from a distance, she could hear her heartbeat tick rhythmically and the rattle as her lungs filled with air and emptied slowly. Her eyes scrunched tightly closed, she tried to understand what the fuck was happening. It seemed necessary given that her body appeared to have clocked out for the day—or night, whatever time it was.

She liked drinking. That was no secret, but it had been a while since she'd drunk this much. A long time, in fact, since back when she drank to forget something. She wasn't even sure what she had tried to forget anymore. That was how long ago it had been.

Cautiously, she peeked an eye open and scowled at the ceiling. There was too much light, which made it feel like her eyeballs had been stabbed with toothpicks. Still, it was ample evidence that the sun was already up, and Sal had told her he wanted to discuss logistics for another trip into the Zoo to collect what he needed to work toward finishing his dissertation. The fact that he hadn't come and woken her to get things moving was either a testimony of how patient he was or how much he'd drunk the night before.

The whole evening was something of a blur, to be honest. They had eventually used Connie as the designated driver and left the AI to control the Hammerhead they'd used to take them home. After getting Anja some blue stuff to make sure she would be in working order the next day, she, Sal, Courtney, Amanda, and Beverly had kept the party going. They had a stash of primo alcohol in their little base, and they had depleted it.

Madigan groaned softly again and found the courage to look around her. She still had her clothes on, which meant she and Sal hadn't started any drunken shenanigans late into the night. More importantly, she was on the couch, which meant beds hadn't been reached. Beverly snuggled against Amanda, who drooled over the edge of the sofa. Courtney sprawled on the couch across from Madigan and snored like a chainsaw.

It made sense that Sal wasn't among them, she decided and finally found the courage to heave herself up from where she'd slept. With the changes that had come over his body thanks to Madie, he would have been the only one capable of walking to his room by the time they were finished.

"Look what the cat dragged in," an annoyingly cheerful voice uttered from the kitchen. "That's what Americans say, right? They do it in movies, but I've never actually heard anyone use the phrase in real life."

She scowled at Anja, who blithely puttered around in

the kitchen. Maybe she should regret giving the woman a taste of Madie the night before. Misery loved company and it hated being in the presence of cheerful temperaments. That was how the world worked these days. She wasn't even sure if Anja knew what they had given her, but the woman looked like she hadn't touched a drink all month. In fact, she looked better than she had since she'd arrived at the Heavy Metal base.

The magic of the blue stuff, she thought and shook her head glumly. Why hadn't she taken any of it? It was a question she had asked herself a few times. Sal had offered but she didn't want to risk anything like that.

In that moment, it felt like a stupid decision.

"How the hell is she so cheerful?" Amanda demanded, her voice a rough growl as she wiped her mouth clean.

Madigan didn't want to think about who they should keep out of the Madie loop. Instead, she merely shrugged, pushed from the couch, and stumbled slowly toward the kitchen, drawn by the enticing smell of coffee and bacon that emanated from the space. Anja grinned, nudged a mug and a plate to her—already filled with coffee and bacon, respectively—and Madigan grunted her thanks. She breathed deeply and took a sip of the coffee first.

"You girls were still drinking by the time I got up, so I have to imagine that your head feels like shit," the hacker pointed out with frank amusement.

"Yeah, you don't say," Madigan grumbled, shook her head, and immediately regretted it. "Just...not so loud. Please. For the love of God."

Anja smirked and slid into a seat across from her.

"Sorry. You really need to get your drinking under control."

She shook her head, determined not to have this conversation. "As a matter of personal curiosity, you didn't happen to notice what time Sal called it quits, did you? I'm trying to get the numbers straight in my head."

The Russian shook her head. "He wasn't around by the time I got up. Sorry."

"Nah, don't be sorry. I'm curious, is all. That guy has one hell of a tolerance level for alcohol, and I wanted to see if we could get some solid numbers on that."

She glanced at the other ladies, who looked like they might be in various stages of leaving their makeshift beds. "Did you guys see what time Sal went to bed?"

Amanda flipped her off, no doubt for the loudness of the question, but the general answer was in the negative. That was unfortunate. She would have to get her numbers some other time. It was annoying too since she usually had a hard time getting Sal to drink. She would get it one day, though, that much she swore.

"You bitches need to get over here and have coffee or I'll claim all of it," she snapped. They uttered their various complaints in low tones and groans and she grinned. They needed to learn to take hard drinking like a champ.

Sal rumbled a protest as he turned over on his bed. He wasn't quite hungover, but the dryness in his mouth and the annoying everywhere ache told him he was on the verge and he needed to hydrate. Now.

He'd forgotten to set his alarm again—stupid damn thing—and he'd likely overslept. Of course, people would say he was entitled to sleep in after the night he'd had, being scientist-napped and all, but he was the one who'd decided to press the snooze button when he pleased. He was the one who made that choice.

Wait.

He blinked his eyes open and took a moment to inspect his surroundings. Sunlight streamed in from outside, the familiar scorcher, but his surroundings weren't familiar at all. It was a prefab building but looked more like a warehouse with a couple of sections walled off for offices or something like that. Shelves were set up across the massive interior, but they were all empty.

His gaze was drawn away from the empty sections of the room to examine the places that weren't empty—and more specifically, the section he was in and who he shared it with.

A little startled, he focused on the barrel of the gun that was currently aimed at him. It wasn't that big but he doubted it would matter. The bullet would still punch through his skull and end his life.

He looked at the man who held the weapon and scowled. It was the same tall redhead who had helped to drag him away from the bar when he'd been drugged.

"Well," Sal grumbled and eased carefully into a seated position, the action slow and measured to encourage the man to not shoot him. "This is a development."

"It's nothing personal, Jacobs," his captor said softly and made an apologetic face. "I'm sorry but you're the best chance we have."

Sal stared at him for a while as his brain tried to assimilate this almost contradictory response. "I…don't understand."

"Allow us to explain." Another man wandered up as a forklift chugged closer to them. "We have a job we need to conduct in the Zoo and we need a specialist for it. Those we were assigned didn't make the cut, so we decided to get the best and that's you."

"I don't suppose you'll tell me why you're going into the Zoo?" he asked calmly and tried to read their expressions. "Or why you need a specialist? And how long have you people been going into the Zoo anyway?"

"We…" The second man glanced at the redhead and the two others who now joined them. "Well, we've only been in the Zoo a couple of times, but we've been adequately prepared for the venture."

"Is that right?" he asked and looked at each of them. "Is that right? Is that why your specialists don't make the cut—which is what I assume is…Brit mercenary code for had their asses killed because you assholes weren't able to keep them alive?"

"That's…a little harsh," one of the men grumbled and looked pointedly at his teammates.

"Oh, I'm sorry. I didn't mean to be harsh on my fucking kidnappers," Sal replied caustically and pushed to his feet. He felt a little more comfortable that they had no real intention to shoot him. "Scientist-nappers? Researcher-na — You know what? It doesn't matter. Is this the new Guedes model? Four-five-two?"

The four men looked a little startled when he approached the case that was hoisted by the forklift.

"Yes, it is," the apparent leader confirmed but glanced at his men as if trying to confirm that engaging with their hostage was the best idea. "How...how do you know about it?"

"I helped with its development," he replied and ran his fingers over the specs, speed reading them. "Mostly the simulator testing of it, but they said they would let me know when it was available for purchase. You boys got it early, which tells me that you have connections. Is this suit for me?"

He had a habit of talking fast in a way that prevented others from getting a word in when he felt nervous. And he definitely felt nervous. At the same time, he was also very curious as to how this new baby would perform. It was one of his favorites, which was why he had put in a long, long list of recommendations to make it one of the best hybrid suits they had ever made. From the looks of the specs, they had incorporated many of them into the finished product.

"Yes," the leader finally said with a firm nod. "That suit is for you."

"Okay, I'll join you assholes, but not because I'm afraid of you." Sal opened the case and began to assemble the pieces. "It's because I intend to keep this suit when we're finished, and I intend to be well compensated for my efforts. Guaranteed cash, and a percentage of the money that comes from this venture. Understood?"

"Of course." Despite his scowl, the tall man responded with a firm nod. "While the circumstances of your joining our team were less than great, we do want to assure you that we are committed to giving you the right kind of treatment now that you're with us."

"Just remember, bubba—" Sal started to say.

"It's Dutch," the man corrected. "Dylan Dutch, at your service."

"Sean Campbell." The redhead introduced himself stiffly, obviously still a little more cautious.

"Andy Smythe," said the man who had been driving the forklift.

"Alan Murphy," added the last.

"Well, I'm sure the pleasure is all yours," he growled and continued his work on the suit. He knew his efforts revealed an aptitude for the task the men watching him hadn't expected from a specialist. "But keep in mind that I'll have a gun out there too, and I won't need even a second to think about it before I gun you all in the back if you try to fuck me over even once. Got it?"

"Absolutely understood." Dutch somehow managed to look affronted. "This is all business, and there's no need for threats like that, Mr. Jacobs."

"Oh, I think there's a need." He attached the assault rifle to the arm of the suit and strapped it on before he only half-jokingly aimed it at the man in front of him to test the sights. "What are you ladies waiting for? I assume you needed to kidnap me because there's a time constraint. Otherwise, you would have contacted me for a hire since I do run a business and would have been interested in getting you motherfuckers in and out of that place without having to worry about drugs."

Dutch nodded. "The man has a point. Let's get suited

up, boys and girls. We're heading into the damn Zoo in twenty minutes."

His team snapped into action and hurried to where the other suits had already been put together. Dutch leaned closer to Sal once they had left.

"I accept that you're mad about what we did," he said, his tone low. "But we need to be able to trust the people we go into the fucking jungle with. Making threats like that won't make you any friends."

"You kidnapped me and now you complain about trust? That's rich." He snorted but remained focused on his work. "Look, once we're in there, we'll have each other's backs. We'll all get out alive so I can kick your collective asses once I've been fairly paid for my work. If you stay focused, we'll get the job done and I'll make sure you boys live to regret this. Understood?"

Dutch nodded. "Fair enough."

Sal completed his preparations, but he surreptitiously studied the group he would go into the Zoo with. They looked competent enough, he supposed. Whether that was merely a first impression or not would have to wait until they were under the trees.

Dutch probably thought his last threat had something to do with the Zoo. As terrifying as the jungle was, it was nothing compared to the hell that would rain on these fuckers when his team found out what happened. Sal only hoped he could sit in and watch with a bowl of popcorn.

Until then, though, he would find out what they were doing there and try to make a profit from it. Running a business out of the Zoo wasn't cheap, after all.

CHAPTER ELEVEN

B reakfast was finished, and Madigan scowled at her plate in much the same way the other girls did. Dishes needed to be done, and those who were familiar with the schedule at the compound knew it was Amanda's day to do it. Of course, she should have been in the French sector by now, and none of them had thought to draft another plan. They had all simply forgotten that necessary evil until now.

And, of course, that was the awkward part. Did you ask someone who wasn't technically a part of the team anymore to take up their former responsibilities if they merely happened to be around for it?

She would have to ask Sal to decide. He was always good at these kinds of domestic disputes. People knew she was all but allergic to pulling her weight on the home front. If he made the decision, it wouldn't be her fault, one way or another. She could grumble about it if he decided she had to take care of it, or she would be blameless if he chose someone else. Better yet, he would probably elect to do it himself and everyone would be happy.

Where the fuck was he anyway?

"Hey, Connie," Madigan called and stood a little too quickly. She moaned as the blood drained and made her head ache.

"How can I help you, hot stuff?" the AI asked with her customary lack of tact in responding to a call. Madigan didn't need to look at the table to know that Amanda had rolled her eyes.

"Could you go ahead and activate the alarm in Sal's room?" she asked as she put her plates in the sink. "We need him for a logistical issue here in the kitchen."

"I could set the alarm off, of course, but the results might not be what you'd want them to be," the AI replied.

"Why the fuck is that?" she demanded irritably. She really wasn't in the mood to deal with the bitch's sass.

"Because he's not in his room," Connie replied matter of factly.

"Well...why the fuck didn't you lead with that?" Madigan snapped and grimaced when Amanda snickered quietly. The armorer stopped and hid behind Bev at the glare her amusement had earned her.

"You didn't ask and I did not think it was vital information." Connie sounded offended.

"Fuck, can you find him?" She rolled her eyes and still refused to start on the dishes herself.

"I'm afraid that will not be possible."

She now had to hold herself back from trying to attack the AI in the server or maybe asking Anja to do so. "Why...

the fuck...not?" she enunciated slowly once she'd unclenched her teeth.

"Because he's not in the facility," Connie replied, and her tone still reflected annoyance at this line of questioning.

"Wait, what?" Amanda asked and looked away from Bev.

"Where did you drop him off?" Madigan asked.

"He was not in the vehicle when I drove you home."

"Oh, yeah, I remember asking you guys where Sal was," Courtney said as she stood quickly. "You said something about him falling asleep in the Hammerhead and then you started pouring shots. Things got...fuzzy after that."

"Wait, when was the last time anyone saw him at the bar?" Madigan looked at each of them and a small niggle of disquiet manifested in a frown.

"We had a heart-to-heart early on," Amanda said. "I don't remember much of him after that but he doesn't do much drinking, right?"

"Fucking hell, I hate this hangover bullshit," Madigan muttered. "Thankfully, we have someone who's an expert at tracking errant scientists these days. Anja!"

She didn't wait for an answer. The hacker had already retired to the server room a short while before, which made it easy to find her. She was talking to someone, but she cut the line when Madigan barreled in.

"What's up?" Anja looked a little nervous of the crowd of women who had suddenly invaded her workspace.

"We need you to track Sal," Madigan said briskly. "It seems he didn't join us when we headed home, so we need you to find out which dumpster he's sleeping it off in so I can kick his ass."

"Your wish is my command." The girl's chuckle almost sounded forced.

"I'm not interrupting something, am I?" Madigan asked, but the Russian shook her head.

"He's not showing up on any of the cameras," Anja pointed out.

"There were cameras in the bar, right?" Courtney asked and looked at her companions for confirmation. "Maybe we can see where he went from there and track him that way."

The hacker nodded and pulled the footage up suspiciously quickly. Courtney wondered if the woman had checked to see if anything embarrassing had been caught on camera and had expunged them of any incriminating evidence. They sifted through the data and their IT guru ran a facial search through the cameras before finally, she found some evidence of Sal.

"That's where I saw him last," Amanda pointed out, and they watched as he waved the woman away and smiled wistfully before he turned to the bar and ordered another beer, having chugged what was left of the one he'd had in his hand. The bartender poured him another, and Sal said something to four men who huddled close by. They seemed to ignore him but a few seconds later, he sagged against the counter and the group converged on him while one left a couple of bills for the bartender.

There was a moment of disbelieving silence as they watched him dragged out of the bar, all four of the men helping to carry him.

"Who are those motherfuckers?" Madigan asked in a voice that everyone else in the room recognized by now. It was her "someone will die" voice.

"I'd like to have a nice long chat with that bartender too," Courtney declared indignantly.

"Those four are…mercs," Anja said as she ran a quick search on the kidnappers. "They arrived recently, made a couple of trips into the Zoo, and had one casualty. What's more, it looks like they've signed on for another trip in—for five people."

"They're taking Sal into the Zoo?" Madigan asked incredulously. "What the hell do they think they're doing?"

"Well, assuming he is conscious and wearing some kind of armor, those four actually signed their own death warrants," Courtney said smugly. "If they make it back, I'll kill them anyway, so it ends the same."

"You'll have to get in line," her friend retorted and stepped out of the room.

Sal had no idea how the four mercs had survived this long. They seemed to have some technical knowledge of what they faced but their instincts were all wrong. They moved toward cover instead of remaining out in the open, and when they were in clear ground, they spread themselves out like they were under fire and wanted to maintain a more difficult target.

It was likely they would probably have handed his ass to him if they were in an urban environment and in a gun battle, but this was his little slice of paradise. If they wanted to survive, they needed to get their asses in shape.

"Stay together, damn it," he snapped through the comm unit as they broke away from each other yet again when the clusters of attackers began to back away. The animals seemed to react with more respect when they encountered groups of people, and it made it much easier to coordinate the lines of fire when they were shoulder to shoulder.

To their credit, the four seemed more than willing to learn from their mistakes and obeyed with alacrity when he yelled at them again.

It didn't really matter, he thought, as none of them followed the protocol he'd committed to memory by now —always check the trees when the animals showed any sign of retreat. Panthers tended to try to snatch a couple of easy kills since they had observed that the humans relaxed at that moment. It was unsettling, the way they could read people in such an uncanny way.

Sal looked up and, sure enough, a couple of panthers had already begun a stealthy descent through the branches. He eliminated the one closest and tracked the second as it launched into an attack on Campbell while the man reloaded his rifle. A couple of his bullets caught its flank and twisted it to land on the merc's shoulder. Sal drew his sidearm and pulled the trigger a couple of times. The beast fell and the venom-filled fangs glistened in the dim light.

"You're fucking welcome." He chuckled and shook his head as Campbell turned to look at him. There wasn't any gratitude on his face, but the surprise was satisfaction enough for Sal to break away and scan their surroundings.

"Let's keep moving," he called and indicated for them to

adjust their heading to the west. They still hadn't told him what they were searching for, but it seemed to be something specific. It also guided them deeper and deeper into the Zoo, and they seemed a little more anxious as they stepped farther into the jungle.

"We're heading in the wrong direction," Dutch said and called a map up on his HUD.

"Unless you want to charge headfirst into those creatures again, I'd suggest we divert around them," he responded lightly. "When it comes to those locusts, they tend to only attack when they're joined by other monsters, not when they're on their own. The only reason why they would choose to attack us without their friends is if we're close to one of their nests. Unless that's what you're here for?"

Once again, he received no answer. He knew he needed to be a little more subtle about his inquiries—or maybe simply listen for them to mention something about the so far secret mission. The latter didn't seem at all hopeful as thus far, they'd made absolutely no effort, accidental or otherwise, to discuss it.

While they walked, he considered his options. There was a reserved transaction applied to Heavy Metal's main account, which Madigan would have flagged by now to give her some indication as to where they were. He trusted these men to not kill him while they were in the Zoo, but that might well change as soon as they got out—especially if they did eventually find whatever they were looking for.

The fact that they needed a specialist for this job meant they had to tell him about it eventually. He would prefer to have the details sooner rather than later. That way, he could decide whether or not he would simply shoot these dumbasses in the back and find a way to get out of there on his own.

Reality dictated that the chances weren't great that he could make it out on his own, of course. Still, depending on what they wanted, it might end up as a calculated risk he needed to take. Some things were best left alone in the Zoo, but he could only make that call when he knew what he was facing.

With all that said, though, he did appreciate the suit they'd secured for him. It took a while to adjust to the added weight, but the hybrid motors in the back more than made up for it once they kicked in. The fraction of a second reaction times were the best he'd ever experienced —even better than in the sims he'd run with it. The company had gone above and beyond to provide the best of the best.

Of course, under regular circumstances, this suit would set Heavy Metal back to the tune of six figures or so, but even his short experience indicated that it would be worth it. The auto-tracking system was bleeding-edge, and the color-coordinated motion sensors and night vision collaboration were wet-dream material. It was like he walked around in the middle of the day.

Of course, it was still the middle of the day but the jungle certainly didn't reflect that. Without his new helmet, everything would be dark with little pinpoints of blue from the sap flowing through the trees around them.

Sal hefted his assault rifle but held it clear from the holster on his shoulder for the moment.

"How do you know where you're going?" Smythe asked and stepped alongside as they continued their march.

"You get a sense of the place when you've spent enough time in it."

"So, you're leading us deeper and deeper into a jungle one needs to have a mythical 'sense' to navigate through." He seemed to put it all together quickly enough. "You make it sound like we wouldn't be able to find our way out of here without you."

"Well, I didn't want to spell it out." He grinned at the man as he guided them to circle once again when he judged they were far enough away from the locusts' nest and could safely resume the direction in which Dutch had led them. "But basically, yeah, you four would crash and burn if I weren't around to pick up after you."

"We've been in and out of here before," he pointed out.

"Sure, but I read the reports that were filed on the missions. They were shallow runs that mostly avoided the prowls of the larger monsters. Those were training-wheel runs. We're in the thick of it now, buddy. I'd like to see you boys untangle from one of those T-Rex-looking mother-fuckers or walk away from the giant centipedes when you stumble into one of their territories. You know, they've expanded a fair distance lately, spreading, procreating—"

"Yeah, yeah, I get the picture," Smythe grumbled and rolled his eyes. "Things are tough. We've been through the sims before. We can kill the critters."

"Well, if you think the sims are a full and accurate representation of the reality you've seen so far in the Zoo, that should be great," Sal said. "Whatever helps you sleep at night."

The merc didn't appear to like that answer and dropped away to rejoin the rest of his group, which left Sal with a warm feeling in his stomach. The whole drug fiasco aside, these guys weren't terrible. They knew what they were doing and so far, hadn't tried to kill him. But drugging and kidnapping him was another matter altogether. They needed to try much harder than a state-of-art suit of armor to offset that offense.

CHAPTER TWELVE

Anja stepped into the garage and paused at the sight of Madigan and Courtney already suiting up for a trip into the Zoo. She narrowed her eyes, her head tilted with curiosity as she watched their preparations. They seemed to be going through the motions with much more enthusiasm than usual—and far less chatter too. She cleared her throat to draw the attention of both women.

"Amanda and Bev have left," she announced when they paused to look at her. "They said they would have a word with the bartender who slipped Sal the roofie. Hopefully, they'll be able to find out a little more about our mercs. That's assuming Amanda leaves the man alive."

"I always did like that woman," Madigan responded smugly. "She knows how to get shit done."

"About that, though..." Anja interrupted her fantasy of the inevitable and very satisfying violence. "I did a little research into the group that took him too. They're buried deep but given that I know how to dig... Anyway, they're all British based on facial recognition—former Royal Marine commandos, tough cookies every one of them, and all retired. They work for different companies and on different continents, but they all registered a payment into their accounts to the tune of a quarter million dollars or the equivalent in euros, pounds, and yen.

"All payments trace back to something called the Phoenix Industrial Group. As far as I can tell, it's a front for something else, but the trail went cold there. The point, though, is that the same group acquired a considerable number of high-end weapons, suits, and equipment for our mercs. More importantly, they recently put in for and received a high-end hybrid suit."

"All equipment required for a trip into the Zoo, I assume," Courtney said as she attached her helmet.

"Correct," the hacker confirmed. "I traced another payment to a Dr. Laurent—a specialist on the French Base —but from what I was able to make out, he was killed on a mission in the Zoo with our four Brits."

"Shit." Courtney looked alarmed. "Is that what they want to do with Sal?"

Madigan shook her head. "Why go through all the trouble to kidnap someone, suit them up, and take them into the Zoo only to shoot them. No, they're looking for something—or someone—and decided that Sal is their best chance to get in and out of there alive. It's interesting how they could be so right and yet so amazingly, fantastically wrong too."

Anja smirked. "Well, if all this armoring up is what I think it is—you two ladies headed into the Zoo yourselves —I really hope you guys rethink it. You're both scary-Mary and all, but how deep do you think you can look for him with only two of you?"

"Not that deep, true," Madigan agreed. She nodded emphatically and dragged her helmet on. "Don't worry. We're pissed, not suicidal. We called backup in—people we've both worked with before and who we know can pull their weight through that fucking jungle. They'll arrive at any minute. Do you have the entry vector for our merc team?"

"I've already forwarded it to your HUD."

Sal had lived out there for a while now, and he could say with some degree of certainty that he had some idea of what to expect from a trip into the Zoo. At the same time, it somehow always managed to throw the proverbial curve ball at those who thought they had it all under control. As a result, another thing he had learned was that people always had to expect the unexpected. This was sometimes difficult advice to follow, but it was something you simply learned to do eventually.

With all that said, what he looked at now was definitely unexpected. He did enjoy being proved right, even when it blew his mind.

From the looks on the faces of the four men he was with, he could tell they hadn't expected to see something like this either.

The unlikely sight seemed almost out of a fairy tale and certainly had no place in the monster-filled Zoo. Streams of water babbled through the open ground where the massive trees gave way to what looked like a meadow in the middle of a jungle. Hundreds of Pita plants covered the ground where there wasn't any water.

He wouldn't have believed this shit if he hadn't seen it himself. Any other team would be drooling at this point, but none of his companions seemed interested in the mother lode they'd stumbled onto. Instead, they all looked terrified by it. Beyond the very real stirrings of his excitement, he found he could understand that fear rather well.

Either way, he had saved all this and essentially everything they had seen since the beginning of the mission on the computer in his suit. There was much more storage space on the hard drive, which allowed him to record an estimated three weeks' worth of data that included film from the HUD as well as everything on the sensors. He'd made sure that everything he had saved was isolated from the other men's suits since he didn't want whoever was paying them to have access to the material he'd earmarked for his dissertation.

"Is this what you are looking for?" Sal directed the question to Dutch.

The man shook his head in response. "No. The last specialist we had in here, though, was very interested. The fool got himself killed trying to take one of those plants out."

"Been there, done that." Sal nodded and inched closer to inspect the larger than usual plants. "On my first trip in, I—" He suddenly realized that he didn't want to share the fact that he actually had a Pita plant at home. "Well, I saw a guy try it. The monsters around us went wild. We set a smoke bomb off to scare them away, and they all attacked him when he tried to run from us. Oh yeah, and there was another time when I pulled a plant deliberately to avoid a firefight and stuck the leader of the attackers with it. I slipped it into his backpack and ran the other way."

The mercs stared at him in stony silence and he shrugged. "What? He was an asshole."

"The man's assholeishness wasn't what we were wondering about," Smythe pointed out quietly.

He shrugged. Did he want these guys to be wary of him? Yes, but not to the point where they wondered if they weren't better off leaving him to fend for himself—or worse, decided to shoot him in the back. They needed him, but if he constantly reinforced that he would kill them, they might simply elect to attack him preemptively. At the same time, though, he also wanted to make sure they didn't think they could try the drug bullshit with anyone ever again.

"Let's keep moving," Dutch called once Sal had taken the time to collect a few of the flowers.

"Be careful not to crush them," Sal warned. "That shit can be painful."

He looked around them and sure enough, his gaze caught something that moved ominously high in the branches. He already knew what lay behind the four eyes that reflected light at him. The monster wouldn't attack yet and merely watched for the moment. Honestly, he didn't like the way it lurked there and spied on them.

A couple more creatures were visible in the light that poured into the meadow, and dozens more lingered outside their range of vision but not beyond the motion sensors. Their silent, waiting presence had him on edge. What were they thinking?

"So...who are these guys?" Anja asked as she studied the group of newcomers who had assembled in their garage.

Madigan patted the closest man on the shoulder. "This is Sergeant Davis—Matt Davis. I ran a couple of times in the Zoo with him. He's a hardy fighter and a canny guy to have around given that he's survived this long."

"Technically, it's simply Matt Davis now," he added while he attached the armor Amanda had prepped for them. "I had my papers signed last week and I'm waiting for an official plane to jet me to the States. I thought I might make extra cash before we head home. Oh...and we have to rescue Sal too."

"Well, it's nice to meet you Matt Davis." Madigan winked at him and turned to one of the other men who wore a hybrid suit. "This here is Corporal Mick Addams... still Corporal, right?"

"Correct." He nodded with a chuckle. "I've taken a little off time. I'm here because I remember and like Jacobs. He's a tough little puppy."

"Tougher still these days," she pointed out.

"And yet we're here, playing the knight in shining armor to his damsel in distress," Addams countered. "Just saying."

"So you all know Sal?" Anja asked, her expression curious as she studied each of them.

"Kennedy, Addams, Monroe, and I were actually there

for his first trip into the Zoo," Davis recalled with a wide grin. "To hear him tell it, he was dragged out of his bed in the middle of the night, and the day after he was dumped here, he was hauled in there with us. He adapted quickly, though, and helped those of us who survived that trip to get out in one piece."

"And what about that guy?" Anja asked and gestured at the final member of the five-man and women team that had been assembled.

"That is former ex-sergeant Nic Xander." Madigan introduced the man, who replied with a quiet nod. "He's worked the freelance circuit for a while since he signed his papers."

"I'm only in it for the money," the burly man explained and looked around at the team with frank honesty. "Sure, I like the little guy well enough. He got us into any number of places and got us out with a ton of cash, so I thought I owed you guys for keeping my prices reasonable."

"It's good to see you've surrounded yourself with people you can trust." Anja grinned. "I need to get back to my day job. Night...job. Anyway, do you have all the details?"

Madigan nodded. "Yep, I do. Have fun. I guess. I still don't know what the hell you do."

"Technical support for the most part," she called over her shoulder, already heading into the building.

"Fantastic." Madigan drew a breath and checked the other members of her team. They all had their suits on and were already mounting up in the Hammerhead. She stepped in with them and let Davis get them on the road before breaking the details out.

"All right, guys and gals, here's the situation." She used their newly minted comm system. "Sal got his ass kidnapped, and we're heading in after him. The people who snatched him are well-armed and well-supplied, but they're not the reason why we need more people on this team. From what Anja was able to make out, they've headed in deep, which means we need enough of a squad to make a deep run after them."

"How will we find him?" Davis asked.

"It's standard procedure to set up an emergency signal if you're separated from your group," Courtney explained. "Sal set his suit to already send that signal, but it was lost, which is only to be expected. On the bright side, we have a rough idea of where they're headed and should we get into the broadcasting range, we'll be able to find them again."

The others nodded without comment. The parameters of the mission were simple. They were all being paid for a rescue mission. The only priority would be to get Sal back safe and sound and hopefully, drill the assholes who took him full of bullets in the meantime. None of that needed explanation. These three were trustworthy enough that Madigan knew they wouldn't do anything stupid and put the priority of the mission at risk.

She didn't like the feeling that things were out of balance and honestly liked to be in control. This offended her on so many levels. She wouldn't be able to control Sal, obviously, but having him around and not kidnapped was something she could control. The geek could handle himself in the Zoo, but—

No, he would be fine, she assured herself firmly. She was merely heading in to make sure she could kick the mercs' asses herself. He would be there to thank her, and they would have fun with amazing "no one needed rescuing and yet someone was rescued anyway" sex. It would be a first, of course.

A couple of hours finally brought them to the entry vector the mercs had taken, and as they arrived in the area, they could see another team already prepping to head inside. Madigan was tempted to bring them along for the ride, but with the two dozen or so of them involved, not only would it be too expensive, but it would also take way too long to coordinate the search parties.

They pulled the Hammerhead to a halt close to where the others were parked, and one of the leaders of the group drew away to approach them.

"No, no, no way," he muttered and shook his head vehemently. "I put too much work into making sure we were the only team heading in today. If you guys want to go inside, you head to the base and coordinate it with the commandant."

"Stand down, soldier," Madigan retorted, her voice edged with menace. "Unless you want to be the squishy thing I have to clean off my boot in a couple of minutes."

The man took an instinctive step back, clearly intimidated by the woman in front of him. The suit she wore gave her almost a full foot of height over him.

"Who the fuck do you think you are?" he asked when he regained his composure. "I have half a mind to report all of you."

A second man jogged beside his leader and placed a warning hand on his shoulder. "Sarge, you do know who that is, right?"

Madigan smirked. It was always good to be recognized.

"I don't care if one of them is the President of the United Fucking States of America himself," the sergeant snapped. "His ass don't mean shit around here."

"It's Sgt. Madigan Kennedy and Dr. Courtney Monroe of Heavy Metal," the second soldier responded smartly. "Everyone knows you don't fuck with Heavy Metal out here. Not ever."

His superior opened his mouth for a moment and shook his head. "Who?"

"Fuck," the apparent number two of the team muttered. "If you're this clueless, I won't go into the Zoo with your ignorant ass. Stand down."

The sergeant shook his head but finally decided not to pick this particular fight, which was all well and good to Madigan. She didn't want to know what the man in front of her thought, but if he tried to keep them from heading in, she would definitely follow through with her threat.

And if the dumbass tried to sabotage their Hammerhead for revenge, she knew who he was. Well, she had his face recorded on her HUD and would therefore be able to track him and personally kick his ass. It seemed that would be a daily routine these days.

"We'll head out now," she said and turned to her team, who were already locked, loaded, and ready.

CHAPTER THIRTEEN

They had pressed on through most of the day, and Sal didn't like the truth that the four men had started to grow on him a little. They had the kind of charm you usually only found in Guy Ritchie movies. Despite their poor tactics, they did seem to be the type who would follow through on their promise to let him keep his suit as well as the money they'd promised him.

He still didn't trust them, obviously, but given how deep they were into the Zoo at this point, they had to be the only humans around for miles. Simple common sense dictated that they would therefore need to watch each other's backs if they all wanted to get out of there alive. Priorities had to be observed. Survival against the hordes of monsters around them would come first. They could kill each other later.

Not even a break for a midday meal delayed their entry into the deep reaches of the jungle. By the time the sun finally set, Sal could only tell from the way the darkness deepened and his suit switched to the motion sensors to compensate.

Over the past couple of hours when they pushed beyond the area patrolled by the teams that made shallow runs, they had allowed him to take point on their little team. He wondered if it was because they really trusted him to guide them or if they wanted to make sure he didn't have the chance to shoot any of them in the back.

Neither would have surprised him. He had laid the veiled threats on thickly, and from the way they'd seen him handle himself, they had to believe he was at least capable of delivering on what he'd intimated.

That said, as night fell, he raised his hand and closed it in a fist, the universal signal to bring the group to a halt.

"Okay," he said and spoke to them over the short-range transmitters so as to make as little noise on the outside as possible. "We'd better put all our shit into the center of a defensible position. Rack out and get some rest. This shit's about to get real, and you don't want to have a whole day of trekking through this place to hold you back when that happens."

The four men shared a glance, and Dutch was the first to speak. "We still have a couple of hours before moving through the jungle becomes really dangerous, and we're using it."

Another one—the one called Smythe—chuckled and shook his head. "Is this guy for real? Some kind of Zoo whisperer?"

Sal shook his head. "Look around you. We've always had something moving around us from the moment we stepped in here. Some kind of animal has kept tabs on what we're doing—watching and following and sometimes attacking. If you'd happen to consult your suits' motion sensors, you'll notice there's nothing moving around us right now, yes?"

The others took a moment to confirm that this was, indeed, the case. It was an interestingly horrifying notion, he knew. The way the monsters seemed to always want to keep tabs on them was unnerving at first, but after a little while, as long as they didn't attack, one might even get used to it. The notion became more chilling when nothing was watching, which meant the Zoo was done waiting to see what they were doing and had decided to act on it.

It was annoying to have to anthropomorphize a jungle like that, but there isn't a better way to put it.

"What comes next, in your experience?" Dutch asked finally, and Sal realized the team had conferred over a private channel—one he wasn't a part of. While he didn't like being excluded from conversations like that, he did appreciate that they seemed to be willing to trust his word.

"Like I said," he grumbled. "The shit's about to go down. It could be hours or minutes, but it's coming soon. We need to be able to defend ourselves and, if possible, get some rest before it starts. It's best to find high ground with as much of a clear view all around as we can. Open and as far away from the trees as we can get."

"We're in the middle of the fucking jungle," Campbell pointed out. "How far away from the trees can we get?"

"Believe me, take as many inches as you can find," Sal retorted, irritated at having to explain himself. "It can mean life or death. Let's get moving."

From their body language, he could tell they had started

another private conversation. It irked him but he pushed the aggravation aside. As long as they didn't see his emergency signal being broadcast, they could have all the private conversations they wanted.

"All right," Dutch stated after a few moments. "You heard the man. Find a defensible position as far from the trees as we can get and set up fortifications. We'll have a quick break for food, stay in our suits, and get as much rest as we can. And stay sharp."

The five men moved quickly and Smythe already had a good idea of where to set their camp up. The defensive positions weren't quite what most would expect as they kept the area as open as possible. Some wiring was set out to establish a quickly-mounted fence with enough electricity crackling through it to fry some of the smaller monsters—smaller, of course, amounted to the hyenas or the locusts the size of dogs. Most of the defenses were set up in a way that wouldn't interfere with a potential line of fire when they needed it.

Sal noted that Murphy hastily positioned two or three dozen claymore mines on their perimeter. There were worries on other missions that this kind of deployment would be triggered by a lone creature that was simply a little too curious for their own good and thus bring on the attention of the full Zoo on their heads. In this case, of course, they anticipated an attack so it wouldn't be an issue. Claymore away seemed an appropriate strategy.

They completed their camp and defenses in under fifteen minutes and prepared a meal to be shared between them. Sal selected diced chicken and vegetables along with rice, pre-prepared in the manner that would usually call for chopsticks to eat it with. All he had was a small metal spork, though, so it would have to be enough. It was warm and it was food, and that was all he could really ask for. Lunch had been a few bites of dried beef jerky and a sip of water.

He seriously needed hot food. Maybe he was a little spoiled by his good lifestyle.

The team remained in their suits and detached only what was essential to be able to eat. Sal could manipulate the utensils with his lighter hybrid suit and only had to remove his helmet. Most of the others—except for Murphy, who had a similar suit to him—needed to remove arm sections to be able to manage their food, as well as their helmets.

The tension among the five of them was palpable and silence reigned. When he had finished his rations, Sal eased away from the team. He'd need less rest than they did, thanks to his method of self-medicating, and he was more than willing to take the first watch. He had a feeling they wouldn't need a second anyway. Let the newbies get their rest. They would need it.

Smythe already knew he wouldn't get much sleep. Whatever his doubts over Jacobs' ability to read their surroundings and anticipate an attack, the lack of animal movement around them was more than a little unnerving. He didn't like it, and it left him irritable.

Therefore, even as he settled and tried to get as comfortable as he could in the heavy armor he wore, he was well aware that he couldn't hope for any actual sleep. He might, if he were lucky, doze off here or there, but he was tired and wired at the same time. Adrenaline had seeped into his system—not enough to leave him off balance but sufficient for him to be ready for a fight when it came.

He wasn't necessarily ready for this one in particular, but combat was combat. His body was prepared to be in a fight for his life. That much hadn't changed, no matter how much alien goop you threw into the mix.

The fact that Jacobs mumbled and talked to himself— audible thanks to the fact that he didn't wear his helmet— made it impossible to rest either. He couldn't make out what the kid was saying. He seemed to repeat words in the same way he did when he talked to them. Smythe had enough trouble understanding what the guy said when he wanted them to hear him. It became absolutely impossible when he talked to himself.

If he was talking to himself. Could he have contacted some of his friends outside the Zoo to come and rescue him? He'd acted like he'd gone along with what they were doing but with a guy like him, how could you really tell? Either way, Dutch seemed to have bought into it, so Smythe couldn't say anything outright about the kid himself.

He sighed softly and shifted awkwardly until he could feel his ribs again, and his hands settled on the assault rifle. Absolutely nothing appeared to be moving toward them, and he now wondered if Jacobs wasn't simply full of shit.

From where he perched, he could make the man out clearly—he used his suit as support so he could stand in place all day. Smythe couldn't decide what the kid was up to. A hint of temptation whispered to pick his rifle up and plaster Jacobs' brains all over the Zoo, but Dutch seemed to think the man was vital to their whole mission.

The scientist suddenly perked up. His mumbling stopped, and he snatched his helmet up and attached it to the suit before he jogged to where the rest of the men still rested. From the way they were quickly roused, it was easy to tell they'd had as much trouble sleeping as he had.

"Trouble's coming," Jacobs stated crisply as he urged them into action. Andy strained intently into the darkness in an attempt to identify a possible threat. Honestly, at any other time and without the warning, he would have missed it entirely.

With how silent the jungle was—so silent that even the motion sensors didn't pick anything up—the reverberations could be heard from farther away. The whispered vibrations were too soft for human ears to pick up but powerful enough for them to tease and shiver the trees around them. Gentle vibrations—that was all Jacobs needed. The guy was messed up in the head but he knew a thing or two about the fucking place.

The team assembled quickly and stepped smoothly into defensive positions, and Smythe finally registered movement. What little light that filtered from the tree cover was picked up by the photoreceptors on his suit and told him, along with the motion sensors, that either something huge approached or a large number of smaller creatures.

He waited until the single shadow separated into its constituent parts. Many smaller creatures, he realized, and as they drew closer, he noted they were four-limbed. They looked vaguely simian and moved like larger apes, knuckling the ground, but they weren't that large either. Large fangs extended menacingly as they roared at the silent, waiting humans.

Andy really, really hoped the fangs weren't poisoned.

The mutants had gathered in large numbers. Dozens of them shambled inexorably closer, and even more circled and emerged from the trees. A cacophony of screeches and roars erupted. Maybe that was their way to communicate with each other, or maybe they wanted to warn the humans to back off and run. Then again, they seemed to have deliberately surrounded the small group of humans, which left very little room for them to retreat.

Smythe growled under his breath. He didn't like this. There were more monsters than he'd ever seen around there before, and even though they appeared to be all the same kind, they weren't anything he'd encountered. Claws extended from their forelimbs, which made them far more terrifying than he'd thought they would be.

"Stay clumped together," Jacobs reminded them. "Stay in a group and they'll be less likely to att—"

He wasn't able to finish his sentence. Campbell was the first to be unnerved by the noise from the aggressive monsters around them, and with a shouted curse in a language Smythe didn't quite understand, he opened fire.

The powerful bullets punched through one of the creatures to fell a couple more behind it as well. The enemy fell silent for a second and Dutch decided to get in on the action. He took advantage of their hesitation to open fire but didn't pause with one round. Instead, he released a volley to cut through the beasts as they hurled themselves as one at their little camp.

Smythe had already prepared his noise suppression for the explosions that would come. He registered the solid thumps when they detonated. The ground shuddered and the lights flashed vividly across the entire jungle around them. The glare revealed that the creatures were pale white, almost albino. Of course, the light quickly faded to catch only a final flash of bright bluish-red as the shrapnel savaged through a line of the mutants. They shrieked and fell back to shake off the explosion. The apparent reprieve was short-lived, as they charged again almost immediately and triggered a couple more of the explosions.

Jacobs gestured at the massive hole in the lines of the monsters, and Andy already knew what he meant. They would take advantage of the gap to make sure they were on the move. Staying in the same place, no matter how well defended it was from ground attacks, generally drew attacks from above. Despite the clear ground they'd chosen, they were sufficiently close to the trees for this to remain a danger and there was no reason to invite any more than they already had to contend with. Jacobs raised his weapon to cover them against the creatures that now launched from above when they realized the ground assault was fraught with peril.

A couple of thuds confirmed how on point his aim was while they maintained the steady stream of fire. Dutch's massive tank of a suit had something that could only be described as a full-on machine gun—barely shy of being a mini-gun, Smythe noted, even though it had three barrels in place so there was less danger of overheating. The huge magazine the weapon carried could also outlast almost anything the rest of the team carried. He assumed the responsibility to provide suppressing fire, and the others picked up the slack when he needed to reload. They were selective with their shots in the meantime to conserve ammo.

Sal indicated definitively for them to change the direction of their controlled retreat. He had obviously seen something approaching from behind them. Murphy was the first to react. He spun, and whatever he saw clearly terrified him. That much was frighteningly clear from the way his vitals spiked for a second as he scrambled to yank something from his pack.

A cluster grenade, Andy realized. The man was famous for saying he would never need something that destructive anywhere in the world. The famously powerful payload and abundance of shrapnel combined to turn anything within a ten-meter radius into pulp. Dutch remained focused on the horde that attacked ahead, but Smythe and Campbell whirled to see what was behind them.

Andy immediately recalled facing something similar in the sim, although research had told him only one of those hulking, gorilla-like monsters had been seen in the Zoo. This one matched it for size, although it appeared to move faster and with far more power. The evidence of its enhanced abilities emerged when it bowled a tree over in its frenzied charge at the group of five humans.

This mutant had two very distinctive differences. The first and most notable was the massive horn that protruded from its forehead, which it used to effortlessly fell the trees in its path. The appendage had the triangular shape and curve of a rhino's horn.

The second difference was the most worrying, though. There were three of them.

A cluster grenade didn't seem like such a bad idea after all.

"Take cover!" Murphy bellowed, yanked the pin on one of his grenades, and adjusted the settings for a delayed explosion. Sal, Smythe, Murphy, and Campbell took that advice without argument and raced away from where the explosive had been lobbed to use the trees for protection.

Dutch either hadn't had the time to react or had all kinds of faith in his suit. He simply continued his attack on the monsters that still swarmed their defenses. More than a handful lay limp on the perimeter fence they'd erected, and periodic thumps indicated that remaining claymores had detonated. Despite the carnage, those behind seemed more than happy to simply climb over their dead comrades.

Smythe closed his eyes and tried to shield them from the explosion that followed, but even his HUD's light and noise reduction software had difficulty coping with what came next. All he could tell was that he had been catapulted away from the tree he'd used for cover, and his ears rang so loudly he couldn't hear anything else.

"Fuck!" he shouted to test himself, but while he could feel the vibrations from his voice in his throat, he still couldn't hear shit.

More worrying, though—or possibly more of a relief— were the chunks of wood that protruded from his armor. He could still move and the vital signs from the rest of his suit told him that everything was more or less fine, but it was still a harrowing sight.

Sal was already on his feet and yelling something at them. Campbell was too, and he raced to where Dutch had fallen to his knees. Chunks were missing from the back of his armor, and while he still looked alive, the gentle flow of something black and thick from the holes indicated that he was hurt.

"I'm fine," he protested, and it was the first sound that Smythe heard over the ringing in his ears. "Get the fuck off me. I'm fine, arsewipe. What the fuck was that?"

"One of Murphy's cluster grenades," the Scotsman explained and helped Dutch to his feet while Murphy ran hasty diagnostics.

Smythe was singled out by Jacobs to follow him, and the specialist almost dragged him away from where the others checked on Dutch. The interruption brought his mind back to the reason why a cluster grenade had been used in the first place. It took him a moment to see where the hulking monsters were, but once he did, it was impossible to not be surprised.

They had been far closer to the explosion than any of the five-man team, having taken no cover, and obviously wore no armor. Despite this, they looked intact, for the most part—except for various body parts strewn on the ground.

And they were still moving.

"What does it take to kill one of these fuckers?" he asked as he followed Jacobs who inched in closer.

"Fuck if I know," the man replied with a shrug. "Although big explosions do seem to be the way to go."

"That's the answer to most things if the truth be told," Smythe agreed. The monsters were still alive but seemed to be in shock over what had happened, and damned if Smythe didn't intend to take advantage of that. He aimed the assault rifle in his hands directly at the temple of the closest beast.

"Don't shoot them anywhere near the spine," Jacobs said and explained hurriedly when he raised an eyebrow at him. "That's where the goop sacs are. Not only are they as expensive as fuck, but if you burst them, it gets a reaction from the rest of the Zoo that's second only to plucking a Pita plant."

"Ah," Andy replied stoically. "Best not, then. It looks like they've given us a small reprieve anyway."

He adjusted his aim to be sure his bullet wouldn't go through the spine and took a step back as the monster jerked a few times when the three-round burst tore through its head. Jacobs had already reached the second mutant and applied the same kind of killing shot. Smythe moved to the third and narrowed his eyes when the other man scrambled onto the back of the creature's head and drew a knife from his pack. No, not a knife—a scalpel by the looks of it. He made an incision into where he had told him not to shoot. His movements were quick but precise, and he withdrew something thick and heavy, about the size of a fist, from the cavity.

"This is the secret of why these monsters get so big without collapsing under their own weight," Jacobs said and displayed the dripping prize. Smythe had to force himself not to retch simply from watching the man manip-ulate the piece before he tagged and bagged it for later.

He'd known, of course, that some animals had the expensive sacs of goop on their spines, even if he hadn't known they were the reason why the mutants grew so big.

He had simply thought...well, big monster. There wasn't much time to think about all this. He would have to ask the kid to explain it later.

They only had time to collect the one, unfortunately. Jacobs scrambled down as Murphy and Campbell helped Dutch get his suit working again. The enemy had broken away after the massive explosion but they would return.

"Do you notice how there aren't any bodies of the smaller ones over there?" the scientist asked and pointed him to where their camp had been. Sure enough, the scars left in the ground from the exploding claymore mines were still easy to make out, but none of the bodies of the creatures they had killed could be seen.

"Well...that's creepy," he said.

"Right?" Jacobs chuckled. "That's the Zoo, though. It reclaims all the organics that result from a fight. I assume it does so to make more monsters, but that's only the creative in me. You never know what will come next. Take the mind of your most demented horror writer, add some alien crazy to the mix, and you might be close to what we deal with out here on a daily basis."

He really didn't want to think about it. Jacobs actually seemed to be enjoying himself out there, which either made him a sucker for punishment or as demented as the horror writer behind all this bullshit.

"We need to radio base," he pointed out to the team as they helped Dutch to keep moving. "We need to contact someone and make sure they at least know where we are."

Sal shook his head. "You won't get through."

Honestly, he was tired of listening to what this kid had to say, all things considered. He was tired and in need of a good drink. Even so, he tried to key their command structure at the French base. They continued their trek and he repeated his efforts to contact them. To the scientist's credit, even though he failed repeatedly to raise anything other than a garbled white noise, the man showed no sign of gloating. It seemed that he was content to simply be right without having to rub it—

Oh, no, wait. There was that knowing smirk.

CHAPTER FOURTEEN

Courtney had made sure that Heavy Metal had the best she could find on short notice to work with. Madigan took point and with the heavy suit she wore, she would be able to bulldoze over virtually anything that crossed their path. It was one of the newer models and had only been used once by someone who had wildly overestimated its ability to cope with G-forces when he'd fallen from a cliff while inside the Zoo. The man had survived to be taken out and brought into a hospital, but the internal bleeding that resulted from the impact had been too extensive and he'd died soon after.

Of course, she hadn't told Madigan those details before she'd presented her with it. Soldiers like her—against all evidence—were incredibly superstitious and there were serious rules about using a dead man's suit. Courtney didn't want her friend to decline perfectly functional armor due to one weird inclination or another. And she didn't want her distracted while she used it, for obvious reasons.

It was simply a white lie of omission, for lack of a better term.

"I'll fucking kill him," Madigan muttered, mostly to herself.

"Which one?" She moved in beside the woman and felt the ground shake every time one of the heavy boots came down.

"Sal," she replied and shook her head. "I'd bet good money he is out here with some of his drinking buddies or some shit, and all they're doing is getting drunk. And he neglected to let us know about his plans before he headed inside. He's idiotic enough to make that a believable situation."

"I know you don't mean that." Courtney placed her hand on the other woman's shoulder, even though she knew she wouldn't feel it through the armor. "So I'll go ahead and forget you said it. Now that you mention it, though, we'll probably have to come up with a way for Sal to pay us back for putting us through all this bullshit. Not to put blame on the victim or anything like that, but I'm sure we can think of something that would pay us back very satisfactorily without pushing the boundaries of what he's done in the past."

Madigan paused and turned to look at her with narrowed eyes.

"What?" she asked defensively.

"Being all corporate has changed you, Monroe. Not that it's a bad thing, but it's something to keep in mind. You were sweet and gullible when I first met you—with something of a dark streak, admittedly, but still. Now, you're all about taking control and thinking ahead. I like it, but I think it's a little terrifying at the same time."

"Thanks. I guess?"

"Take it however you please." Madigan grinned. "Now, let's talk about how Sal will repay us for all this trouble. I'm fairly sure that saving his life if it's in danger or not killing him ourselves if it's not should demand a high price. Maybe we should make him give us a hefty bonus out of his own commission."

"I thought something a little more...horizontal." Courtney chuckled. "It's not like I need the money."

"You would think that." Madigan rolled her eyes, but a hint of a smile tugged at her lips.

Davis pulled back when he heard what the two women were talking about. They had kept it out in the open, which meant they weren't worried about keeping the topic of their conversation a secret. That said, there were some things that were best left to the imagination, especially in this case.

He glanced around to see Xander and Addams talking as well. They had also left their conversation conducted on their suits' speakers out in the open. Given the topic, Davis wondered if they shouldn't have kept what they were saying to a private comm channel or something too.

"Did you ever tap that?" Xander asked as Davis came in closer.

"Which one?" Addams queried.

"Either?" Xander shrugged. "Both, maybe? They seem close and so maybe they're open to the concept of a threesome. Just saying."

"I never got close with Dr. Monroe," Addams responded. "She never seemed the type to hang around with simple soldiers like the rest of us. Kennedy, though? She seemed to be the kind of woman who would get it on with her fellow soldiers. She and I had a little something going. It never got physical, and next thing I knew, she'd moved on and wasn't interested. It was weird, but a guy has to move on from setbacks like that. It's what makes him a man, proper."

Xander nodded as if Addams had said something very deep and profound before he turned to Davis. "How about you, Sarge? Would you ever want to get in with either of them?"

"Not for a million bucks," he replied almost immediately. He'd known the way the conversation would turn and had his response ready.

"Interesting," Addams cut in. "Would you care to explain?"

He shrugged easily. "They might be hot, sure, but it's still a hell no from me. I don't need that kind of 'love'"—he made the air quotes for effect—"behind a gun aimed at me out here in the Zoo. My ex-wife would have accidentally shot my ass and kicked me at a killerpillar while I was still bleeding out or some shit like that. Sal is definitely a braver man than I am. Or plain fucking crazy."

"Wait," Xander called. "Are you saying Sal is dating both of them?"

"I'm sure it goes beyond simply dating at this point, but yes." He nodded. The other man's response was fairly predictable, he supposed. He looked surprised, a little impressed, and then, as he suddenly came to the same realization that Davis had about fifteen minutes earlier, a little terrified.

"Now he gets it." He grinned.

All three men ducked as the sound of sudden and very loud gunfire cut through the comparative silence that had been pervasive in the jungle before that moment. The series of shots came in almost too quickly to register as more than one. A couple of stinger-tailed locusts thudded from the top of the trees above them.

Instinctively, his gaze turned to the tank of a suit Madigan wore and more importantly, the small, Gatling-like canon that had raised from her shoulder piece. The woman hadn't even looked up from her conversation to aim properly, which told Davis some kind of automatic targeting and triggering system had enabled her to shoot like that.

"In case you haven't noticed, that there is a scary woman," he pointed out and took care to keep his voice low. With the new and fancy suits she and Monroe sported, there was no telling what they might hear him say. He'd heard they were impressive, but this was on a whole new level. What the fuck did they have on call and why did they think they needed three extra hands on deck for this mission?

They were either playing it safe or they anticipated considerable trouble. Neither answer comforted him much. He had resigned his post there to avoid these deep runs into the Zoo and keep himself alive to enjoy the hefty pension he had put aside for himself. Coming in there had been a bad idea. He absolutely knew it.

That aside, he had a crazy, suicidal streak to him, was all. It was the only reason he'd stuck it out this long.

CHAPTER FIFTEEN

It hadn't been a particularly long day. The previous commandant of the US base had essentially allowed the corporations on the facility free rein. They conducted missions with military personnel as much as they pleased and only bothered to put the paperwork in when it was required by the people who ran the show in the Pentagon.

In the early days, when people were still adjusting to the idea of an alien jungle miraculously appearing in the Sahara, that might have worked. But as with everything in the world, the bureaucracy would eventually catch up with it. Audits into the mess that was the base had ended with the former commandant relieved of his command.

After a brief period, they'd decided another commandant was needed and put Lieutenant Colonel Franklin Bernard Evans in charge.

It had taken a long couple of weeks to bring everything into working order again thanks to the mess left behind by both his predecessor and the successive failures of the people who had tried ineffectually to restore order and efficiency. Bureaucrats were good for one thing and one thing only, and that was to keep the wheel of civilization well-oiled. There wasn't very much civilization out there in the Zoo, which meant they all had to keep themselves busy making everyone else's life busy.

The first order of business had been to involve the auditors. A firm hand was needed. They would allow the people making money to keep making money since that was how the base was funded, but only as long as they did so in an organized fashion. Patrols were given pay increases to run through the jungle without taking time out of their trips to try to find something to supplement their income. Making sure that anyone who wanted to make a run into the Zoo out of their base signed up for it at least three days in advance had been another thing. Keep it simple and keep it organized had been a positive strategy.

There were exceptions, of course, which was why Evans really didn't feel good about the paperwork he had in his hand when he tracked his assistant down.

"Hey, Lieutenant," Evans snapped, caught the young man by his shoulder, and turned him to face him. "What the hell is this?"

The younger man peeked at the paperwork. He was a lieutenant only in name, of course, and acted as a liaison for the various intelligence agencies that didn't want to commit their people to the Zoo but still wanted to keep a finger on the pulse. Evans had decided to make the kid useful given that he would hang around the place anyway and had all but made him his personal assistant.

"That's an emergency entry request form," the lieutenant replied after a short pause. "I thought you told me to keep them off your desk and out of your mind by handling those myself."

"Yes, by denying them." Evans shook his head. "You authorized this one. Where the hell do you get off?"

"It was a permission form put forward by Heavy Metal," the younger man said with a nod. "Sergeant Madigan Kennedy herself lodged it."

"Again, I ask you why the hell you thought it would be a good idea to allow her—of all people—to go into the Zoo without my express authorization?" He rubbed his eyes as if the gesture could somehow erase the offending document. These people would get him killed, and not only by the monsters that could be found out in the jungle.

"There's a reason statement at the bottom," his assistant replied with a small smile and pointed at a small portion of the form set aside for the reasons why the request was made. The commandant hadn't even noticed it. In all honesty, he was used to ignoring that section and categorically denying all emergency requests.

He decided to give this one his attention and narrowed his eyes when he read the reason.

"A kidnapping?" he asked. "Are you fucking serious? Salinger Jacobs…kidnapped and taken into the Zoo. Please tell me this is a fucking prank. I love pranks."

"Are you asking me to lie to you, sir?" the young man asked and looked both wary and confused.

"Shit," Evans snapped. "How many teams do we have in that area right now?"

The lieutenant checked the logs on his tablet hastily. "Only the one, sir. They are doing a sweep along the outskirts and are scheduled for a satellite uplink in about three hours."

"Get them out of there." He had already begun to walk to his office. "Get them out of there right now. World War Fucking Three is about to break out in the fucking jungle, and we can't afford to lose any more people."

"Sir, do you really think Dr. Jacobs would be capable of causing that much trouble?" the young man asked, his expression now skeptical.

"Jacobs?" the commandant asked and quirked an eyebrow. "Not a chance. He's one of the brightest minds we have still willing to go into that fucking place. Kennedy and Monroe on the other hand... Get another team together—the best of the best available on this kind of short notice. Put in time-and-a-half pay and I'll cover the expenditures."

"To...help our team get out of there?" Confusion reigned once more on the young man's face.

"Nope." Evans dialed a number on his phone. "To handle the shitstorm that will come when those women find Jacobs. And maybe even to get his ass out of there alive if they're pissed to see him. I need his damned brain and if they shoot that all over the trees, he won't be around to help us in the future. For fuck's sake, I can't believe the idiot let himself get taken."

The lieutenant nodded—reading the signs if not their full significance—and backed out of the office.

"Sir, there is news."

Ryen Solaratov didn't like people to interrupt his afternoon naps. He'd spent a couple of years working in an embassy in Spain and had acquired a taste for their usually forgotten ability to take a siesta in the middle of a day. Getting all that work in one's system was exhausting, and there was nothing quite like taking a break for a little shuteye to let one's mind rest and mull over everything it still had to do for the rest of the day.

He had been leaning back in his comfortable office chair, his feet propped on a nearby ottoman, and had dreamed of a chilly evening around a fire with roast pork, liberal vodka, and loose women. His wife didn't need to know what his dreams were as long as she had access to his credit card at home.

The men who worked for him knew better than to interrupt his traditional afternoon nap with something that couldn't be handled by someone else. The people who hadn't followed those simple instructions had found themselves on the patrol detail—the deep patrol detail.

Ryen wasn't above being petty and liked his base to run precisely the way it was meant to be run. It was, after all, his base to order as he saw fit.

"What's the matter?" the commandant demanded and quirked an impressively bushy eyebrow at the tall, lean man with a hint of Mongolian in his bloodline and a sergeant's bars on his shoulder. Lebedev, he thought he was called.

Lebedev—yes, that was his name—shut the door quickly behind him, placed an action report on the desk, and turned it for him to look at. "It's about Salinger Jacobs. I know you've met the man, and I thought you'd want to know he was kidnapped from the French base and dragged into the Zoo by four mercenaries of unknown origin."

A wave of disappointment washed over him. This was what amounted to news these days? This was what had interrupted his afternoon nap? This was why he wasn't back in his dacha taking shots from perky models' belly buttons?

He didn't need to be vindictive this time. Lebedev had been an admirable soldier in the past, if a little excitable, which was why he had survived the three trips into the Zoo he had been sent on.

"Why do I need to know this?" the commandant asked and shook his head. "We all know Jacobs can handle himself. You've seen it for yourself. Or heard of it, anyway."

"Of course, commandant." The soldier appeared to regret having come in there at all. "We also thought you should know that intelligence has picked up that Madigan Kennedy and Dr. Courtney Monroe have assembled a small team to go in after him and hopefully rescue him."

"Oh." Ryen grunted. That was news. "Why the hell did that imbecilic *cyka* have to go and get himself taken? If he can handle himself so well, you'd think he would be able to keep himself out of the hands of simple kidnappers, wouldn't you say?"

"Of course, Commandant," Lebedev replied, although Ryen thought he might not, in fact, say quite that. "What do you want us to do?"

"There isn't much we can do." He shrugged. "Move the teams and give their vector a wide berth. With that said, I would like us to have a team in the area willing and able to help Jacobs should he come in our direction."

"Will he need help to escape?"

"Possibly, although my thought was he might need time and space to let Kennedy calm down once everything is said and done." Ryen leaned back in his seat again. "Let us be a buffer between that poor kid and whatever it is that's coming for him. We owe him that much."

"Yes, sir." Lebedev nodded and saluted sharply before he about-faced and left the room. His superior kicked his feet onto the ottoman once more, smiled, and let his eyes drift shut. There really was little chance that he would have any more sleep at this point, but all this seemed like the kind of problem he usually passed along for someone else to deal with.

It was, after all, one of his strengths. Ryen Solaratov was great at delegating tasks.

Brian wasn't usually much of a gambler. It was the one vice he now never allowed himself to have. It wasn't a holier than thou attitude where he felt better than the people who engaged in gambling. There were many gamblers out there who were great people.

No, that wasn't it at all. If anything, there was a hint of a gambler's problem still in him—something that had taken most of his time in the Zoo and more than a few hours of court-mandated therapy to empower him to overcome his addiction. Of course, the easiest route was to simply acquire another vice that took all your time and money instead. That way, you would at least not have to deal with the withdrawal symptoms without a little something here and there that could provide much-needed endorphins.

It wasn't a perfect system, of course, but there were very few perfect things in the world these days.

Drinking was one such vice, and there were more than enough sources to indulge that particular need. The Bar in the base had more than enough booze to satisfy even the most demanding of patrons, which Brian wasn't. He merely needed his alcohol to be strong, taste good, and not give him too bad a headache the next day.

Most of the men in the bar with him at that time suckled from the same proverbial teat, of course, although they lacked his restraint and ability to avoid games of chance. In all fairness, his game of choice was, and always would be blackjack. Maybe poker too, if he needed a break.

He'd been able to count cards for a while—since his teenage years in fact—a skill that had earned him a fair amount of money and a black mark in all the casinos in Atlantic City. That unfortunate experience had taught him to pace his need to win and so far, he'd only been to Vegas a couple of times and was still welcome to step onto the gambling floors.

Most definitely, his gambling preferences leaned toward better things. All this betting on people's lives and shit simply felt crass.

They were betting on a guy named Salinger Jacobs. Although he'd only been around the base for a couple of weeks, Brian knew the name. There were always intriguing details associated with it and he had never been able to tell which of the stories were true and which were fiction. Either way, the young researcher had ended up drawing more attention than he could probably handle with his actions in and out of the Zoo.

His name and picture were still in place above the bar, along with his record of twenty shots in rapid succession which was damn impressive—and true, by all accounts. A handful of people still talked about it after the fact, claiming the bet had been with another gunner over who would go home with Madigan Kennedy that night. There were pictures of her—or so it was said—but those weren't in the bar.

"What's your money on, Brian?" one of the other patrons asked and slapped him hard on the shoulder. He wasn't sure where he knew him from but he smiled and turned to face the man who already reeked of the alcohol he'd consumed.

"That depends, good buddy," he replied, unable to help himself. "What are we betting on?"

"Well, there are reasonably even odds that Jacobs will survive," he responded with a firm nod. "The real money can be found on the opposite side of the coin. Whether he'll get himself killed by something in the Zoo, whether the mercs who kidnapped him will kill him, or if one of his Heavy Metal ladies will have the privilege."

Heavy Metal ladies. Not quite a band name, he thought inanely, but it was close.

"What are the odds split between the two ladies?" he asked and sipped his drink to lubricate his hesitant thoughts.

"Well, so far, it's twenty-three to one that Kennedy gelds him," the man replied, his words slurred but edged with humor. "Thirty to one that Monroe dissects his genitals."

"And why would his fellow teammates want to kill him in such a memorable fashion again?" He couldn't seem to move past the single section of the story that didn't add up.

"For letting his ass be kidnapped, of course," his informer grumbled before he burped loudly, tacked on a barely intelligible "excuse me," and shambled to the bar. Brian still couldn't quite wrap his head around why Kennedy and Monroe would want to kill the researcher when he was the victim of the whole devious plan, but who was he to say what these people were up to in their spare time?

The least he could do was make money from his intuitions. What good were they simply lying around with nothing to do?

Brian smirked, shook his head to focus himself, and eased from his seat to stroll over to the men who handled the bets.

CHAPTER SIXTEEN

Anja could feel her eyes drying out with every second she spent glued to the screen. She couldn't help it, not really. Too much time had already been spent in front of the damn thing, driven by the inner impetus that constantly told her she needed to keep on working until she dropped. Now, there she was. A drop was imminent, but she had to somehow stave it off a little longer.

The mission with Savage was over and Sal was out in the Zoo, kidnapped and now also hunted by a couple of vengeful Valkyries in the form of Madigan and Courtney. All she could do at this point was to sit around and wait.

Sure, she had a couple of buns in the oven she could work on. These constituted facial recognition, infiltrations, and bugs she already had behind enemy lines that constantly fed data to her. She needed to sift through it manually since most algorithms, even the ones she wrote, wouldn't be able to find what she needed on their own. But it was all busy work, nothing she could stay focused on for too long without boring herself into an inevitable bedtime.

She sighed softly and finally managed to pull herself back from the almost nose-on-the-screens posture and rubbed feeling back into her eyes. The damn things had been open for so long that tears were prompted by the simple act of closing her eyelids. It was a satisfying feeling but not worth the damage it would cause to her vision. She couldn't help another drawn-out sigh of relief when she dragged herself from her seat and stretched her legs. It was time she came up with a daily schedule. Then again, maybe at a time when she wasn't helping people who ran operations from across the globe, both in the US and there in the Sahara Desert.

Also, she needed to talk to Sal about a raise. Or maybe Courtney. She wasn't entirely sure how the chain of command worked yet. It seemed he ran the operations that took place in the Zoo but she was in charge of what happened in the States. Maybe she could leverage herself something from both of them.

No, that wasn't fair. She wasn't in this for the money. It certainly made things simpler to have available cash to spend on her work, but it wasn't why she did this and she had all the funding she needed anyway. Of course, at some point, she would want to go somewhere else. Maybe not Russia since she was reasonably certain she had slammed that particular door very firmly behind her, but there were other places she could call home. She'd liked it in Boston.

Maybe then, she would work so she could buy a house and start a family—something that had never been too high on her list of priorities. Still, it had always been there somewhere, waiting for her, or so she thought. Ending up alone was not among her plans.

She looked around for a moment and was distracted when her phone buzzed. It took a second to remember where she'd left it—in the kitchen. Anja didn't have the energy to trundle all the way there to get to it. And since the line would probably cut by then, she merely dropped into her chair.

"Hey, Connie, please patch my phone to this computer," she instructed.

"Right away, Anja," the AI replied. She was the only one Connie didn't give a hard time to. Well, she didn't annoy Sal as much, but that was probably because he was a guy and she seemed to be programmed to annoy women in particular. Either way, the AI seemed to know that Anja was actually in a position to rewrite everything she didn't like about her and was more than willing to play nice in order for that to not happen.

The line came live and displayed on the screen to reveal Amanda, calling from wherever she was at the time. The French base was the only detail Anja had heard, and she hadn't been able to really keep track of what was happening out there with all the other things taking precedence.

"Hey there, Amanda." The hacker summoned a happy face as the camera feature of the conversation came live. "How's tricks?"

"Tricks? Really?"

"I've been up for about thirty-six hours and it doesn't look like I'll get sleep anytime soon, so yes, tricks is what you'll get from me," she insisted. "What's up?"

"Well, I just finished a conversation with the bartender responsible for drugging Sal," the woman grumbled with a vindictive glance over her shoulder. Anja thought she could hear a soft groan in the background.

"And how many pieces did this conversation leave this bartender in?" she asked, grinding her jaw in a mixed response of pissed-off and very amused.

"Well, one...for the most part." The armorer glanced down and appeared to nudge something with her foot. Or someone, rather, based on the sound he made. "I still had to send Bev away for the worst of it. Seriously, the woman dissects animals all day and every day for a living and she can't take a little violent exchange of information?"

"Did you learn anything?" she asked and made a valiant effort to stave off the need to snap. Those hours had really taken their toll.

"Nothing much. He said the four men involved were recent arrivals but had been regulars since they'd arrived and spent most of their time outside the Zoo drinking. They had money to throw around and were decent enough tippers. Oh, I also learned that our friend here is known for being able to provide roofies for his regulars when they happen to need them. Helpful little fucker, isn't he?"

Which explained why she had gone so hard on him, the hacker mused. She didn't blame the woman. While her own tactics would have been a little more subtle, she always wished she had the guts to go the more direct route of beating the shit out of assholes like him.

All that aside, she hadn't learned anything they didn't already know. Regular roofie provider aside, she had been able to keep an eye on the financial transactions and could tell he didn't make much more than was to be expected from a bartender at the French base and had sincerely doubted that they would learn anything new. It was still a lead they had to follow up on, of course, but she wasn't surprised that it proved to be another dead end.

Thankfully, they weren't all out of leads.

"I've done a little digging from my end, and I think I've come up with some interesting shit." She pulled up a couple of files she'd earmarked on her computer. "I've researched a little deeper into this Phoenix Industrial Group—PIG, of all the stupid acronyms—and I found very interesting oddities in their financials. A considerable amount of money has been invested in paying for talent across the globe, including our four mercs as well as researchers and specialists, living and dead."

"What's hinky about that?" Amanda asked. "Many companies create foundations to pay for personal talent that doesn't get tied directly to them."

"Well, I traced the money back a couple of months." She scowled and squinted at the files to refresh her tired brain. "They've gone through a tiresome trail of hoops, but I eventually found a definite link to a very interesting company name."

"You know I don't like to be kept in suspense," the other woman stated petulantly.

"Pegasus. The money all came from Pegasus and has been funneled into the Phoenix Industrial Group for years. It looks like they've used it to send money into the Caymans and then pay it back to the executives as bonuses. It was usually only used for tax evasion, but over the past few weeks, much more funding has gone into the accounts and either remained there or been paid out for talent like the four mercs."

"These are Pegasus thugs?" Amanda demanded indignantly. "I thought we were done dealing with those motherfuckers around here. Wasn't that why Anderson was sent to the States?"

"Well, we'll obviously have to deal with them around here for a while longer." The hacker shrugged. She'd had a little more time to adjust to the reality and tried for patience. "So, how do you feel about tackling a couple of those motherfuckers while you're there on the French base?"

"Like I've waited my whole life for this." The response was immediate and enthusiastic. "Send me the address of where they're stationed. I'll call in a few friends, get suited up, and show these asshats what they're messing with. Well, remind them, I suppose. They clearly have memory issues."

"That sounds like a plan. I've already texted you the details. Happy hunting."

"Thanks." Amanda's grin was pure evil. "Tell Connie to jump up her own ass and die for me, would you?"

Anja laughed as the other woman hung up. She thought the constant bickering between Amanda and the AI was charming if a little odd. Humans and AI getting along was never a good sign.

She peeked into the camera feed from the bar, not entirely sure she wanted to see what had happened before. The bartender was still alive and conscious, which was a start, anyway. He'd managed to find his feet and scowled while he held a steak to his head to reduce the swelling. Amanda ignored his passive insults as she strapped her armor on. There were rules in the French base against walking around decked out in a full suit of combat armor, which explained why she only attached the power arms and shoulder supports. Nothing in the rules prohibited her from wearing pieces of it, after all. It really was fun to circle the rules with impunity.

The Russian shook her head and wondered if coffee would help. This was simply one more mission she would have to provide support for. Living the free life had its drawbacks, she decided as she pulled up the security feeds across the French base to assist Amanda. Connie would play her part too, and it wasn't like either of them had anything better to do.

"You heard what she said, right, Connie?" she asked.

"I did, yes," the AI replied. "And you can tell Miss Gutierrez that the sentiment is well-received and returned in kind."

She couldn't help a small smirk in response.

CHAPTER SEVENTEEN

S mythe had officially begun to regret the whole stupid fucking endeavor.

It wasn't that he was cowardly. There were things he'd done and times when he'd put his life on the line that many would even consider heroic. He'd never subscribed to that attitude, though, and had simply done his job. The difference was that at the time, he had done those crazy, stupid, and heroic things for Queen and country, or so he'd assumed, and there had been a reason to do it. If nothing else, even during the last couple of years when dissolution had seeped into him, he'd done it for the men who relied on him—his brothers in arms.

He was still protecting some of them. It had all changed, though, by virtue of the fact that they hadn't been ordered out there. Instead, they took money to do this, and a good chunk of money besides.

That said, there wasn't enough cash in the world to get him out there again, not when he knew the kind of hell that waited for him.

The creatures had become an endless nightmare. He couldn't even begin to speculate where they all came from, but they seemed to almost evolve on the spot. The deeper the small team ventured into the Zoo, the more the enemy appeared to change and the more of them that died. Ammo would soon be a problem if the flood didn't stop.

Of course, the real problem would be the people who still needed to shoot. Dutch was injured, and his suit wasn't at a hundred percent so he couldn't bulldoze them out of trouble when the monsters tightened the circle as they so often did.

They pushed on through the night and the monkey-like creatures—Jacobs had already named these but Andy had difficulty in remembering said name—maintained their constant harassment. After a few hours, though, changes in their physiology were very evident, even to him and he wasn't a scientist or even a local in these parts. The scientist would most likely monitor these changes himself and probably recorded them on the HUD of his suit to keep for posterity.

Wait, no—these specialists were paid for additions to the databases held by the US base. He'd read up on that during the flight over there. Maybe the kidnapping would be forgotten with the unexpected windfall of a veritable flurry of new creatures that manifested continually before their eyes.

With his weapons ready for combat again, Smythe stepped into the line that was held in the center by Dutch. His suit was slow as a result of the damage, but it was still the sturdiest. It seemed odd that they hadn't equipped everyone with the massive tanks. Well, aside from the cost and the fact that they were far slower than the others and could probably be swarmed by the monsters that attacked them.

Still, the idea of all that heavy-duty protection had its appeal.

He pulled the trigger and eliminated a couple of the creatures that launched from trees above them. A trick Jacobs had taught him was to time them from the point of their jump to about halfway to the ground and use those as a point A and point B. The kid had gone through the details of it, but the science talk had all but put Smythe to sleep. It was basically calculating trajectory, something they taught in long-distance shooting training, which meant there was a much simpler way to explain it.

The dude did seem like the kind of person who liked the sound of his own voice. While he gunned these mutants down like a pro himself, he could do all the talking he pleased—which, given his track record, would undoubtedly be a hell of a lot.

"Oh, shit!" Campbell's shout drew Smythe's attention to the treetops. He gaped in the split second he'd had to see the massive creature climbing effortlessly through the branches. Something that big had no right to climb trees so quickly. Four eyes and a massive tail presumably made it easier to negotiate the upper reaches of the canopy.

It wasn't really relevant, he thought stupidly as the monster swooped into a concerted attack focused directly on him. Reflexively, he pulled the trigger on his assault rifle and the weapon responded comfortingly. The seconds before the mutant impacted with him were enough to see no visible reaction to his attempted defense.

Smythe tried to avoid the creature but was only partially successful. It caught him in the chest and hurled him hard into a painful slide across the jungle floor, one stopped only by a sizeable root that seemed to pack a comparable punch of its own.

"Fuck!" he managed to shout, and he scrabbled and flailed in an effort to find his feet. He could see the holes left in his suit from its claws, although nothing had driven through to his chest, thankfully.

The battle, however, was far from over. There seemed to be no apparent injuries from his rifle fire, so he simply resumed the strategy. He had a couple of smoke grenades in his pack, but he doubted they would help much against something with four fucking eyes.

Which, he realized with a kind of vague horror, was what had killed the specialist on their first run. What was his name again? Dr. Laurent? The critter's tail had taken his head right the fuck off.

Honestly, the kinds of thoughts that came to your mind when you were about to die were fucking weird.

An overpowered hybrid suit boosted up the tree he was backed up against and thankfully diverted his mind. Jacobs shinnied a little higher but the monster, even with its four eyes, only saw him at the last second and way too late. He flung into action and landed on the creature's head with his knee in a perfect three-point landing, pushed his rifle into his target's upper right eye socket, and pulled the trigger three times. Nine bullets proved to be enough to kill the critter, which immediately sagged and went limp.

"You have to keep your eye out for these fuckers," the scientist said with a grin and offered a hand to help him up, which he took gratefully. "They like to move in the treetops and wait for an easy meal. You'd think they'd be right in the middle of things given that they're practically bullet-proof. I guess they've developed serious intelligence during their time here."

Smythe looked around, still a little shell-shocked, as they gravitated to the rest of the team. "Did you really do a superhero landing to kill that bastard?"

"How cool was that?" Jacobs asked with a chuckle. "The guys in the simulator think I only do that in the game. The bastards forget that I like to bring my work home with me."

"What does that even mean?" he asked, not entirely sure he wanted the answer.

"I don't know. It sounded cooler in my head." He shrugged and added with a grin, "I'll take the coolness, though. I get time to practice in the simulators, and if it works, I try it in the real world. Enjoying your work is half the job around here."

"What's the other half?" From what he'd seen from the kid so far, he already knew what the answer would be.

"Surviving," Jacobs answered in an overly dramatic, raspy voice and punctuated what he'd said with a couple of shots into the veritable line of monsters that now launched a concerted attack.

Yep, he'd known that was coming. And honestly, he didn't really mind. The kid could talk all he wanted and make all the jokes he wanted if he kicked ass like that.

They had made a slow start. There was no telling where Sal and his kidnappers were headed so the team had to rely on a guess based on the fact that there was far more chatter about what happened with the patrollers around them than about any mercs with an unwilling specialist in tow.

"Did you hear about that?" one of the radio contacts asked after they had raised them to ask for information. They hadn't had anything to share and were either very happy to play with fire or merely stupid enough to not realize they were talking over the open radio.

Courtney knew more than her fair share of the men and women who made up the armed forces on the various bases near the Zoo, and she could say with a good degree of certainty that either option was more than likely. All things considered, these guys tended to be either that stupid or that inconsiderate, and in some cases, a little of both.

"Hear about what?" one of the others asked. From the amount of static, it was clearly someone from another team close enough to be heard clearly but not in their little group.

It hadn't been all that long ago when they weren't able to get any radio signals thanks to the goop in the trees releasing what everyone still hoped was harmless radiation. Sal had been instrumental in helping to develop comms that could pierce the problematic Zoo. They'd succeeded up to a point. There were some things that simply blocked every signal but still, they were now at least able to communicate fairly reliably over distances of up to five kilometers. The white noise started beyond that, which meant the second team was outside that range.

Then again, even that wasn't guaranteed. The Zoo would seem to behave for weeks and sometimes months on end before it once again interfered with even basic comms along with everything else. It was like it simply waited for them to get comfortable before it harassed them once again. Still, it was working for now, which might or might not be a good thing depending on your perspective.

"Salinger Jacobs had his ass kidnapped," the first team leader said and sounded like he tried to contain his laughter. "He was roofied on the French base and dragged out here."

"Isn't he the guy who can drink anyone on any of the bases under the table?" another voice from the second farther away asked, the tone a little skeptical.

"That's what I've heard anyway," said the first man. "It seems that tolerance doesn't extend to whatever drugs they used on him."

"Yep." The second teamer laughed. "There are a couple of pots going at the US sector and the other bases over whether he'll make it."

"Seriously, I've seen that guy's reports. Him surviving in the Zoo shouldn't bring any amount of money in a betting pool. Who's taking those stupid odds?"

"The kind of people who know he has two girlfriends who know their way around their guns and suits and are known to have temper issues." The man chuckled. "It seems the higher odds are that he survives until they get their hands on him and they end up killing him themselves."

"Hey, assholes," Courtney interjected over the comm

system and shook her head. "You do know you're on the open channel, right?"

A moment of silence indicated that either they didn't know or had apparently hoped the Heavy Metal team would be too far away to hear what they said.

Either option was equally likely.

"Ye-es?" one of them finally ventured and ended the prolonged word with what sounded like a question mark.

This wouldn't be the brightest moments for the men in the armed forces. But not the darkest either, she thought with a soft smirk.

"If you guys are putting money on someone who's saved your collective asses, one way or another, directly or indirectly…" Courtney said. She knew she had their attention since these assholes seemed to think that she and Madigan were bloodthirsty psychopaths. "If that's what you dumbasses are thinking, maybe you should also think about talking about it on comms that won't give us your names and addresses on base, right?"

When no answer was forthcoming from them, she didn't care if she'd hurt their feelings. She didn't even care if they would lock their doors more carefully over the next few weeks. They didn't deserve to sleep comfortably and securely.

Courtney glanced at Madigan. She had to be the one to take this the hardest. While Sal could take care of himself, she knew the woman took her role as the gunner of Heavy Metal very seriously. If something happened to one of the members, she would feel it was on her, regardless of the fact that it had happened outside the jungle. And if something happened to Sal while he was out there in the Zoo, she would feel even worse about it.

Telling her it wasn't logical to feel that way and that what happened to Sal was no one's fault but his captors' wouldn't change how she felt. She was a smart woman, and she would have put that shit together a few hours into this mess.

Nothing about this was logical. She felt the same way her friend did, and she would have to deal with that too. Knowing Madigan, though, she assumed dealing with it would end very poorly for the kidnappers.

"I have something on my motion sensors," Addams called, took a cautious step forward, and peered into the underbrush. Something large moving in their direction was never good but not necessarily the worst either. Courtney still believed the worst thing to happen in the jungle was the living vines that snatched people off the ground and hauled them somewhere that was dark, dank, and digestive.

"Bearing south-southwest but approaching fast," Davis added. He drew his assault rifle and checked the weapon visually, even though it was supposed to be connected to his HUD. There was something about not trusting the suits they used and having to confirm shit with their own eyes that were so very military in all these men. They were used to their weapons and armor being made by the lowest bidder. Simply trusting them to work was a mistake most men didn't survive.

Of course, they were currently working for Heavy Metal, and while the gear they wore wasn't the highest quality, it was still better than what they were handed by the government when they went on one of the patrols or acquisition missions into the Zoo.

Courtney stepped in to stop him from moving forward. Madigan had altered her course, and with the mini-gun-equivalent strapped to her shoulder, there wasn't much she couldn't eliminate on her own, one-on-one.

"She needs to vent a little on that poor, unfortunate critter," she explained on a private channel, one that excluded Madigan for the moment.

"Are you sure?" Davis raised an eyebrow and she simply nodded as the group turned to watch the woman march her eight-foot-tall, three-and-a-half-ton suit to where one of the T-Rex mutants lumbered toward her. The fact that it hadn't already attacked meant it probably hadn't planned to. They had most likely intruded on the damn monster's territory and it wanted to see what kind of idiot was stupid enough to do that.

Madigan came to a halt in front of it and the two adversaries studied one another in silence. After a few seconds, the monster took a step forward and roared loudly enough that Courtney felt the vibrations through her suit.

The woman barely flinched, though. She turned the speakers on her suit on to deliver an equally impressive roar of her own. The ploy seemed to have little effect, however, and rather than retreat, the animal prepared to charge.

The mini-gun on the woman's shoulder swiveled and opened fire, not at the monster but at one of the nearby trees. Hundreds of bullets chewed through the wood to fell the tree so it dropped onto the back of the now enraged dinosaur. The enormous bulk toppled, and Madigan vaulted up, powered by the jet packs on her boots, and landed with a hard punch delivered to the creature's muzzle. Its roar of pain was cut off when one of her boots impacted hard on its neck. It wasn't enough to break the skin but a loud crunch made Courtney flinch.

Madigan hammered a couple more punches aimed at the monster's jaw and eye before it managed to pull itself from under the weight of the fallen tree. By this time, it had no interest in a prolonged fight. As it heaved itself to its full height, she drew the massive assault rifle holstered on her back and the mini-gun arced to aim at it the beast as well.

The creature was smart, however. It knew the fight was over and that if it pushed the human's patience anymore, it would be turned into the Zoo's variety of Swiss cheese.

It tried to intimidate her with a weak growl, but she simply repeated her roar in response. The mutant took the hint, turned quickly, and shambled off in the direction from which it had come. It favored its right leg, but more impressive was the way its head slumped almost to the ground. Either Madigan had done serious damage to its spinal column or its spirit was thoroughly crushed.

Either one sounded likely, but she had no desire to know more.

"Do you feel better?" Courtney asked and walked to where Madigan wiped ineffectually at the blood on her suit with an armored hand.

"It's a start," her friend replied with a firm nod. "A small start."

CHAPTER EIGHTEEN

This shit would not let up, Smythe realized. They were deeper in the Zoo than most of the teams usually went these days, and the jungle seemed to know it. The creatures didn't follow any kind of steady attack formation. Instead, it was as if they were sent in waves like the Russians had done in the Battle of Stalingrad. They seemed to know that the humans couldn't be defeated without a fight but also that they would run out of bullets eventually.

"Save your ammo," Dutch called from the center of their little line. The Gatling on his shoulder had run out a couple of hours before, which meant all he had to fight with was his assault rifle and the heavy fists of his suit. His armor had a knife large enough to be a machete attached originally, but the damage he had taken included the knife and left it as nothing more than a useless hunk of metal fused to the sheath that was supposed to keep it sharp.

Smythe checked his assault rifle. He wanted to visually inspect the bullet count attached to his heavy right arm.

There were six, maybe six and a half magazines' worth of bullets to be loaded into the empty mags plus the two he had already lined up for easy access. He also had the knife on his hip and a couple of smoke grenades that had been handed to them on their first entry into the Zoo.

It wouldn't be nearly enough. They were still a good distance away from whatever Dutch knew they were looking for, and if they wanted to make it all the way back, they needed to consider packing up, turning around, and getting the fuck out of Dodge.

His concern was shared by his teammates. They had fought through most of the night, and the fact that dawn was coming soon wouldn't change much of anything. These creatures didn't seem to have an aversion to sunlight and even if they had, it was doubtful that much sunlight would actually reach them on the jungle floor.

Dutch looked exhausted. The first aid functions in his suit had sealed off whatever had been bleeding, but there was still internal damage that needed treatment. Even though the man wouldn't admit it, he was one bad hit away from the big goodbye.

Most of the others remained somewhat intact. Campbell and Murphy's suits were still in good shape, although they had complained about some errors that popped up here and there. Smythe scowled at the holes left in his from when the huge creature with the four eyes, claws, and whiptail had almost had him for lunch before Jacobs had played the hero.

The scientist was the only one of the five who looked like he was enjoying himself. He chose his targets well and the way he moved made everything seem easy. His suit still seemed to lack any defects or damage, and his conservation of ammo meant that, from what he could see, the kid could keep going for days.

Hell, he'd probably done way more at some point. This was most likely only a milk run compared to what he usually had to do. Smythe had seen his file and the number of his contributions to the databases.

"I still remember the time when these locusts didn't have tails," the scientist said while he lowered his weapon and drew a long blade from his back. It looked something like a sword and was used like one to smoothly chop the stinger from the tail of one of the monsters under discussion. "Back on my first trip in, they were mostly peaceful little creatures, curious about what the fuck we were doing in here. They only got violent when you plucked a Pita plant or something like that, and even then, were mostly used as cannon fodder. Dangerous in large numbers, sure, but they didn't even have anything that could penetrate some of the older suits of armor."

"Huh." Smythe struggled to maintain his position in the line as they proceeded. The kid's nonchalant attitude to all this death-dealing had really begun to wear on his morale.

Jacobs raised his rifle and activated some kind of auto-targeting and firing mechanism. It continued to fire as he stopped to pick up the stinger he'd cut off. The monster, suddenly missing its primary weapon plus a piece of its body, struggled to rejoin the others that pushed forward aggressively.

"The first time we ran into one of these, the venom they had was a very strong and concentrated dose of hemo-toxins—like rattlesnake venom, but much more powerful and fast-acting," the scientist explained as he inspected his sample. Crazily, his assault rifle still rattled rounds into the creatures attacking them. "But after a couple of months, we had to do more testing after they stung a couple of people and they died despite having anti-toxins applied. We found neurotoxins had been added. And ever since then, we've noted changes here and there to the biology of the venom they make."

Smythe looked at the kid in the brief moment of silence in which his assault rifle reloaded. "Who the fuck are you talking to?"

He grinned. "Well, excuse me for assuming you dumb-asses would want to know what is trying to eat you and kill you dead—in that order—but since you ask, no, I'm not talking to you. I'm recording all this stuff for posterity, as is my right as a specialist on a team heading into the Zoo. So if you don't like it...well, watch me not give a fuck."

Smythe glanced aside and knew he would see Campbell grinning at him. That was one of his favorite jokes. It had something to do with the Flash, but he'd never been a fan so most of the time, he never enjoyed the joke unless Campbell was around to enjoy it with him.

Which he was, thankfully. But Andy wasn't in the mood for jokes today. He needed to stay focused on not becoming alien monster excrement. Which was difficult when there was a young specialist who liked the sound of his own voice while he proved exactly how much better he was at this than they were.

It wasn't fair. The rules that applied to combat every-where else in the world simply didn't apply in this little section of the planet infested with alien monsters. How were you supposed to prepare for something like that? Simulations certainly helped and he knew for a fact they would all be dead several times over if they hadn't had that time for preparation. But it didn't alter the fact that they had still entered the play woefully unprepared for the reality of their current situation.

"Do you mind if I continue to educate you on the dangers of what you're facing?" Jacobs asked. His head tilted in what might have been a challenge and he'd resumed firing at the monsters, almost like he didn't need to actually look at them while he did so.

"Whatever, jackass," Smythe muttered under his breath.

"I'm sorry, I didn't hear that, kidnapper," he snapped in reply. "Remember who brought whom on this little mission."

Ah. That explained it. He was being intentionally irritating and apparently knew exactly what buttons to press to make sure they remembered the lengths they had gone to in their attempt to bring him onto the team. Regrets suddenly ran high.

"Oh, shit," Andy shouted, his attention yanked to the matter at hand when a comparatively small creature suddenly erupted from the trees directly ahead. It tilted its head like it was curious and wings flared around its neck. The jaws opened almost ninety degrees and spat a glob of liquid at him. He'd seen these little beasts in the sim, and while he'd never thought he'd actually run into them, he quickly remembered what he was supposed to do with them. Exactly what you did when you caught on fire.

Drop and roll. The acid from that little mutant's mouth could melt through his armor like it was Styrofoam. He couldn't be sure if any of the droplets had hit him, though, and annoyingly, Jacobs was back in form. The scientist lunged and stabbed his blade through its spinal cord from behind. It jerked spasmodically before it fell.

Smythe checked his suit for smoking holes and, finding none, turned to the other man who, predictably, wore a knowing smirk. "You can't have that beastie melting your arm off, Smythe. You need that shit."

He chuckled despite his irritation and accepted the kid's offered hand to help him up before they rejoined the rest of their party. The team had drawn to a halt when the animals appeared to have had enough blood-letting—at least for the moment—and melted slowly away from the group of humans.

Smythe checked the visual perimeter and his motion sensors, and everything seemed to confirm that the animals were, in fact, withdrawing. He noted that Jacobs was quick to check the treetops first before he relaxed somewhat and turned to face the team.

"What's next, boss?" Campbell asked. Smythe couldn't tell if he was talking to Jacobs or Dutch, although the talkative scientist was the first to answer.

"We're running low on ammo and resources," he pointed out and sounded more serious now than he had during the firefight. "It's time to head back. If we stick around any longer, this place will throw the really nasty critters at us, and I don't want to be around here when that metaphorical shit hits that metaphorical fan."

The group paused and shuffled their feet. They'd listened to the specialist but now waited for word from Dutch. Even in the massive suit of armor, their leader looked like he was about to keel over, and he nodded slowly. "That sounds like a sensible plan. Lead the way, Jacobs."

The researcher nodded and chose not to gloat as he looked around and checked the map and compass attached to his HUD. It seemed that as yet, the Zoo hadn't chosen to fuck with compasses. Of course, the only way to discover it had would be to discover one was horrifyingly lost. "Follow me," he said and chose a more northerly route away from the French base where they had started.

No questions were asked, though. The exhausted men simply wanted this nightmare to end—or at least offer a small moment of reprieve. Smythe swore he would take a week-long nap if they ever made it to base.

They hadn't covered much distance before Jacobs raised his hand and called a halt. Andy tensed and anticipated a horde of mutants poised for attack, which was what usually happened when he paused their advance. When nothing displayed on the sensors, he turned to where the specialist knelt over a small plant with blue leaves. After a few seconds, he checked the earth around it with his hands and turned to Andy. "You have some space in your pack, right? Pick that and seal it."

"Why?" he asked but moved forward to do as he was told.

"It's new and therefore profitable." The response was clipped and matter-of-fact. "Something like that could bring up to seventy-five grand if you find the right buyer for it."

That was good enough for Smythe, and he eased the plant out gently and slid it into a sealed container. "Seventy-five thousand? Are you kidding me? Why the fuck is a glorified dandelion worth that much?"

"Who knows?" Jacobs shrugged. "Some rich old dude wants parts of his anatomy to work again like they did when he was in his thirties, and there's a chance this plant has the hormones or chemicals that can do precisely that. It's as probable that it doesn't, but stranger things have happened out here."

"Stranger than finding out that a plant is the fountain of youth?" he asked and grimaced as he tucked the treasure into his pack. "We're not being paid enough for this shit."

"Trust me," Jacobs replied with a suddenly serious edge to his voice. "That might be the smartest thing you've ever said. I'd recommend you guys have your contracts canceled, but I don't suspect there's anyone around here who can accept your resignation, right?"

He knew better than to answer that question, and when the other man resumed the steady march forward, he allowed himself to fall back down their line to where Murphy helped their leader keep up with their pace.

"Spit it out, Smythe," Dutch commanded, never one to beat about the bush.

"Do we really trust Jacobs?" he asked and fell in beside them. "How do we know he's not fucking with us? Or leading us into a trap?"

"We have to remember that he can't get out of here on his own and he knows it," Dutch pointed out. He sounded winded, which for him was a point of concern. "Hope, really. We won't get out of here without him."

"If you say so." His doubts reflected in his tone, but he agreed with the statement. They wouldn't make it out of the damned jungle without the little specialist's help and therefore had to hope he felt the same way about them.

Amanda had no idea why she'd so willingly stepped into this. She wasn't someone's hitman or anything like that or a fan of violence for its own sake. Generally, if some kind of fight was demanded, she always preferred to leave it at the point where the other party was willing to call uncle. She wasn't a violent person by nature. At the same time, she also knew it was sometimes necessary that people understood who they could push around and who they couldn't.

It was personal this time, of course, which definitely made a difference. Sal being kidnapped meant they thought Heavy Metal could be pushed around, and that was something she wouldn't tolerate. Even if she would no longer be associated with the brand, the people were her friends—and, dare she say it, family. Given that her own family had less than warm and fuzzy things to say about her life choices, the family positions were mostly vacant. Her Abuela was essentially the only one who still held a very permanent place in her heart.

She stepped into the location to which Anja had sent her. Some of the buildings in the French area were being used, but not fully. As she moved through the doors, she realized there weren't many security measures in place around her, which confirmed her decision not to enlist backup. She would have called the hacker to help her with those anyway, assuming the half-suit she wore could still connect with her.

If the defensive measures were any indication, she was unlikely to need assistance in the building itself.

Her entry revealed a couple of recently opened cases that usually contained suits of armor. She'd assumed the mercs were newcomers, of course, but the fact that someone was willing to drop millions of dollars on suiting them up meant there was something fishy afoot.

"Who the hell are you?" someone shouted from the other side of the warehouse. She turned to see a tall, lanky man in a lab coat with a pack of cigarettes in one hand and a lighter in the other.

Amanda didn't bother to answer. He didn't seem to be armed, but there was no point in making assumptions she couldn't verify. She sprinted across the room and covered the fifty or so meters in under five seconds, thanks to the power functions of the armor she wore.

She tried to be gentle given that the lab rat didn't seem the type to be involved in fistfights. Her efforts spun both lighter and cigarettes to the ground in a single motion and bowled him into the wall, which he bounced off to land with a strangled groan on the floor.

"*Putain,*" another voice said from inside what looked like a small office. "*Pas si fort, connard!*"

The second man stepped out and looked equally as shocked as the first.

Before he could do anything, Amanda had her sidearm aimed unwaveringly at him.

"Don't do it," she warned and shook her head decisively. "Whatever brilliant idea came to your mind, I can assure you that you'll be dead before you can enact it."

"You'll...kill me anyway?" He'd meant it as a statement, given his expression, but the hope in the tone added the sense of a plea.

"Nope, I'm only here to ask you a few questions." The armorer hauled him closer to shove him down beside his comrade. "I think you know what about."

"No, we don't," the first man protested. He seemed to have shaken off a little of the shock of being attacked.

"Your idiot mercenaries kidnapped a friend of mine," she said and shifted her weapon to aim at one, then the other, for emphasis. "Does the name Salinger Jacobs ring a bell with you idiots?"

"That's who they grabbed?" The lab rat looked genuinely surprised and even horrified. "Those fucking idiots. Is Sergeant Kennedy after them?"

"Yeah," she said and lowered her weapon, although she kept it handy and her guard up. They seemed to genuinely not be in the know about this. "And Courtney Monroe too."

"Shit." The first man groaned and shook his head. "We need to get out of here. Now."

"What?" she asked, a little distracted by the unexpected change of subject.

"We won't survive Sgt. Kennedy coming after us," the second man agreed.

"And you think you'll survive me?" Amanda asked and injected her annoyance deliberately into her tone.

"Well, you did say you wouldn't kill us."

"Right." He had a point. She cast a cursory glance around the room they were in. It had appeared to be an office at first glance, but it was actually a server room much like the one Anja had at the compound.

"Okay, boys, here's how this will work," Amanda said and fixed them with a hard stare. "You give me the passwords to all this, tell me how to operate it and get it running, and I won't hand you over to Kennedy."

They shared a quick glance that suggested compliance.

"We'll need an hour's head start to reach Casablanca," the second man said, his expression a little panicked.

"Get me into everything without needing to call my offsite specialist," she replied with a smug grin, "and I'll give you two hours. Oh, and you'll need to fix that shit right there too. I think one of you crunched it."

She pointed out the spot on the wall against which she'd thrown lab rat number one. It had looked like a regular structure but turned out to be hard drives mounted against drywalling. The man in question groaned.

"That was me," he said and probed his side gingerly. "Well, when you threw me into it."

"That's a great story." Her laugh drew a frown from her captive. "Tell me more about it while you fix this shit and get it working."

CHAPTER NINETEEN

This was pure unadulterated bullshit.

Having a mission put together this quickly wasn't in the rulebook, and the commandant knew it. Emergency missions could be called, of course, but only in the event of an actual emergency. And when said missions were called, the reason why they were pulled out of their R and R was usually included in the briefing.

No such luck this time. All Sergeant Alex Diggs was told was that they would conduct a rescue mission. For some unfathomable reason, no one would reveal who they were rescuing or where they were.

Of course, the suits provided answered the 'where' of the question, if only vaguely, but the details remained infuriatingly scant. The fact that the team was expected to move out as soon as they assembled was what worried him most of all.

Diggs had been torn while selecting his team. He didn't want to risk the really skilled members of his pool on a run they knew absolutely nothing about. That said, given that he would have to run the operation, he needed to find the people who would watch his back when things went bad in spectacular fashion—when, not if, his thoughts insisted.

With his suit on, he adjusted the shoulder straps and scrutinized the assembled group. The ten men who now prepared to venture into the most dangerous place on earth were representative of the types of soldiers available in the Zoo. There were those who looked nervous, including one or two newcomers and a couple of veterans. The latter, of course, cracked jokes in their usual laconic manner. This wasn't because they weren't as nervous as well but because they knew the best way to head into tense combat situations was to be as calm as possible.

"Do we have the details on the mission yet, Sarge?" one of the newer members asked. Despite his obvious nervousness, he still appeared to regard this with the utmost professionalism. That particular tendency wouldn't last much longer.

"It's coming in now." Diggs shook his head in frustration as the slow HUD worked through the mission brief that was currently uploading. "It looks like we're being sent in to help defuse a hostage-slash-kidnapping situation involving— Oh, shit."

"Oh, shit." The echo from one of the other members of the team had a hoarse edge. He recognized that it belonged to one of the older ones who knew who Salinger Jacobs was.

"Who is this Salinger Jacobs?" a recent arrival asked and looked curiously at the team. "And why the hell would we go there to save him? Kidnapping is bad, obviously, but if he's heading into the Zoo, is risking all our lives really the right choice?"

The sergeant flicked his gaze from one man to the next in sequence. Some seemed to share their comrade's doubts, but the others—mostly the veterans of the crew—knew precisely why they were going out there.

"For one thing, if Jacobs got his ass kidnapped, it means the rest of his Heavy Metal team is heading in there to break him free and then, very likely, to break him." Diggs chuckled when he recalled the stories around the somewhat colorful characters of Madigan Kennedy and Dr. Courtney Monroe.

"Huh." The young soldier looked even more confused than before. "That makes less sense. If there's already a team going in to save him…"

Diggs let the man's voice trail off before he answered. "Heavy Metal has a reputation for tearing shit up in the Zoo. And secondly, Jacobs has—either directly or indirectly—saved all our asses. Yes, even the ones who haven't met him yet since his work gave us the technology that has saved your lives at one point or another. We owe that specialist a trip into the Zoo to keep his girlfriends from murdering him after saving him. The little dude will owe us drinks for a fucking year."

"Girlfriends?" another one of the newbies asked, his eyes wide.

"Yeah," the sergeant snapped. "Girlfriends. But we really don't have the time to go into the details of this. Get yourselves ready for action. We'll leave as soon as the Hammerheads are gassed up, and I'll write anyone who's late up for...something that will lose you your commissions for the next six months."

He doubted he could do that but the threat must have been believed as the entire team spurred into action. Having to risk their lives in the Zoo without the cash bonuses paid for their efforts was the one thing that could get everyone moving like their lives depended on it.

Something intangible but frighteningly real permeated the Zoo. Madigan wasn't sure what it was, precisely, but something happening in the jungle around them made the hairs on the back of her neck stand on end. It was a particularly annoying sensation when she was encased in a damn nuclear-powered suit—one she still felt uncomfortable with, even if it hadn't shown any signs of defects.

She kept the mini-gun mounted on her shoulder on an almost constant swivel. The animals around them acted far more aggressively than usual and attacked them rabidly, no matter how many there were or what size the creatures were. Usually, they would avoid the humans to the point of circling out of their motion sensor range unless there was something that actively drove them to attack like the pheromones released by the Pita plants when they were pulled. Otherwise, they were either hunters hoping for an easy snack on unsuspecting prey or were simply not interested.

But not today. Even the tiny simians that didn't often venture down from the treetops threw rocks, pellets, and what Madigan knew had to be feces down at them.

It was like the whole damn Zoo was angry at something. While the focus didn't appear to be them, they still faced the flak from it.

"Goddammit, Salinger," Madigan grumbled under her breath and focused on a pack of hyenas that launched into an attack. The beasts were suddenly joined by a new kind of monster, powerful gorilla types with spikes protruding from their foreheads.

Despite the noise and the violence, Courtney had the time to look at her with her head tilted in query. "Is everything okay over there?" she asked and sounded genuinely concerned. Madigan didn't like that at all. They were friends and everything, but ever since they'd started out on this damn trip, the woman had hovered constantly over her like a maternal fanged panther.

"I'm fine," she snapped and yanked her assault rifle up. The heavy weapon kicked despite the power in the arm that carried it.

"Don't take this the wrong way, but you don't sound fine," her friend pointed out as she moved in beside her to cover the flank the mini-gun couldn't reach. The enemy numbers increased steadily, and they had no time to talk as they were thrust suddenly into the middle of a fierce firefight.

Their attackers had managed to isolate them from their team, which left Davis, Addams, and Xander cut off. They all had extensive experience in similar conditions, though. Even under pressure, both isolated units of the same team knew to connect with one another. Coordination, calm, and precision were the only things that had kept Madigan —and Heavy Metal by association—alive for the whole of their time together, and damned if that didn't show.

The jungle seemed to be able to tell when you panicked and there was little you could do after that except retreat and regroup, all while knowing that casualties would be sustained. Which begged the question, of course, of why she had thought a team this small would be enough to find Sal.

Madigan had begun to ask herself the question with brutal frankness, and just as honestly, she had to answer that she had really hoped they would have run into him by now. She would give him a punch, ask how he thought he could get away with something like this, imply that the way to pay her back for her efforts wouldn't be easy—and rather sexual in nature—and lead them the fuck out. A team of six would be more than enough to get the job done.

Well, that was the usual consensus. But the very distinctive but still elusive something different happening in the Zoo today raised her doubts. For one thing, Courtney had already pointed out at least five different animals that were new as well as the fact that some of them seemed to evolve into bigger and deadlier monsters before their very eyes. Not literally, of course, but the apes had only appeared with horns on their heads about a half-hour before.

They finally received a reprieve when the horned apes clambered hastily into the trees at a speed they had no right to be capable of and the motion sensors confirmed they were heading away. There were still a couple of stragglers hanging around, but the mini-gun could handle those. She hurdled the bodies they had left and even had to push a pile over before she reached the three men huddled together.

The evidence didn't look encouraging, she realized and pushed into a jog. Her overpowered suit would shake the ground with every step and a woman less secure with her self-image would feel conscious about that fact. She merely felt delighted by the power that came with the weight.

Addams knelt but she noted that he wasn't the one who was injured. Xander, the foul-mouthed patrolman she and Sal had gone into the Zoo with in the early days, had a deep hole in his hip. It looked triangular, like a rhino's horn had gored it, if smaller than she'd expected.

"One of those fucking monkeys," Davis said and brought her up to speed on the situation. "The critter attacked, ignored the bullet holes all over its body, and hammered its horn into him. It broke its own neck doing that, too."

Madigan knelt beside the medic. The man had retrieved his first aid kit and now treated the wound. It appeared that the horn had driven through the armor and into his hip to leave a massive, bleeding gash.

"Yeah, these fuckers get suicidal when they're riled up like that," she said and studied the injured man casually. He put on a brave face and gritted his teeth while their teammate worked, but a sheen of cold sweat on his forehead and the general paleness of his features told her how much pain he was in. He wasn't the kind to act like he was more injured than he was, she recalled. That meant he was hurting badly.

"Fuck," she snapped. "Can he stay on the move?"

Addams looked sharply at her, about to question why she had said that, but paused when he realized what she meant. If he couldn't move forward, they wouldn't leave him behind. He wouldn't make it back on his own either. They had some hard decisions to make.

"I can't tell," he replied after a short pause and returned quickly to his work.

"We only need to stop the bleeding, boss, and I'll be good to go," Xander said with a firm nod.

"No offense, but I wasn't asking you," she replied. "It's getting dark. We're in as good a defensible position as we'll find around here. Well, maybe we could get away from all the bodies to make sure we don't run into anything that will rush in to have a midnight snack. But we'll set up camp here. Monroe!"

"I'll be right there!" Courtney shouted back. She stooped to inspect a plant she had noticed.

"We're killing animals left and right around here and you're worried about plants?" Madigan asked and approached when her curiosity got the better of her.

"All the plants with blue on them have some kind of connection to the goop," Courtney reminded her. "It's always worth it to at least collect samples or something. Just get it in there and make it work."

She sighed and rolled her eyes. "Fine, but we need to get set up."

"I will keep it in mind." The other woman smiled but had already retrieved the devices she needed to collect her precious samples.

He never thought he would see the day when Russians would gather to help an American out of a mess. It was heart-warming, it honestly was, even if the group that had gathered weren't exactly the best of the best.

The commandant had told him he could take a team in to help Salinger Jacobs out of the predicament he'd been dumped into, and while the man owed the life of his son—as well as his current position—to the American researcher, there wasn't much he could do in terms of his power. People in the Motherland didn't like their local bureaucrats having too much weight to throw around. He could authorize the mission, but he couldn't sign off on it being an official operation. This meant they couldn't order men to join the mission. All those who went in had to be volunteers.

And again, having someone volunteer to come along and help an American scientist who had gotten himself kidnapped wouldn't be a popular call in most circumstances. Salinger Jacobs wasn't most researchers, however.

Most of the men had met him during his visits to the Russian base along with Kennedy—his gunner-in-chief—and Courtney Monroe, another researcher. The core group of Heavy Metal made their way to the base often to ensure that the watering holes on the other bases had enough prime-stock vodka.

Most of the two dozen or so men now assembled had either had their lives saved by the trio—or the lives of someone they cared about—or owed them enough that they would be willing to take on an underpaid mission to head in there and help them out.

Gregor, for his part, didn't believe in very much. One of the things he did believe in, of course, was in repaying the debt he had incurred when Jacobs and Kennedy had saved his neck when no one else would. It seemed odd, though, that it meant saving one's neck from the other.

Yes, he didn't doubt that Kennedy would be unhappy about what had happened, but having met the two of them and seen them interact, he doubted she would do much more than to leave him with a bruised shoulder. Or maybe a black eye. They fought like cats and dogs on meth but seemed to genuinely care for one another.

And Gregor was always a sucker for stories about true love.

"You all know why you're here," he announced when the last of those who had signed up finally arrived and began to put their combat armor suits on. "Nothing new—Americans need Russians to step in and help them out of a hole they dug for themselves. In this case, a man who has fallen in love with two women and now, those two women are coming for his balls. And maybe his cock."

The assembled men chuckled. The fact that Jacobs was romantically involved with both women was no secret. It wasn't like they'd tried to hide it or anything.

"You all know the only reason you're doing this is because you'd want people like us to assemble and help you if you were ever in a similar situation," Gregor continued once he'd connected the group of twenty-five, himself included, on a group comm line. "Not that most of you would be, but that's beside the point. We all have dreams, yes?"

They all agreed. Rescue when the chips were down was one dream most of them seemed to share, for some reason.

"Let's load up and bring our man out of that hellhole alive—and as intact as we can," he called. The challenge was greeted with a collective cheer and the team clambered into the APVs that had been authorized for their use. There were only four of them, but the Russian models were bigger than the American versions, for some reason. It would still be a tight fit with their numbers, but they didn't have all that far to go.

It would be worth it, he thought as he slid into the driver's seat of the lead vehicle and gunned the engine. He could joke all he liked but getting Jacobs out of that place alive—and again, mostly intact—would be a start to repaying what he owed the little man.

"One hell of a start," he muttered, shoved the huge vehicle into gear, and rolled out.

CHAPTER TWENTY

The bar wasn't quite as upbeat as he remembered it being. The place was still packed and people continued to talk loudly about the only situation that seemed to be on everyone's minds, but the atmosphere was more subdued, somehow. He doubted it was because of the lack of alcohol.

Bets flowed, hot and strong, on how the situation with the American researcher kidnapped on the French base would end. The pot had to be in the tens of thousands by now, and the people running the bar knew it was one hell of a draw. They were probably selling like crazy.

Other stories had begun to filter in as well, and he'd already heard a couple that made him smile rather than piqued his real interest. As he made his way to one of the barstools, he heard one of the local mercs talking to the bartender. Being an intelligence officer wasn't always a breeze, of course, but the fact remained that it was still his job to eavesdrop on conversations, whether he was interested in them or not. In this case, he was more than interested.

"The sensors we helped set up went crazy," the man said and the slur in his voice indicated he was four or five drinks in and nowhere near finding the bottom. "The specialists went wild about it. Something's happening out there in the Zoo. Something big."

"What do you mean?" the bartender asked and took his time to pour the man another drink.

"Something weird," the merc said with a firm nod but suddenly seemed to remember a need for caution. "I...I can't tell you what's going on. Only that—"

"It's weird, I got it," the bartender interrupted with a chuckle.

He nodded and leaned back a little in his seat. The word of something happening out in the jungle was still supposed to be confidential. There were numerous people spread across the variety of bases that had been set up around the Zoo, and news like this was the kind that would make people panic, and nobody wanted that. Especially not the people who would panic. If something concrete came from it, they would have to share the news and the appropriate measures would be taken. Otherwise, people who didn't need to know wouldn't.

"What's happening?" one of the other men—a soldier, judging from his garb—asked and leaned toward the talkative mercenary. "Another Surge?"

"It hasn't been quite like the Surge," he admitted cautiously and straightened a little defensively. Someone needed to take control of the narrative before people got the wrong idea. "Think of it more like a perfect storm of shit happening. Three groups sent in by the Chinese have trouble in their section, and one from the Israelis has gone dark."

"The fucking shit's about to go down," the bartender said with a chuckle and poured the officer his usual tall glass of lager.

"Something like that, yeah," he replied with a chuckle, took his glass, and raised it to the merc.

Most of the men seemed to lose interest in the narrative and returned to their own conversations. Thankfully, this wouldn't be the spark that ignited a flame. People tended to not listen to tales of doom and woe unless they started them or had nothing better to do. It seemed that Sal might well have—inadvertently, of course—saved the day with his entirely more appealing drama.

"Dammit, Jacobs," he whispered softly and took a long sip of his drink while he studied the blabbermouth out of the corner of his eye. "Why couldn't your ass have been kidnapped next week?"

"What do you mean, you have some experience with this already?" Dutch asked.

Sal shrugged. "Given that I was dragged out of my apartment in SoCal, flown all the way out here, and suited up to head out into the Zoo the very next day, you'll have to forgive me for drawing comparisons between this situation and my first trip out here."

Smythe nodded. The stories definitely had parallels. There had been less drugs and kidnapping in the original story, of course, but that didn't change the general tone.

"Of course, on my first trip, I wasn't nearly as familiar with how this place operates," the researcher said and helped to put the motion sensors up as he talked. "I was sent out here without so much as a pistol to defend myself with. The Zoo was a much safer place back then than it is now, but still.

"There was actually this time when we found a spring and this idiot took his helmet off to drink and maybe dunk his head—oh yeah, I know it was dumb. I was attacked by a fanged panther. It was the first time I saw one and thankfully, one of the gunners who was with me appeared at the perfect moment to kill it. The second one attacked him, though, and none of the others were close enough to help. What I ended up doing was pull a scalpel from my gear bag and attack the beastie with it. I didn't expect it to do much, to be fair, but fuck me if I didn't manage to kill it and save the gunner. Lynch—a total asshole. He died a couple of days later after trying to solo a Pita plant out of the jungle."

Smythe studied the man speculatively. That little speech was more than he'd said all afternoon while he'd guided them deeper into the Zoo, headed due north now. He wouldn't assume the man wasn't leading them into some kind of trap, and his suggestion that they set up camp seemed even more suspicious.

Even though it was getting dark, none of the crew were crazy about the idea of spending another night in this monster-infested place. But Dutch seemed to have put all his eggs in the trust Jacobs basket, and Andy couldn't do much but follow his lead. It wasn't like his judgment was all that good anyway, given that it was what had brought them there in the first place, so he really had no better alternative to offer.

They completed the temporary camp a few minutes later and retreated into the center of the nest created by the motion sensors and what claymore mines they still had left. Preparing the food was a dismal affair and was accomplished while Murphy helped Dutch out of chunks of suit that were broken and made an effort to repair them.

Silence settled around them while they ate. It was an uncommon sensation, Smythe realized. Jacobs had talked their collective ears off for the past few days. As the younger man pulled his helmet off, Smythe noticed lines of worry he'd not seen on his face before.

Holy shit. He'd almost forgotten how young this kid was—in his early twenties but he appeared younger, thanks to what was likely his Hispanic genes.

The fact that he looked worried wasn't a good sign. He'd put on a solid front for the group since they'd started and even he had to agree that the researcher, despite his irritating side, had been good for morale. Knowing that even the veteran—in Zoo terms, anyway—of their team didn't like what he saw was enough to send any hearts plunging to their stomachs.

Jacobs stared into the jungle, his hand on the sidearm he seemed to always have close to him. The sword that had been a part of his suit was clasped in his other hand. It took Smythe a couple of seconds to realize what he heard, and that only came because he still had his helmet on and his HUD scanned for the soundwaves automatically.

A low roar was followed by what could have been gunfire—or could have been chattering from the hyenas that seemed to follow the larger monsters around for a free meal. It was weird how they were the only creatures Smythe hadn't seen evolve much since his arrival.

It was weirder still how the researcher had heard something that he had needed his HUD scanning for sound waves to pick up.

"Well, damn," Jacobs said and narrowed his eyes.

"What's up?" Dutch asked when he noticed both men looking around. "Do we need to load up again?"

It took the younger man a couple of seconds to respond, and when he did, he settled onto the ground with a shrug. "No." He sighed and shook his head. "But the Zoo isn't pleased. Someone's getting fucked up tonight. On the bright side, I don't think it will be us."

"Why is that?" Smythe asked, ever the skeptic of the man's abilities as the Zoo Whisperer.

"Call it a feeling." He seemed unconcerned by his companion's doubts. "A hunch, if you will. Get some rest. I'll take first watch."

"You took first watch last night," Campbell pointed out. "And are therefore the only one who didn't get any rest."

"And yet I'm the one who still doesn't need it." Jacobs chuckled wryly. "Don't worry about me, big guy. I can handle myself. Get some rest. Consider it an order, if you like."

Campbell backed down quickly, and Smythe assumed it was because the man really did need rest. Dutch was already nodding off, probably thanks to the painkillers Murphy had supplied to help him with his wounds—which looked to be healing nicely—before he continued to fix what he could on the man's suit. That left Smythe at something of a loss. He didn't feel ready to sleep yet, so he moved to where Jacobs inspected a small plant that grew inside their camp.

Weird. Andy didn't recall seeing it before.

Jacobs turned suddenly, his hands on his weapons, and Smythe took a step back.

"Oh… Fuck, don't sneak up on me like that." The researcher laughed and turned to the plant again.

"Sorry." He meant it, which surprised him a little. "What's on your mind, kid? Why are we heading north? That's away from the French base and you know it."

"My first thought was that we would be heading in the direction where my team would come from if they were to mount a rescue operation," the researcher replied, his attention still fixed intently on the plant. "If not that, we would still be heading into territory I'm familiar with. I know the Zoo changes considerably on any given day, but if you stick to one section long enough, you can start to predict how it might change."

Smythe nodded, even though he didn't understand fully and probably never would. "Do you really think they'll come for you? Your team, I mean?"

Jacobs shrugged. "I hoped they would when we first started out. A while after that too, if I'm honest, but seeing the kind of shitfest we have around here now… I actually hope they're safe somewhere else."

He grimaced and part of him hoped the same thing.

They'd never intended to involve others in the crazy mission. The researcher flashed him a glance that seemed encouraging.

"Seriously, get some rest," he said and patted him on the shoulder. "I'll wake you in a couple of hours. I actually do need some shuteye."

CHAPTER TWENTY-ONE

There was an upside to having a fifteen-man team join you on a trip into the Zoo. It wasn't only because there was safety in numbers out there, although that did play a major role in it. For the most part, the more people you were with, the more the monsters of the Zoo that wanted your ass dead avoided you. They were smart, in a way—at least in the way they knew they wouldn't be able to take a team on without a serious numerical advantage. And that advantage had to be multiplied categorically with each new member of the team they attacked.

Which...no, not quite fifteen men, Lance Corporal Ben Wu acknowledged as he studied his team. Three of them wore the light army-issued specialist gear that was basically glorified hazmat suits with hard drives attached to them. Well, they had a couple of powered features, mostly around the legs, and they issued them with weapons too. These were mostly sidearms but did make them a little less helpless out there in the Zoo.

Which meant they counted for...maybe half of a fully

suited and armed gunner? Maybe? In effect, he was in the jungle with what was essentially a thirteen-and-a-half-man team, but the beasts and monsters around there didn't know that. They would hopefully see fifteen humans and steer clear.

All this was the basis for his annoyance when their orders came in through their satellite link-up, which thankfully did work in some areas, although the quality couldn't always be described as good. The commandant ordered that they make contact every twelve hours, and the latest command was to pull out of the Zoo as quickly as their spindly human legs could go.

There was no reason attached to that order, of course. There never was. But this was one of the oddest he had ever received. Seriously, why did they want a team that did in-depth research deep inside the jungle to withdraw before they were scheduled to return? It wasn't like they were in any kind of serious trouble or anything.

Wu had reluctantly issued the order for them to turn back to the APVs but damned if they would rush to comply. The specialists found new plants and specimens to collect every couple of miles, and the entire team would receive cuts from the commission that would come from those. Having this split fifteen ways would be marginal, at best, which meant they would only pull out when they ran out of discoveries to document.

The officer was quite content to allow the specialists to geek out over all the new flora that popped up like weeds. He was in this for the money. His kid had been approved to attend one of the upper-end private high schools in his region and the institution was as expensive as fuck. Reality dictated that his wife couldn't cover the tuition on her salary as a teacher, so it was all up to him.

They pushed on through the underbrush again once the specialists had finished taking their samples. They looked genuinely excited about what they discovered and collected. He wasn't sure why they were happy about fucking plants and honestly didn't care. The only reason it had any relevance in his mind was that it made other, richer people much happier and more willing to part with their unearned dollars.

He loved his job. Well, no, loved was a strong word. He liked to be able to earn a little extra scratch while doing it. And it wasn't that much more difficult than regular army tours as long as you kept your head low and knew what sections to avoid.

"Elcee, we have something approaching from the west!" one of his men cried and gestured a warning for the team to slow. Wu scowled and directed his scanners to the west. Sure enough, significant movement crept in their direction but not a worrying number. Not yet.

With any other team, he would have told them to get the heck out of the area and let the monsters have whatever they were coming for, but they had extra orders to work on for this trip. Besides the Pita plants and the new plants too, they were also offered a little bonus if they were willing to test some of the new firepower that had been handed down the chain. Knowing the pencil-pushers at the MSS, these things were probably a couple of years removed from the top of the line but it was still better than five years down from there. Or six, depending on where you fit into the hierarchy.

"Form up!" Wu called and twirled his power-armored hand to indicate that they should create a small circle with the specialists at the center. Hopefully, the non-combatants would still be able to assist with covering fire but not be put in danger thanks to the almost nonexistent armor they wore.

Seriously, hazmat suits would be more useful at this point. At least the men would be able to run faster.

The group huddled around their specialists and held their guns trained toward the west where the numbers of their would-be attackers steadily increased. Wu ground his teeth as he positioned his assault rifle and watched the targeting reticle appear.

"Incoming!" one of the specialists yelled, and Wu spun to catch a glimpse of a couple of fanged panthers that attacked from the treetops. As if they had actually planned it, the monsters gathered beyond the edge of their view surged into a combined assault. Their ranks, for now at least, seemed limited to what he thought of as the regular animals—locusts and hyenas—and a couple more of the fanged panthers launched into another attack from above.

Wu focused on the felines as his team unloaded a barrage of opening fire on the monsters that surged balefully toward them.

One of the gunners pulled back, removed a piece from his armor, and set it on the ground in front of them. He attached a bullet feed hastily and stepped away. When he moved, the mechanism activated, and an automatic targeting system swung the barrel to face the enemy. This was a new addition to the armory.

Automated turrets were something they already had on

the wall but having them powered by the new suits was an interesting addition, if a little flawed. They still needed to be wired up to the suits they were connected to and lacked their own power supply. Also, they ran out of bullets far too rapidly. In this case, where they had to defend a location, they would need as many extra guns as they could get so every small contribution helped.

Besides, he'd need to include in the report he would send to the people who developed these weapons the intriguing fact that the animals seemed very interested in attacking the turret rather than the people who controlled it. That was troublesome, given that someone needed to be connected to the damn thing, but it was an interesting development. Maybe they could come up with one with its own power supply as well as considerably more bullets. They would be able to set up camps with them and would be able to rest easy in the future.

Assuming Wu managed to get the report back to the developers.

"What do you want us to do?" one of the specialists asked when the fighting had settled into a hint of a break.

"Stand back and we will hold them," Wu replied. He reloaded his weapon and slapped a grenade into the launcher under it. "For our children, so they don't fight these monsters in their sleep."

As the mutants rallied, the officer stepped into position, launched the grenade under his barrel into the massed adversaries, and smiled when the explosion ripped a hole in their advancing line. There were too many of them to deal with individually and the turret was running out of bullets.

He did a double-take a second later when he registered the reinforcements they now faced. His so-called regular animals were joined by something considerably larger. The new additions resembled apes to some degree with pale skin, white hair, tusks, and a horn protruding from their heads. Their overall appearance, however, suggested the inclusion of a reptilian DNA. What would this fucking place come up with next?

The ground shuddered ominously as the massive creatures lumbered toward them. They were huge, even by the Zoo's elevated standards, and shambled forward on four legs. If he had to compare them to anything, he would have compared them to some kind of unholy combination of a Komodo dragon, a gorilla, and a rhinoceros.

He didn't like that, not in the slightest.

Wu highlighted the massive creature quickly on his HUD and linked to the other members of his team. Five of his men turned to face it and all had similar reactions as he had when they saw it.

"Shèngjié de gǒu shǐ!" one of them shouted, and the small force released a vicious fusillade at the first beast as it shuffled toward them. It moved with a single-minded purpose and trampled other monsters that happened to be in its way. The aggressive and almost arrogant disregard suggested it either didn't care or that there was some kind of hierarchy amongst the monsters.

While the soldiers maintained a concentrated stream of fire, it was difficult to tell if the bullets made a difference since the creature held its approach unwaveringly with no apparent injury or hesitation. The bullets seemed to have no effect on it at all.

"I know what will hurt you." Wu shoved another grenade under the barrel of his gun and locked it into place, pulled the trigger, and sent the payload in a determined streak toward the target. He missed the head, unfortunately, but the ordnance pounded home in the flank.

As he'd hoped, it did appear to have an effect on the creature. The effect, however, was not at all what he had hoped for. His expected solution didn't appear to do much other than bruise it and make it angry. The irate beast surged forward at a terrifying speed with wild roars of rage and defiance. The effort to vent its fury opened its jaws at an almost ninety-degree angle to reveal large, red glands beneath the ugly blue tongue.

"Get back," Wu shouted in sudden panic. "Get back now!"

His warning came seconds too late. A green, foul-smelling liquid spouted from the glands he'd seen and arced toward the gunner who tried desperately to reload his turrets. Smoke and his horrifying screams pitched above the sound of the battle as the acid covered his whole body, melted through the armor, and rapidly located the easily roasted flesh within.

It was time to bring his A-game. Wu hastily selected an option on his HUD as he dove for cover, away from the acid-spewing monster.

As he bounded to his feet, he could see that about six of his team had come up with the same idea has he had. It had been well reinforced that the rockets mounted on their shoulders were expensive and were only to be used when things were really, really bad.

He decided this surely classified as really, really bad.

Six of the soldiers launched their rockets at the same time. They were fairly small but the proprietary chemical blend inside delivered a significant concussive force. The tip of the missiles contained shrapnel to hopefully maximize the kill zone. He had been told they were supposed to be a kind of bunker buster, which was why it was perfect to test against these monsters.

The projectiles pounded into the beast at almost the same time and the resulting impact actually tumbled a couple of the gunners and one of the specialists with its force. Wu was able to see very little, but what he could make out—something very big and heavy walking around in the cloud of smoke— told him another volley was in order.

His men needed no encouragement, and another assault careened into the smoky target, harder and louder than the first. This time, Wu flailed and stumbled a couple of steps back from the effect of the explosion. They hadn't been kidding about the concussive force of them.

He moved in closer when the smoke started to clear and held his weapon trained on the massive figure in front of him. It lay on the ground, but with something that could spit enough acid to coat him in a layer of death, he definitely wouldn't take any chances.

After a moment of cautious scrutiny of the unmoving form, he approached and prodded the massive head with the barrel of his weapon. He narrowed his eyes and waited, poised to respond against a possible attack.

A quick study of the now confirmed corpse revealed clearly what had happened. Even with the explosive power of the rockets, they hadn't broken the tough hide. The bulging eyes, however, indicated that while the skin wasn't broken, the blasts had shaken the internal organs enough to kill it since they weren't half as durable as the creature's skin.

"Well," Wu said smugly and nodded approvingly at his team. "At least we know our rockets kill these monsters."

"That's the good news," one of the men said with a nod. "There is bad news, though."

Wu's gaze slid in the direction in which the man pointed, and he scowled when he saw three more of the monsters gather speed for a determined assault.

"That and I don't think we have any rockets left," another man said.

"Motherfucker," Wu snapped. "We retreat."

They didn't even pause to collect the dead man's dog tags. Assuming, of course, there were any left after the acid. Things were simply that desperate.

He didn't like running away from a fight, but discretion was the better part of valor. They would live to fight another day. Hopefully.

CHAPTER TWENTY-TWO

G regor had to admit he didn't know what the hell they were looking for out there. The Zoo had grown to massive proportions, and when it was both a dense jungle and changing all the time, there was really no way to tell where their quarry would go and why.

They needed to come up with a better plan than merely scanning the area as much as possible. The chances of them accidentally tripping over Jacobs and his kidnappers out there amongst all the possible monsters they could face were astronomically small. The contradiction in terms seemed entirely appropriate.

His men dismounted from their ATVs and inspected their surroundings. They had all joined this rescue mission on the assumption that Gregor would lead them, and as he stood there, he suddenly realized he didn't have a fucking clue about what they could do.

Fanning out wasn't an option. Splitting up wasn't either, not if they wanted to survive. They needed to come up with something better—and fast, before they ran out of time. Jacobs could be dead already for all they knew.

Gregor doubted it, though. If anyone could survive the Zoo, it was the little scientist. Hell, he had probably taken command of his kidnappers and now helped them get out alive. If so, they were probably all on the way to the American base and hopefully, extraction. Which wasn't technically a bad thing. They were close enough to that location and could easily set an intercept course.

Night was starting to fall. The monsters around there were notoriously more active as the darkness crept in, but they still needed to keep moving.

"We'll head toward the American base from here," Gregor announced, distracted for a moment when he realized his motion sensors had gone wild. "Our target will probably and hopefully head in that direction."

"And we should start moving now," one of the other members of his team said with a nervous scan of their surroundings. "Because it looks like the Zoo will try to kill us at any minute now."

"*Mudak*, I know that," he snapped and gathered his bearings while the men opened fire as the monsters barreled from the underbrush in ambush. It wasn't a large force but enough for them to have to constantly watch their backs and keep their lines of sight clear, lest they suddenly be overwhelmed.

Those defensive tactics were also better done while they were on the move.

"Form up!" Gregor shouted and eliminated a couple of panthers that tried to sneak up on them from above. "Lines of two. Have the heavier hitters on the ends and keep your firing lanes clear. Don't let anyone get too far ahead of you, and always make sure not to fall behind. I don't want to say that anyone who falls behind gets left behind, but you know it will happen anyway. Keep up the pace and we won't have to be in this fucking place for too long."

No one bothered to answer as the men fell quickly into their assigned formations and pushed ahead. He took position near the rear since he had the kind of tech in his suit that would keep track of the monsters that attacked them. More importantly, he would be able to fire at them with auto-targeting weapons mounted on the shoulder of his suit.

Jacobs had his own problems, so it didn't feel right to blame him for this, but damned if the kid wouldn't owe him big time for this. To the tune of about a year of free drinking?

Yes. That did put a smile on his face.

When conducting a rescue mission in the middle of very hostile territory, it was an extremely bad thing to be forced to stop. That was, like, rescue mission 101 and especially when time was of the essence and your target could be dead and shat out of a monster's rear end by now.

There was still no word on the open radio from Salinger Jacobs, and Diggs had nothing more than a generalized location to work with. It wasn't ideal, but then again, he had been sent out with less intel in the past and had gotten the job done. All he really could say was that there were no promises and they would try their damndest.

Well, maybe scratch that last part out. Being ground to a halt wasn't exactly trying their best, let alone their damndest.

He evaluated his team as they recovered slowly from the most recent attack. A handful were down. One of them was dead—one of the new guys. The team took a moment to locate the dog tags in the middle of the bloody, mangled mess that was his corpse after he'd been dragged into a melee with various creatures.

No, this wasn't a good development. A couple more were wounded and needed treatment before they resumed their march through the damn jungle. The team would definitely not proceed until they were patched up, and that was assuming they weren't embroiled in another battle before that happened.

Diggs made another quiet study of the vegetation to ensure they were alone for the moment before he jogged to the men who were receiving attention.

"At this rate, we'll probably need to be rescued," he grumbled under his breath and started to regret not having picked a full team of vets for this mission. Having new soldiers out there was like weak links in a chain. It made it difficult to keep moving effectively.

"How soon can you boys be up and running again?" he asked and searched the faces of the men present.

"You mean…" one of the medics started to say. He hesitated and glanced around before he continued. "What are our options?"

The sergeant shrugged. "We're on something of a timetable here, so if they can't be on the move in the next five minutes, we'll have to split the team. One group will continue the mission while the others stay here to escort the injured parties to the base once they're ready to move."

"We're ready to move in one minute, Sarge," one of the younger team members said with a firm nod. His arm had been bandaged and a teammate assisted to attach the suit to him again. Diggs nodded. He didn't want to have to leave anyone behind. It was a shitty thing to do, even when it was the right thing to do. None of the men liked doing it, and it was a killer for morale.

At the same time, death was an even bigger morale killer, one they would all prefer to avoid. They already had one man down and didn't need another.

Less than five minutes later, the men were all ready to march again, and Diggs heaved a sigh of relief at not having to make a hard choice about what they would do next. For now, they could keep moving and mourn the dead later. He felt they'd already hung around in one place for too long.

"And not a second too soon." One of the veterans echoed the sentiment as he shouldered a rocket launcher, strapped it to his suit, and connected it to his HUD so as to allow it to be fired automatically.

He'd barely spoken when a group of the mutants appeared as if out of nowhere and immediately made their aggression felt. Diggs simply couldn't understand it. Nowhere in the world were animals so willing to throw themselves to their deaths. He had to assume there was some kind of revival attached to it.

Perhaps that would explain why the bodies seemed to disappear minutes after death and how there were so many of them all the time, even when they were obliterated in such colossal numbers. It would be an interesting thing to investigate if they ever had the time or inclination to do so. A real-life application of the mostly Asian-religion belief of reincarnation—although, in this case, if you were killed, you were brought back as something that had taken a couple of steps up the evolutionary chain.

He locked and loaded and prepped his suit for combat again. Experience and training clicked in and he made sure to pull their team up and into a more compact formation this time to avoid having anyone else singled out and attacked.

They pushed on and thrust through the jungle as quickly as their suits could carry them. The team worked well together to eliminate those few animals that were able to keep up with them, although most hoped and prayed they weren't racing into some kind of trap. Stories abounded of the Zoo animals herding the unwary into an ambush.

And, Diggs reminded himself, they could only hope and pray they were headed the right way to find Jacobs, Kennedy, and Monroe. Preferably before any one of the three was killed by the other two, all of whom were top contenders for either fate.

"I still don't get how a guy like him can get two women like that," he said with a chuckle and shook his head.

"What was that, Sarge?" a newbie asked, his breathing a little hoarse.

"Nothing, keep moving," he snapped in response. The curt tone was a little unfair, but he didn't want anyone to realize he was actually jealous of a specialist.

Smythe couldn't decide if it was simply that Jacobs' tales of woe had started to tell on him, or if he had somehow become more attuned to the feelings and processes of the jungle around them. He sat quickly and kept an eye on the motion sensors that enabled the team to get some rest. Despite the apparent calm, he couldn't shake the unsettled feeling that hovered around him. His best description was that it resembled the stuffy air that settled in before the lightning storm of the century.

It wasn't something common where he was from, but a few of his American friends had told him it was a regular occurrence in the Great Plains that constituted most of the central part of their country.

No. A better description, he decided—or at least one that was the most relatable to the other members of their party—was the way a body would tense up immediately before a massive sneeze.

Yep, that was one way to take the power away from the Zoo. Imagine it gearing up for a fight as one big sneeze.

He toyed with the weapon in his hand and tried desperately not to either fall asleep or tinker with stuff to stay awake. With things this tense, even the slightest noise would wake his teammates. He wasn't normally the kind of person who paid too much attention to rules like that, but when it came to sleep, that shit was sacred. Especially after the day they'd had. Hell, make that the fucking week.

Nothing triggered on the sensors, but something didn't seem right to him. They had set their little camp on a hill left bare and close to nearby Pita plants, which gave them a rather fantastic view over the rest of the jungle around them. The location had enabled them to set up a small and well-defended position, and nothing could attack without being seen. Any assault would face a significant load of lead.

Of course, there were monsters out there that could, in fact, soak up an unholy amount of firepower, which meant this was an entirely temporary measure.

A soft noise made Smythe turn to where he could see Jacobs push up from where he'd slept.

"Christ," he whispered. "Why don't you get some sleep?"

"I haven't needed as much lately," he replied with a chuckle. "I don't feel a hundred percent rested, of course, and by the end of this, I think I'll need a week-long nap. Maybe a month, who knows?"

"I can sympathize with that sentiment."

"But yeah, this is as much rest as I'll get while we're out here," the scientist grumbled and attempted to roll the stiffness from his neck. "It's not the best, but better than nothing. Any movement?"

"Not even a little," Smythe said. "If things are this calm, why the hell aren't we moving the hell out of here? Shouldn't we be on the move instead of waiting around here like sitting ducks?"

The scientist flashed him a quick glance before he stood, pulled himself to his full height, and stretched. "Do you feel the tenseness in the air? It usually means something's about to happen and you really don't want to move randomly through the Zoo when that shit goes down. We're in a well-fortified location with lines of sight all around, which means we can have some rest before the worst of it starts."

"Don't take this the wrong way," he said after a moment and looked the kid squarely in the eye. "But I actually thought you were trying to get us killed out here."

Jacobs laughed. "Don't think it didn't cross my mind. But between you and me, I won't get out of here on my own. I need you gents to stay alive so I'll do my best to return the favor. As long as you don't plan to shoot me in the back, of course."

Smythe nodded and was about to respond when his companion suddenly tensed and scanned their surroundings.

"I feel it too," Andy said a few seconds later. The sense of pent expectancy seemed to evaporate from the air, which meant the metaphorical sneeze was about to start.

"Start waking the team," the scientist said and immediately reverted to the man who did his best to get them out of the Zoo alive. "I'll give our perimeter one last check before everything goes to shit."

"Aye, aye, Doctor." Smythe smirked and gave him a mock salute.

"I'm not…"

"Not a doctor. Sure, whatever. The way I see it, you've earned the title. I won't call you that again, though, so savor it."

"Will do." The younger man smirked before he moved to their perimeter, careful to avoid the claymores.

CHAPTER TWENTY-THREE

"What are you looking at?" Courtney asked.

Madigan didn't answer immediately. She wasn't sure what it was she saw, to be honest. Still, if she had to put money it, she would have bet something along the lines that a firefight had happened there.

None of the bodies were around, of course, which was fairly standard for a jungle that always seemed to reclaim its dead, but there were other clues. Sap oozed from the trees that had been impacted by the shooting, the ground had been scuffled, and a hundred other different signs all indicated that someone had sprayed and prayed in this area, and not too long before.

It was hard to tell in the dark but at this point, all she really had were assumptions.

"Do these fighting tactics look...uh, familiar to you?" she asked and pointed to a slashed section of a tree trunk—it really did look as if it had been made by a damn sword—and a couple of boot prints on the bark of another tree.

"Someone's climbed all around the trees," Courtney

agreed, her eyes narrowed as she searched for additional clues. "That sounds vaguely…"

"Yeah, vaguely like Sal," Madigan completed the sentence she'd allowed to trail off. "He does like cavorting and doing his stupid if admittedly awesome superhero landings whenever possible. Which, speaking of…"

"Yeah." The traditional tracks of a three-point landing were repeated two or three times across the ground.

"So, this is Sal?" Madigan sounded like she was afraid of getting her hopes up. "Is this the first trace we have of his whereabouts?"

"I'd give that a tentative yes."

"That motherfucker." She looked relieved for the first time since they'd started on this trip. "You know, I'd bet he had the time of his life around here, you know? Just running and gunning and showing off to the new guys or something."

"You know, I think you're right." Courtney chuckled, her own irritation balanced a little by amusement.

"I will fucking kill him." Madigan tensed and straightened to look around at the seemingly quiet jungle. A hint of movement displayed on her motion sensors, which told her they wouldn't be alone for very long.

"No, you won't." Her friend nudged her playfully in the shoulder. "Although I do think he needs yelling at for putting us through this. I know it's not his fault he got kidnapped. But the fact that he's run around with these guys, kicked ass and taken names without so much as bothering to try to find us himself, or get away by his own means? He needs a little reaming to…remind him of what's important."

She smirked. "I like you, Courtney. I think I might keep you."

"Lucky for you, I've considered staying already," she replied with a half-smile and a coy head-tilt.

"We keep moving," Madigan said and raised her voice to call the rest of her team in. Xander was recovering well but he couldn't move quickly. She toyed with the idea of leaving him behind for what felt like the hundredth time, but she knew Courtney wouldn't stand for it. None of the members of the team would. They wouldn't tolerate leaving people because her priorities were elsewhere.

They desperately needed a tug in the right direction.

She stepped in beside Xander and offered him her shoulder to help him along a little faster.

He made as if to reject her, but the way he limped and tried to stay on his feet meant she wouldn't be refused for long. After a moment's hesitation, he scowled and put his free arm on her shoulder. The other held his weapon firmly.

"Thanks," he muttered and managed to move a little quicker now. "I could move on my own, though. They repaired my suit and the first aid is working really good."

"It's no worry." She forced what she hoped was a non-threatening smile. "We need to keep moving, though. When we get to Sal, he'll have some special stuff that'll get you working in no time."

"You don't mean his—" Xander started to say but stopped when Madigan glared at him.

"Do you want me to drop you?" she asked. "Because I will."

"No, I do not," Xander replied.

"Sal has medicine and I've tried it. It works wonders, and it will not require that you and he be in any way naked or with each other. Do we have an understanding here?" she demanded and fixed him with a hard look.

He nodded quickly.

"Good." Her expression settled into a smile. "Okay, we need to keep moving and stay with the pace. We'll shoot anything that gets in our way and avoid most of the big fights. Got that? Everyone?"

There was no reason to not agree with that. They had a trail to follow now, and there would be no point in finding any other trouble. It wouldn't get them to Sal any faster.

Jacobs finished setting their fortifications up quickly. There wasn't much to add, although he had suggested Murphy hand over his heavy-duty grenades to be passed around to everyone so they would be able to push back any attackers that got through the claymores and the electrical fences.

Smythe still wasn't a fan of standing their ground. It felt suspiciously like a last stand they wouldn't walk away from but which would be sung about in ballads for years to come—and maybe turned into a film directed by Michael Bay. They would hopefully get an actor who was British to play him.

The scientist held his assault rifle in one hand and his long machete-sword in the other, and his gaze scanned the area ahead of them. The rest of the team had already made sure they had all the approaches covered. The lack of trees above them would make it a little easier to defend since they didn't have to always keep one eye above them to ensure that a panther or ape wouldn't try to pounce for an easy kill.

"What are you doing?" Dutch asked as he pushed a couple of rounds into the Gatling he had mounted on his shoulder. It wouldn't be much, but thanks to the fact that his assault rifle shared the same type of rounds with the weapon on his shoulder, he could spread the bullets around a little. They definitely had to conserve ammo, which begged the question of why Jacobs now attached tracer rounds to their ammo pool.

"We don't want to advertise our position here, mate," Campbell protested. He seemed to jump at the chance to correct him, but the young researcher merely rolled his eyes.

"Look, I'm no happier about this than you are," he snapped and fixed them with a hard look. "This shit was a fun walk for me until last night, but I think we can all agree that we're in deep shit and we should, in fact, advertise our position to anyone who might see it. Either I can put a flare up, or you will all die while we fight shit and I'll simply do it myself when you're gone. Either way, the tracers and flares will go up to indicate a vector to anyone close by to move into comm range. With our ammo running as low as it is, we'll stand a better chance of surviving the next few hours until dawn if we have more guns on our side."

Smythe looked around. The kid had a point and none of them liked it. They were low on bullets, and none of them wanted to enter a fray like the one they would inevitably face with nothing but sidearms and blades to protect themselves.

Dutch exchanged slow glances with each team member and nodded, telling them to do the same. They didn't like having tracer rounds, especially in dark conditions like this, but they did as they were told. There wasn't any time to debate the point, fortunately, and they all assembled again hastily when the motion sensors activated to alert them to approaching company. The warnings signaled all sides too, and there was no doubt in their mind that they were being converged upon.

Smythe still couldn't make out what they were looking at. The enemy was too far away and too jumbled together to be able to make out any details.

"We're setting the flares off every sixty seconds for ten minutes," Dutch called over a private comm channel. "I'll keep an emergency signal going out to help with that too. Just in case."

Andy nodded. He had felt taut and nervous all night. He was exhausted and his attitude wasn't helped by the kinds of problems they had going in before they'd even fired a shot. He breathed deeply and willed himself to focus. A sudden calm settled over him and brought his heart rate down. The control freed him to concentrate as he set up to cover as much of the line of approach he was responsible for as he could with as little movement as possible. This was what they were trained for. Not this specifically, but combat was combat.

"So," Jacobs said, took his place beside Smythe, and checked his flares and tracer rounds. "You don't know the women who are coming after me, so I thought you might appreciate a heads-up. When they get here—yes, when—I suggest you four shut the fuck up and let them yell at me and vent all their fear and frustration. Then, let them take their anger out on the Zoo. Believe me, they will be worth it. If you value your nuts, don't draw their attention before they've had the opportunity to offload their killer instincts onto someone else. And for the love of everything holy, don't piss them off."

Smythe nodded and leaned back to give him a punch on the shoulder. "Hey…good luck, mate. I hope you make it."

"Me too. I mean…yeah, I hope you make it too. Mate."

He smirked and looked away with a small shake of his head. Seriously, he was still a kid, this guy.

CHAPTER TWENTY-FOUR

Courtney still wasn't sure how Madigan could do it. They had managed to avoid most of the heavier fights, usually by moving around where the monsters seemed to have gathered in the largest numbers. This enabled them to flank them, thin their numbers to discourage an attack, and push on. Her friend was good at coordinating them to maintain a constant march through the jungle and the ever-increasing ranks of mutant animals. All while helping to keep Xander on his feet, she realized, no small feat in and of itself, given their circumstances.

And then they'd careened into a group of panthers—maybe a nest or whatever they called it. Burrows? Courtney thought she saw a couple of young rush away, but after a few seconds, she realized that they were actually smaller locusts without the stingers on their tails.

Did these monsters raise each other's young too? She would have to file that under the 'nowhere else on Earth does this shit happen' paper. For now, she simply raised her rifle.

Madigan had no interest in scientific observations. The woman looked pissed and damned if she didn't act it too. She used the size and power of her suit and fired both her weapons on all the creatures ahead of her as Courtney, Xander, Addams, and Davis covered her flanks.

She backhanded the first one that attempted an assault. It catapulted into one of the nearby trees with a soft crunch and the beast dropped without so much as a whimper. Courtney assumed it had been killed by the backhand before it ever saw the tree.

It was an impressive sight. Madigan treated her suit like it was an extension of her body, even with the extra appendages, and in their dangerous situation, it was all too easy to simply watch in wonder.

And cover her flank. No matter how impressive she was from the front, she was still vulnerable from the sides and the back. Courtney stepped in when she saw a couple of the creatures dart in from the side. She eliminated them quickly and precisely to make sure all her friend had to focus on was what she took her anger out on directly ahead of her.

Madigan pulled up after a couple of seconds and looked around. She pivoted her mini-gun in the opposite direction for maximum coverage to confirm that no other creatures lurked in readiness for another attack.

"Do you feel better?" Courtney asked again and this time, felt safe enough to laugh. The other woman smiled but no more than that.

"A little," she said and narrowed her eyes to focus on

something over Courtney's shoulder. It was an odd look and she turned to investigate. Lights flashed and flared in the distance. Out there, in the dead of night and in the darkness, when all you really had to guide you was motion sensors and night vision combined, they illuminated the jungle floor like they were neon.

"What the fuck is that?" Addams asked and helped Xander to limp forward.

"Those look like tracers," Madigan said, her gaze intense. Courtney was about to zoom in to make sure when she was almost blinded by a much brighter, long-lasting light that appeared on her visor. She took an involuntary step back and blinked a few times while her pupils adjusted to the sudden influx of light.

"And that's a flare." Madigan looked grimly at the team. "It looks like someone's in desperate need of help."

"Something isn't right." Addams frowned at Madigan, waiting for her order. "It could be a trap."

"Okay, far be it from me to put what the Zoo is capable of into a box or anything," Courtney said and looked at each one in turn before she continued. "But I don't think what we're looking at... Well, I don't think the Zoo is capable of anything like this."

"Someone's calling for help," her friend said, and her tone told them all clearly that her word was final in this case. "It could be Sal or it could be someone else. Either way, we'll head in to help."

They all agreed it was the right thing to do, but Courtney couldn't help a cold feeling in her stomach as they changed direction toward where the flare arced into a slow descent from the sky. She gritted her teeth and nodded. They were doing the right thing. And if that was Sal calling for help, so much the better.

He didn't need to overthink it this time. There were occasions when he had to peer into the depths of a place to see where the patterns were. Those were usually the moments when there was a high risk that he wouldn't make the right call. It was something that came with the business. When your job was studying people, you were bound to be wrong a fair amount of the time.

Lieutenant Brian Keys didn't need mistakes right now, though. Overthinking it would bring him nothing but hurt, and too many people like him would try to overanalyze a situation they were in. Inevitably, they would make it more than it really was. Besides, intelligence officers like him weren't usually paid to be big thinkers. They were merely supposed to collect data out there and transfer it to the people who were paid to think—people called analysts.

He'd been sent there to glean insight as to how the people felt around the US base, and his task was so much easier when done while with the people in the bar. Alcohol had a way to make it a little easier for all parties concerned.

Tonight, the feel he had was much less vibrant than he had experienced before around there. The last time, he would have called them subdued. Right about now, though, the word he would go for was somber. Anyone who hadn't managed to drink their eyes closed looked at the TV set up over the bar.

Satellite TV wasn't a common luxury in the base, even

in the bars, but it had been a splurge the commandant had felt was necessary for morale. Keys could respect the sentiment, at least. People who were stuck there were bound to start feeling antsy with all the developments starting to come out of the Zoo, and it wasn't a pleasant thing to see them lose their will to be there.

Not even a couple of weeks before, the entire crowd had been drinking and laughing and talking. The presence of the Zoo was there and large enough in their minds to make them drink more, but there was hope along with it. They were at the cutting edge of science and it carried them along on the crest of its weird wave.

Morale only started to dip when they realized that science had something of a cutting edge too.

Keys leaned back in his seat, content to wait for his drink as the bartender made his rounds. He attended to the regulars first, those who tipped the most.

"Did you see what happened with the Chinese guys?" one of the men at the bar asked his comrades. They might not have met each other before, but a kind of bonding experience came into play while they sat there, trying to forget their problems over drinks and a couple of football games being transmitted. The volume was kept low to allow for conversation between the men assembled.

Those seated around the counter turned to look at the speaker as he sipped his beer.

"What happened?" someone asked and finally gave in to the suspense.

"A group of fifteen were in there and tried to get out on orders from on high," he said and leaned forward on the bar top. The attention was gratifying, and he didn't want to waste a moment. "They were attacked from all sides and huge new monsters showed up to test them. They were running out of ammo, so what they did was to form an attack team and escort the three scientists on their teams—squishies, they call them there—all the way home. When the going got tough near the end, they formed a line and stopped the animals from attacking and let the three specialists escape unscathed. Well, no, not unscathed. I think one of them is still in the hospital, but…it's better than being dead, am I right?"

He wasn't wrong, apparently, as his small crowd hurriedly agreed. Injuries were usually better than being dead.

"Here's to those damn fine soldiers," the first man said and raised his glass and his voice to make sure that every man and woman in the bar could hear him. Out of respect, the whole bar quieted. Not that it was terribly loud to begin with, but the change was noticeable. "Those men gave their lives up for their fellows, and while they might not fight alongside us, they will go to that shiny place in the sky where all the heroes go. I don't care what religion you have, or if you're an atheist, and don't mean to offend nobody neither, but everyone's got that special place, right?"

There was a general noise of assent as glasses were raised throughout the crowd.

"Bless those guys for holding their line so their squishies could get out," the man stated and nodded to the crowd who still maintained their serious demeanor. "Here's to them. May we all have that kind of courage when the time comes to defend our fellow soldiers."

"Hear, hear," came the chorused call of the people assembled as they all raised their glasses to celebrate the fallen and the survivors. A short silence descended as people took long sips from their drinks.

Keys chuckled as he raised his glass as well. While morale was at an all-time low, there was a degree of brotherhood among all these people, even those who weren't on their own bases. They might not be at their highest point, but he wondered if the commandant wasn't a little foolish to think that people would be antsy. They were professionals—most of them anyway—and would take the good with the bad. They were in the armed forces, whichever division that might mean, and these men and women would stand their ground with the rest, no matter what the news around the Zoo.

He finished his drink quickly. The truth was that he felt a little maudlin and didn't want to feel that way while out in the open and drinking with others. Let them enjoy their time off without some scumbag from Intel spying on them. Just this once.

They were much closer now. Davis could tell because they could hear them and see the tracers that still slewed through the darkness. The flares had long since stopped, but Courtney had mentioned they had caught a couple of emergency signals coming from a location they estimated to be about two or three klicks away. There was still some interference coming in, but the fact that two emergency beacons had activated was an encouraging sign, apparently.

Sal was supposed to have his pinging in the background since he'd first triggered it to sound the alerts so the team could hopefully track him.

They finally moved close enough to hear the transmission properly, and Madigan joined the rest of them in listening to the message.

The first was a fairly standard emergency call to state the location and that it was an emergency in a dull, stale, and robotic voice. The second was a little less orthodox.

"Hello," said the familiar voice of Salinger Jacobs. "If you receive this message, it means I am in some kind of life-threatening danger. It also means I need someone to come and rescue my bony ass from what I can only assume is the Zoo being an absolute dick. All that to say… Help me, insert your name here. You're my only hope."

"And that's on repeat," Madigan said, and from what Davis could tell, she tried to repress a chuckle. "Nope, not even close. Getting me to laugh comes nowhere close to making up for all the shit he's put us through."

"Still, though, he has to know, right?" Courtney asked.

"Yeah, we'd better double-time it," Madigan said with a nod. "He has to be in some serious shit right about now."

"Right, let's get going people," Courtney said as the two women immediately picked up the pace.

Davis realized that both Addams and Xander were staring at him, waiting for an answer. It wasn't like they didn't already know that Jacobs was in deep shit, but the fact that he had the emergency beacon activated seemed to spur the two women on to make it there even faster.

"Come on, it's not that complicated." Davis gestured

irritably for them to pick up the pace in pursuit of Madigan and Courtney. "Seriously?"

"Just fill us in," Xander said. Although he still struggled noticeably, he managed to keep up with the rest of them. "We don't have time for games around here in case you haven't noticed."

"Right." Davis chuckled and decided it might be safer all round if he simply clarified things rather than run the risk that they might misunderstand and inadvertently add fuel to the fire. "Well, the long and the short of it is that Sal wants his women to join him there. He has to know they'll be as pissed as fuck thanks to them having to track his ass through the damn Zoo. What it means is he's somehow more terrified of what he's facing right now than he is of facing them. Ergo, he's in deeper shit than he would be with them."

"Ah." Addams grunted understanding. "I guess it means we'd better get our asses in there too, right?"

"Correct," Davis acknowledged. He'd also noticed that they hadn't run into any of the monsters on this last stretch through the Zoo—an indication of something he'd have preferred to avoid but which was all too clear. The tracer rounds were picking up, which meant there was probably a massive concentration of beasts ranged against Jacobs and his kidnappers. He glanced at Madigan and Courtney who, thankfully, had stopped. Their expressions suggested they had arrived at the same conclusion he had.

"We can't charge in there," he said, out of breath. By now, the mutants displayed rampantly on their motion sensors and things definitely didn't look good for any human who would be caught in the middle.

"What kind of heavy-hitters do we have?" Madigan asked. She obviously had the mini-gun on her shoulder, and he thought he'd seen a couple of rocket launchers connected to her arms, although he wasn't sure.

"Rocket launcher, right here," Xander said and patted the shoulder of his suit. "Plus a grenade launcher in my assault rifle."

"Same," Davis affirmed. "On the grenade launcher, not the rockets. How the hell do they fix rockets to these suits anyway?"

"We don't really have time for a chemistry and metallurgy lesson here," Courtney reminded them when the shooting escalated in intensity ahead of them. "Just know that Addams' suit has a rocket launcher but not a grenade, since his assault rifle is fitted to have a couple of shotgun shells. Mine doesn't have any of that."

"How—" Addams was about to ask but her quick look cut him short.

"I bought the damn suits, genius. I know the specs by heart," she snapped. "Do we have a plan?"

"Are we going for something a little more sophisticated than blow a hole in the monsters and cut our way through to Sal with excessive violence?" Davis queried with no attempt at any kind of humor.

"Nope, that works for me." Madigan tucked a grenade into the launcher. "One volley from the rockets to get their attention, grenades to kill as many as possible, and then it's a free-for-all-slash-all-you-can-kill buffet."

"Except we're not taking any shots at the person we're here to save, right?" Courtney reminded her with her hand on the other woman's shoulder. She had to reach up, thanks to the difference in height on the suits, but there was nothing small about the gesture itself. It certainly had the power to bring a measure of calm to the other woman, although she remained as determined as before.

"Don't worry, I won't...kill, Sal," she promised begrudgingly. "I can't say the same about the assholes who kidnapped him, though. Honestly, I might send a couple of stray bullets into someone's belly when we get there. Accidentally, of course."

Davis wanted to say he didn't feel overly happy about the plan, but it was better than no plan and certainly better than sitting around, waiting for shit to happen. He prepped his weapon and, less than a minute later, they pushed into a fast jog toward the rising crescendo of the next wave of the battle ahead.

CHAPTER TWENTY-FIVE

"What the fuck is that?"

This time, the specialist finally chose not to remind Smythe that he would have to pay for so many shots when they got back to one of the bases, they would probably have to spread it over a couple of days. The upside of that meant that Sal would probably transfer the drinks owed to him to Madigan. It might be the only incentive for her to let them survive this trip—assuming she was the one who got to make that choice.

Despite the fact that these assholes had kidnapped him, he still didn't want them to die in the Zoo. That was something he wouldn't wish on his worst enemy, although Courtney obviously hadn't felt the same way when she'd faced the woman who'd tried to destroy, then kill her. Having Madigan and Courtney go after them was another thing he wouldn't wish on anyone. Besides, during his time with the four British mercenaries, he realized he wasn't sure he wanted them dead at all. Drugging and kidnapping aside, they were rather competent and, in the right company, could be kept from making such poor decisions in the future.

It was premature, he knew that, but he was a big-picture kind of guy. If they all got out of there alive, these four might be a good team to work with in the future, assuming they would stick around the Zoo for a while.

Damn. He had a habit of letting his mind run free while his body simply went through the motions. What Smythe was referring to, of course, was a creature he had never seen before, and yet something of a pattern had begun to emerge in what honestly seemed little more than random mutant chaos. It wasn't easy to discern the pattern, of course, but if you paid attention, you could see the Zoo pick and choose the various genetic traits and infuse them into a variety of different animals. He recognized it now. The Zoo very clearly elected to run with certain traits and pushed them into the future generations while dropping others.

The bullet-proof carapaces on giant arthropods seemed to be the latest fashion around there, and Sal didn't like it. These new creatures were about four feet long and a couple of feet tall, with armor that seemed to encase their entire bodies. They looked like millipedes, with hundreds of smaller legs that worked furiously beneath the shell. He hoped this area would be the weak spot in their defense. The bullets they fired at the creatures didn't seem to have any effect on them. A stinger on the back was fortified by a pair of claws, no doubt a handy mechanism to drag prey into the sting. The fact that the poison-filled weapon wasn't at the front meant that it could be a weak spot to strike at as well.

"I fucking hate these stingers," he grumbled belligerently. The bullets definitely wouldn't do much, so there was no point in wasting ammo. He would need to step in there and do real damage up close.

A trio of eyes popped up to look at him as he approached.

The first wave of creatures had been mostly obliterated by the claymores and the team had only needed to make sure that nothing had found a path through. Firing the flares hadn't elicited the kind of attention they had hoped for, which meant they might be all alone out there. When the first wave was driven back, hope had surged among the four men, and Sal had wisely kept his optimism to a healthy minimum as he could see another horde already on the way. More of the ape creatures were among the new arrivals, although he couldn't see any of the larger ones in the front ranks. They had possibly chosen to hang back, or perhaps they were busy elsewhere.

For all his knowledge of the jungle, he still didn't know the details of how it worked. He had a couple of theories, of course, mostly revolving around the reproductive cycles being heavily influenced by the goop in the creatures, which forced the evolution in the formative stages of their development. But with the lack of actual knowledge of what happened to the animals when they weren't trying to kill people, all he had were theories. And knowing the Zoo, he could be right one day and wrong the next. It was always best to keep an open mind.

He stepped in closer and focused as the millipede twisted in an attempt to bring its stinger around to strike at him. Sal knew better than to waste too much time on analysis. He yanked the sword from the sheath on his back and lunged in quicker than the creature could react to sting him. His boot caught it squarely on the broad side and heaved it over onto its side.

The stinger reared to attention in another attempt to strike at him, but sure enough, the underside of the creature was unarmored, probably to allow for all those legs to move. He wasn't sure if the appendages had stingers too, but there was no point in risking it. With a guttural yell, he stabbed the blade down three times into what he sincerely hoped were the internal organs. Sure enough, a hiss of pain issued from the creature and it curled hastily to try to defend itself.

Sal evaded the now sluggish stinger and grinned smugly as the blood soaked into the jungle floor. The monster itself wouldn't be much of a threat, but there were more of them coming and they were all out of claymores.

He moved the team out of the defensive positions they were in. They couldn't rely on the ring of fire they held, and he didn't want to have to move out of their position. The trees only yards away still teemed with life, a measureless mass of killers that waited for them to try to make a run for it. They had a difficult enough time keeping their little section clear of the monsters on the ground. It would be impossible to do the same while on the move and trying to keep them off their backs from above as well.

A number of the millipedes had passed under the electrical fence—which had to be almost out of charge by now—and shuffled slowly but relentlessly toward the group. Smythe, Campbell, Dutch, and Murphy gave up on wasting ammo on the enemy and decided to use their volleys as cover for him to attack the creatures in a melee fight.

He focused on the mutant closest to him and came in fast to duck under the stinger swung at him by the surprisingly agile beast. In a hasty thrust, he slipped the blade between the carapaces and severed a couple of the legs in the strike. The steel was hard enough that it didn't bend when he used the power armor to force the blade up and flip the millipede onto its back. He used his pistol to deliver two shots into the soft underbelly.

There was a need to save ammo, but he also needed to clear these mutants as quickly as possible if he wanted to collect any samples. He had filled the storage in the suit's hard drive to about half of its capacity—which was an impressive enough feat—but he wanted to have as much physical data as possible to bring back.

While he already had more than enough for two or even three dissertations that would have jaws dropping, he still wanted to be overprepared. Besides, anything that wasn't submitted to the committee could be monetized, and damned if he wouldn't get as much cash as he could out of this.

Provided they could get out of there alive, of course. His doubts had begun to increase as the Zoo seemed to build to what might be a grand finale for them. The softer targets had been sent in first to soak the bullets up. He'd been around there long enough to know that this kind of sacrifice was how the Zoo learned the best way to try to eliminate something they wanted to destroy. It was like there was some kind of hierarchy among the monsters. Some were regarded as inferior and therefore more expendable, while the more powerful, stronger creatures held back and waited until their prey was weak and exhausted.

Sal hated the idea that a culture had begun to develop among the creatures. They were mostly less than sentient, but there were some that teased at the edge of a sentience that would allow them to make quick work of the teams that went into the Zoo. The horrors this encapsulated aside, he was rather curious about what would happen next.

The next millipede tried to reach him and he dodged hastily before he lobbed one of the frag grenades between its legs. The device caught on the appendages on the other side and bounced lightly under it for another second before the explosive turned its insides to mush. Nothing showed on the outside of the carapace, though.

That was worrying.

He stepped back to regroup and checked to make sure he still had bullets before he quickly cleaned the blood from his sword. With no obvious target at hand, he dropped back to where the rest of the team were. This was a small reprieve and unlikely to last long. The arthropods seemed unwilling to risk themselves at the hands of the human team. Sal wondered briefly how high they were on the food chain.

"What's up?" Sal asked. Murphy had dropped back, which forced Campbell to cover his sector.

"I'm getting something on the comms," Murphy replied. "It looks like someone's answered our distress call. Finally."

"Which one?" he asked and immediately caught his mistake as the four men eyed him oddly.

"What do you mean, which one?" Dutch asked with a suspicious scowl.

"Nothing, doesn't matter, not important," Sal said quickly and shook his head. He reminded himself acidly that they didn't know about the call he'd sent out since the moment they'd stepped into the Zoo in hopes that his Heavy Metal team would know where to find him once they came into range. "What kind of response are you getting?"

"It's an automated response directed at us." Murphy looked at him instead of Dutch. "It's giving us their vector and asking us not to fire on them as they approach. Northeast is the bearing I see here."

"Well, let's not shoot the friendlies," he said and nodded vigorously. "We have enough of these bastards out here trying to kill us and don't need to add ourselves to that list."

Sounds of gunfire rumbled faintly from the north, and Sal felt a little disappointed that Courtney and Madigan weren't the first to reach them. But hey, he couldn't exactly be picky about the people who came in to save their lives.

"Can you get me on the horn with them?" he asked, and Murphy nodded before he patched him quickly into the connection with the team that slowly moved in.

"Hey there, we have you in our sights," he called and identified some fifteen members of the new party that pinged across his HUD. "Do you need us to clear your approach vector?"

"That would be very appreciated from this end," said a man's voice with an American accent. "This is Sergeant

Alex Diggs from the American Base. Hey, Salinger Jacobs, is that you over there?"

"Yes," he said, a little confused. "Were you looking for me?"

"You have no idea, Jacobs." The sharp response sounded rather too gleeful for his taste. "I have a little bet with the commandant over whether we could reach you in time."

"In time to…save us from the monsters?" he asked, a little distracted by the fact that the enemy began to surge forward again.

"Sure," Diggs replied with a chuckle. "But there was also the issue of getting to you in time before Kennedy and Monroe killed you."

"What?" Sal snapped. He raised his weapons at the creatures but held his fire until they were closer. Conserving ammo was still something that had top priority.

"Don't worry about it. It's nothing you have to think about now," the sergeant said. "But try to keep us out of your shooting lanes as we approach, understood?"

"No, I think I still want to hear about what the hell you are talking about with a bet," Sal said and fired at the first rush of mutants, mostly the locusts and panthers that plunged in to absorb as much of their fire as possible. A few groups of apes held back, ready to sweep through when the advance guard fell.

"Oh, well, the bet is over whether we would find you first, or if we would find you savaged by all the beasts surging all over the damn Zoo, or if Kennedy and Monroe would have attacked you first," Diggs explained. Gunfire now peppered in the background as the new arrivals pressed closer to where the small team made their stand.

"I know you guys are coming in to help us, but that's a dick move," Sal grumbled. "Seriously, though, thanks for saving our asses out here, guys."

"Let us know if you want us to 'accidentally' gun those kidnapping mercs down during our approach," the man replied cheerfully. "I figure we all owe you one. Well, a couple if we're counting."

"That won't be necessary." Sal shook his head firmly. "Besides, these guys are harmless once you get past the whole...uh, drugging and kidnapping of specialists. Besides, that decision will come down to...well, uh, you know?"

"Kennedy and Monroe, got it." Diggs chuckled. "Right. I can see your tracers now, so we should be close. We're slowed here by the damn monsters for some reason, even though they seem to be focused on you guys."

"I'm not sure but we might have killed one of the head honchos around here."

"Really?"

"How the fuck should I know?" He laughed and yanked his sword out while his assault rifle reloaded. A couple of fanged panthers tried to rush at them, but they dropped away when he brandished his sword aggressively to push them back. "Tell your men to take cover. I'll open a way for you."

"Will do." Diggs apparently didn't bother to question his orders as the command immediately went out. Sal retrieved the grenade Murphy had given him. The power of it wasn't forgotten, of course, which was why he planned to hurl that bastard as far as he could into the thickest cluster of animals. The hope was that enough of them would absorb the blast so the newcomers wouldn't be caught in it.

There were no guarantees, though. He didn't particularly like the plan much, but even with the fifteen men working as reinforcements, they wouldn't last long if the mutants swung behind them. They needed to push forward now that they had more forces.

Sal timed the grenade for five seconds before he pitched the ordnance deep into the thickest huddle of animals. He knew what was coming, having remembered what it did the last time, and they would need to take cover.

A slight difficulty, he realized too late. They were out in the middle of the goddamn open.

"Brace for—" The blast knocked the air out of him with a painful whump that made it impossible to draw breath for a moment. Even with the suit on and most of the explosion absorbed by the mass of flesh that made up the various monstrosities the Zoo had to throw at them, the concussive blast of Murphy's grenade was still enough to knock him on his ass.

The rest of them were better off, of course, having braced for it before he had called for them to do so. They had heard most of the conversation he'd had with the newcomers, after all.

When he looked up, the team of fifteen men filed through the hole punched in the line of monsters. They moved briskly and efficiently and maintained their fire until they converged on the area where Sal and the mercs had set up their defensive perimeter.

"Jacobs?" the leader asked as they pushed through the

electric fence that had, in fact, run out of charge as he'd predicted.

"That's me." Sal raised his hand, still a little winded.

"That's some ballsy shit you pulled there." Diggs chuckled, took his hand, and shook it firmly. He could feel the strength even through his suit. "But I think that ballsy is your go-to, right? Given your choice in women?"

He rolled his eyes. "Sure, that's my life. I'm attracted to strong and insensitive women."

"Isn't that redundant?"

"What, the insensitive part?" He brushed the dirt from his suit, a fruitless exercise but it kept his hand busy. "Because I wouldn't know. I've only ever been with the two women."

"You do have a way to pick them, that's all I'm saying." The sergeant shrugged and turned his attention to their defenses.

"It's more like they picked me," Sal muttered but tried to refocus as the new team worked to set out heavier defenses. They had more mines, for one thing, and took advantage of the brief respite bought for them by the massive explosion that seemed to drive away even the most dangerous of the predators.

"Let's share some ammo around," Diggs called to the rest of his team. "Yes, even with the kidnapping bastard mercs. I want every gun out here firing on all cylinders, and from the way the Zoo is acting up, I think we'll need it. Besides, your ass will be grass by the time Sergeant Kennedy gets her hands on you."

"Who?" Smythe asked with a startled look at Diggs.

"She's not one of ours anymore, though," he replied and

handed the man extra magazines. He gestured with his head to where Sal stood. "It's one of his girlfriends. The other one is Dr. Monroe. She's equally as crazy and lacks the former's...shall we say, goodwill?"

"Wait, girlfriends?" Campbell asked and drew in closer to them. "Did he say girlfriends, plural? I'm sure he said that."

"Who the fuck is this guy?" Dutch shook his head in evident disbelief as he slapped the extra bullets into his supply. He ventured an enquiring look at Sal, who shrugged and smirked. The answer had to wait as it seemed the Zoo had regathered its strength and replenished the numbers that had been shredded by the grenade with hundreds and hundreds more.

And every last one of them looked pissed.

"It looks like we're in for a long night," Sal grumbled under his breath. He stretched and eased his back while he prepared himself mentally for another battle.

CHAPTER TWENTY-SIX

The ground itself shuddered as the enraged creatures swept through the mines the team had set up. He couldn't help but wonder why the concept of the mine hadn't evolved from the claymore. The explosives were bigger, of course, and the payload had been made deadlier, but it was still the front-toward-enemy device that had been developed with the same kind of mistrust for the people who would handle it. Who was it who said to never bet against human stupidity again?

And honestly, that wasn't the point. Sal dragged his concentration to the hordes of creatures that were now only moments away.

"This is what you've dealt with all night?" Diggs asked and looked at Dutch, who simply nodded. "And this is your first trip into the Zoo, yeah?"

"Well, not the first trip but...yeah, sure, it might as well be." Sal wanted to smirk and make a smarmy comment about how they wouldn't have made it this long without him there to guide them. He'd chosen to manage his sense of humor more cautiously to make sure they had enough to last them through what looked to be a very long night.

It was like the jungle knew help had come and didn't like it. The Zoo had, for some reason, singled them out for an assault. It couldn't have been for Pita plants that might or might not have been damaged in the fighting. The hordes had begun the attacks long before they'd set up the location of their last stand. In fact, Sal couldn't help being tempted to merely take a couple of the plants anyway since things around there couldn't get much worse.

But he was more than strong enough to resist that temptation. If there was one thing he'd learned not to do, it was to underestimate the amount of shit that could come at them in this fucking jungle.

He shouldered his assault rifle, took a deep breath, and let his mind drift a little so it wouldn't get in the way of what his body had to do.

Dammit, he'd forgotten to collect samples from the millipede creatures and the bodies would be long gone by now, with their kind of luck. He shook his head. *Stay focused, dammit.*

An eerie ambiance was created by the cutting-edge night vision software provided with the suit and paired with some of the best motion sensors. These were brought together with some nifty coding to deliver a high definition, real-time image of what they were looking at. It was more than effective and very useful, but it coated the world in an odd green hue that was unsettling. He simply couldn't shake the notion of it being ridiculously alien. It appeared they were on an alien world, surrounded by alien plants, and attacked by alien monsters.

And only one of the above wasn't the truth of the matter. They were indeed weird times they now lived in.

Sal checked his ammo as the monsters galvanized into action once more. They had lost most of their cannon fodder to the mines and would now bring the big boys in to fight. He had about fifteen mags worth of bullets, which in these conditions could last him anywhere between fifteen minutes and three hours. Despite the much-needed replenishment, they still had to play it safe with their ammunition or risk engaging with the creatures with nothing other than their sidearms and what melee weapons they had on hand.

He made a mental note to bring up whether the big, tank-like suits couldn't be outfitted with some kind of power-enhanced war hammer. His head envisaged something straight out of a video game but with the kind of concussive force that would ignore the armor these monsters were developing. He'd already suggested they add concussive rounds to the ammo store, and their response had been to remind him that there was no such thing and to stop calling them at three in the morning, goddammit.

Sal did feel bad about that, but they needed a reliable alternative that could provide a solution to the sudden spurt of creatures with bullet-absorbing or shielding carapaces. They would be torn apart by any more creatures that could shrug gunfire off with such ease.

The defenders formed up again and released a hail of bullets at the monsters that rumbled forward in a concerted attack. Each man checked their firing line to make sure they didn't overlap anywhere. Sal marked his section, cleared it, and verified that his assault rifle was set at a semi-automatic capacity to keep his kills at one or two rounds max. He'd learned to play this game. It wasn't foreign to him.

Efficiency. That was something taught to him by Madigan and had kept him alive this long. His brains had obviously come into play a couple of times too, but for the spectacular to take the stage, the ordinary needed to play its part. He wondered if she was proud of how far he had come. With almost twenty team members out in the Zoo, all trained and skilled in the arts of combat, he held his own among them. He was a far cry from the kid who had needed to be carried out of the Zoo the first time in.

And while people appeared to have forgotten about that, he never would. He would let it drive him to ensure that he was never in a situation like that again if he could help it. It stood to reason that he couldn't always avoid it, but so far, it had been one of only two times in which he'd been carried out. Too many, in his opinion, but he would continue to work to make sure that remained the record.

"Reloading," he called and yanked his sidearm clear of the holster. He used it to keep the beasts at bay as he stepped a little out of the line and tried to at least estimate where they would concentrate their attacks next. He wasn't sure how he could tell but it felt like the right move.

He pointed at Dutch and drew the man's attention to the tree line. Sal couldn't tell what it was, but something moved there that was different from anything he had seen all night. He couldn't say he'd never seen anything like it ever—given the sheer number of different creatures he'd seen out there, that would be a ridiculous claim—but there was something different about this one that made it oddly significant.

The other man nodded and appeared to set his shooting to something like an autopilot as he called up one of the last flares they still had available. He fired it into the air in the direction of the creature Sal had pointed out.

A pair of wings flared out, the first thing Sal saw, and he couldn't help the need to suddenly change his assault rifle to full auto as the appendages flicked ominously.

His mind raced to absorb what details he could. It had to have a ten-foot wingspan, which made it much larger than any of the birds he had ever seen or heard of. The wings were illuminated by the flare that still arced upward, and it was obvious they weren't feather-based but extended skin like a bat's. Fur covered its body and made it difficult for him to make out the exact biology. The head, though, resembled a bat with massive ears spreading out and up. Large eyes with huge pupils were set high in a head that reared into what looked like a pterodactyl's crest.

"How fucking beautiful are you?" He gasped and stared at the monster in both awe and something close to terror. The mutant watched the flare and it seemed to respond to brightness as an attempt to hurt it or scare it away. When the light trailed downward, the creature saw it as an attack and soared up from the branch it had perched on to watch the fighting.

The massive wings flapped as it climbed smoothly into the air with a low yet reverberating screech. The sounds of both the wings and the defiant scream resounded across the clearing, and from the way the animals flinched and tried to pull away, he could tell they heard and felt it too.

The other members of his team weren't similarly affected, though.

"Do we shoot it?" Dutch asked and waited for Sal to say something. He honestly didn't know what he could say. The monsters out there seemed to have paused to wait for the winged creature to move clear of the battle. Something that could be described as reverence had settled over their body language, a sure indication that they would probably attack if shots were fired at it. For once, he truly didn't have an answer.

Another powerful flap of the colossal wings batted the flare away and into the trees to die quickly beyond the battleground. Where it couldn't hurt the beast's eyes anymore, he thought.

"Do we shoot it?" Dutch repeated the question and when he moved in closer, Sal realized that his mind had drifted. He wasn't sure where to, but he needed to snap out of it. The beasts around them had held back their attack, but they were more restless now the giant winged...bat whatever had returned to its perch above the battle. It simply sat in indifferent arrogance as if content to watch and wait for something.

He had no clue what it could be waiting for or why it was this close to the conflict without engaging. All of the larger, more powerful monsters knew to stay away from the fighting for a while before they got involved, and it seemed like the Zoo itself somehow protected them from injury to the point where killing them would send the beasts into a rage.

There were so many things he didn't understand, and

he wanted to understand. Unless he did, he wouldn't know what it was doing and why it watched them.

"Sal!" Smythe shouted to attract his attention. He realized that he had actually taken steps toward it and shook his head at his own distracted stupidity. Worse, the beast had now settled its full focus on him.

"Shoot it," he instructed, his tone harsh because he didn't want them to hear the tremble in his voice as he pulled into their defensive perimeter. "Shoot it now!"

Dutch nodded. He had no more rockets for his shoulder launcher, but there was still the possibility of using the grenade launcher under the barrel of his assault rifle. Sal didn't have one of those, and it didn't seem like any of the others did, but they could always obliterate the mutant with bullets—or try to.

The merc quickly calculated the grenade's trajectory over the animals as the rest of the team laid down covering fire to ensure the monsters that had already coalesced into a new frontal attack wouldn't be able to intervene. Sal tried to keep an eye on what Dutch was doing while still covering his line of fire. The man used the heavy armor to launch the grenade into a high sweep that thumped heavily into the tree.

It wasn't a clean hit and the flash of light made Sal blink and look away. When he turned back, pieces still fell from the tree after the explosion, but a hint of movement told him the beast had pulled away. There was also no sign of any change in the temperament of the creatures around them, so it was hard to tell what difference the assault had made, if any. The enemy pressed more intently than before, which meant he had less time to watch the skies when they were forced to tighten their formation to reduce the lanes of attack.

He forced his mind to focus on the creatures that surged and ebbed in a concerted wave. The onboard computer selected his targets for him using software Anja had helped them to develop, if a little indirectly. He thought about her and hoped she was having more luck than they were out there.

With Amanda gone and Madigan and Courtney hopefully coming in to save his bacon, she would be alone on their little base. With Connie, of course, so not that alone. He recalled what the AI was capable of with the base's defenses, so she wouldn't need to worry for her safety. Her sanity, on the other hand—

Sal ducked instinctively and stumbled from the impact of a series of explosions that rocked the ground beneath their feet. He looked roughly due north or maybe a little northwest as the team turned to where the explosions came from. His first thought was that the Zoo had somehow found a way to develop explosives.

It wouldn't be the first time in nature, of course. There were those bombardier beetles that had somehow developed a chemical formula that, when mixed, would cause a small explosion—although not small for the beetle, Sal mused, but still. Biologists were baffled regarding the evolutionary history of the creature that would lead to it develop something like that, which still kept his hopes about humans evolving into superpowered mutants somewhat alive. It wasn't likely, but hey, there was a beetle out there that had found a way to eject explosives from its ass.

But no, it wasn't likely that the Zoo creatures had found

a way to make things blow up. Not impossible, but very unlikely.

It could only mean they were looking at another team of humans coming in and coming in hot.

Sal realized there was a message coming through the private emergency channel he'd opened.

"I don't know if you're listening to me, Salinger Jacobs," Madigan's angry voice yelled. "We have your location and are heading in now. If you're dead, I'll literally kill every living thing in a five-mile radius, and that includes the trees. If you're alive, I'll simply kill you, and to be honest, that sounds like far less work. So you'd better fucking be alive, you dumb-shit scientist."

He chuckled. While he hoped she was joking, at this point, it was so good to hear her voice all the way out in the middle of the Zoo. He was more tired than he'd ever been in his life—he had no idea how he was still on his feet—and hearing her voice, knowing that she and the we she had made mention of were coming for him was enough to raise his spirits.

He felt something interestingly similar to hope and he didn't mind it at all.

"We have friendlies moving in from the northwest," he called over their comms. "I doubt you need to be told where but if you do, it's where all the explosions are coming from. We need to open a path for them to reach us, or maybe for us to reach them. With more members on our team, we might be able to start a concerted push out of here and not have to simply defend ourselves."

The American newcomers looked relieved at the news and appeared to already know who approached. There were only so many people out there who would be willing to bulldoze into a tide of monsters like that. Three, in fact, and Sal was one of them.

The other two were probably the ones on the way.

"Friendlies for some of us, anyway." Diggs cackled. He apparently had little sympathy for what the British mercs could expect, and honestly, Sal could sympathize. The four exchanged a quick look, and all Dutch could do was shrug.

"If they kill us, they kill us," he said with a wry chuckle and shook his head. "Let's clear a path, boys."

"Aye, sir!" Smythe responded and the tasks were quickly broken down. Half the members of their conjoined team would concentrate their fire on clearing a path for the new arrivals. The rest would have the job of making sure their position wasn't overrun. It was made easier by the fact that the animals seemed to turn to attack the new threat, challenged by the aggressiveness of the team's approach. There was a reason why most people in the Zoo didn't launch an attack like that. It was a good way to draw the attention of way too many nightmare creatures and make them determined to destroy you.

It worried Sal, frankly. Madigan wouldn't have made this decision for anyone outside of Heavy Metal. Damned if he would let her kill herself to save his life.

CHAPTER TWENTY-SEVEN

Madigan scowled and glowered at the line of retreating monsters that had begun to fall back against the small team's relentless push forward. It wasn't like them to back away from a fight, not when they had gathered in these kinds of numbers. No, they probably weren't retreating at all.

The likelier explanation was that they would regroup to attack the new threat. She could only hope they had drawn some of the heat off Sal and his team. He still hadn't responded to the message she'd left him, although that was par for the course with the man. When he was deeply engrossed in his work, he was the kind of guy who wouldn't respond to messages.

Or deep in Zoo monsters trying to kill him. Or if he was dead.

No, she wouldn't allow herself to think like that. Nothing good would come from that train of thought. Sal was still alive and he was merely being a dick who chose not to answer. How selfish did you have to be to choose working on saving your own life instead of answering your girlfriend's calls?

She was being facetious, of course. Despite what people seemed to think around there, she had no intention to kill him. Instead, she would demand reparations for all the shit she'd pulled to get him back.

The dumbasses involved in kidnapping him, though? She had every intention of murdering the shit out of them.

Madigan recoiled as one of the explosions caught on a tree and splinters erupted to fill the air with shrapnel that wouldn't do much damage to the suits they wore. Still, she reminded herself, there were no guarantees in this place. It was always better to be safe than sorry, and she would have to do a little cleaning up before she got herself back since she could see more than a few splinters in the outer sections of her armor. Although only a millimeter or so, they would do far more damage to the creatures that weren't armored. Sure enough, the dead and wounded in the area meant a substantial number of the mutants would not be part of the night's festivities.

Addams stepped in to fire another grenade into the mix. The ordnance cleared a small section of the monsters and drove them aside as the team moved quickly to fill the void and gain more ground.

The defenders were visible now where they'd established themselves in an open area. Knowing Sal, he probably tried to use the Pita plants in the middle of the clearing as some kind of protection since the animals weren't too keen on damaging the fucking plants. There was also the thought that they could keep the areas above them clear. Madigan hadn't really cared much about that since they moved quickly and caused damage to the trees. This aggressive approach usually forced even the bravest of the panthers to steer clear of their trajectory.

Despite this, it was still a tough fight. They were out in the open and in some respects, vulnerable to any significant attack that went beyond the average Zoo battle fare. The new ape creatures were a case in point. They were smarter than the other monsters they had encountered, and when they noticed that charging the humans blindly didn't work, they decided to gather rocks and sticks and hurl them from above instead. It wasn't all that effective but was still something to keep in mind among the hundreds of other things they had to think about.

She studied the clearing quickly. Someone in light, hybrid armor waved his arms, probably getting orders out, and the team around him seemed to reorganize and take up new positions as if about to break out. They focused their fire immediately on the creatures between Madigan and them.

Sal finally got her fucking message, she noted. And damned if he didn't do all this in that new suit. She didn't remember the name, but she did remember him raving about it after a couple of test runs in a simulator. They had outfitted him well, as it turned out. She hated the idea that she might be even slightly impressed by drugging kidnappers.

"Keep moving forward!" she called and gestured with her hand into the hole the suddenly focused fire had created in the enemy line. It wasn't much, but if they played their cards right, it would be enough. She rolled out a couple of rockets from her shoulder—the last two she had—then primed and launched them at the clusters of animals that tried to reform where the hole had been made. A couple of grenades were thrown in too from both sides. It was a perfect pincer movement, and despite the tough fighting, it seemed it might work.

Something changed, though, as if an unseen ripple eddied through the massed animals. The mutants appeared to pull themselves back. While a group remained to harass and try to isolate Sal's team, the others drew away from the battlefield to what she would describe as a watchful distance. Fanged panthers, tailed locusts, hyenas, huge millipede monsters that Madigan couldn't begin to name, and more seemed to have withdrawn to make space for something else to happen.

It was more instinct than reflexes that made her look skyward. Something flickered around her vision as the motion tracker immediately lurched in response and the mini-gun tried to track it. The software was simply too slow. An enormous shape swooped in and thrust Madigan's suit a couple of steps back, although the gyros compensated quickly. Courtney had no such luck and was literally hurled down by what felt like only the air displacement from something so enormous moving incredibly quickly over them. The unknown monster felt like a damn airplane flying over them, and the team stumbled and fell or flailed to catch their balance.

Xander was the least lucky. The monster closed on him quickly and the massive wings folded for a brief moment before the curved, lethal claws gripped him firmly by the shoulder and dragged him off his feet. He screamed in pain and shock as he dangled between the branches. His assault rifle fired when the claws appeared to drive through his armor and find the flesh beneath.

Madigan wondered for a moment if the winged creature would take him off and away to a nest to feed its young, but those thoughts were quickly destroyed when it banked slightly and hammered the man into a nearby tree, then another. His screams ceased, and when he was finally dropped, his body was set upon by a group of hyenas before it had even fully landed.

She gulped and fought to regain control. There was no way she wanted to stick around for that motherfucker to come back for them, but their distraction had proven costly. The mutants now resumed the attack and with considerably more intensity than before. She turned, drew her mini-gun back into action, and held the line for them. The hole was gone. All they could really hope for was to be able to hold their current position until the raging tide ebbed a little.

Courtney stepped in beside her, a worried look on her face. Madigan hated to have to think like this, but of all the members of their team who could have been lost, Xander was the best for them. The guy was wounded and had already slowed them. Addams, Davis, and Courtney were all up and kicking. She was vital to the team, if she did say so herself, and they wouldn't allow the monsters to make any more surprise kills. If that critter tried another aerial raid, she would nail it about a hundred times with her mini-gun.

Just try me, you piece of shit. It wasn't easy to focus on the battle at hand and still keep her eye on the area above them. She couldn't see where the beast had disappeared to, but she had the feeling it would come back for more. They were a man down too and needed to get to where Sal was, and fast.

It truly was ironic that the man they had come to rescue needed to help rescue them.

"What's our next move?" Courtney asked. She wore the same wary anger that stiffened her spine. The enemy seemed to have decided to circle them and strike from behind, and it wasn't a nice place to be in.

"We push forward." Madigan shook her head as the mini-gun drove a group of hyenas and locusts back, cutting through them easily with the powerful rounds.

Something moved out from where Sal's group stood. She wasn't sure what it was at first, but some kind of reaction emanated from the beasts in the line. They looked perturbed and almost angry. She wasn't sure how on point her summary of their body language was, but it definitely seemed they were agitated.

A couple of grenades pounded into the beasts as they tried to back away. The explosions and the shrapnel decimated their ranks and broke their attacking strength.

And there was Sal. She grinned when he raced toward them from their relatively well-defended position with his new suit and—motherfucker, was that a sword? It certainly looked like one, not quite katana-esque but long and sharp and could be manipulated with one of the armor's gloves while he held the assault rifle in his other hand.

She couldn't make expressions out in the darkness and couldn't see much more than his fusillade aimed at the creatures in front. He no doubt looked crazy, given that he had erupted into what could only be described as a suicide run. The rest of his team seemed to pick up on what he was doing and tried to provide covering fire, but Madigan narrowed her eyes and watched him move. She'd never seen him do that in the sims. There had been one time when they'd fought with the Russians, but not since then.

He literally dove in and reloaded his assault rifle quickly as he rolled over his shoulder to find his feet in the middle of a circle of panthers that tried to lash out at him. Sal was quicker, though. One dropped away, decapitated, and he twisted quickly to cut and slash at a second and third and drive them back. A hyena tried to hurdle the carcasses in an effort to catch him by surprise, but he whirled and pounded it back with a powerful, crunching roundhouse kick.

Curiouser and curiouser, she thought and shook her head to force herself to not be distracted by the man's new moves. Whether it was about the new suit or he had held back on her—or maybe he hadn't had the opportunity to show these moves off in the past—didn't matter. If he fought his way toward them, she would return the favor and try not to shoot anything at him at the same time. She might get a couple of wingers in to remind him how pissed off she was, but only once they were in the clear again.

For now, though, she kept track of his movements out of the corner of her eye. He continued his onslaught against the line of beasts and rapidly gunned down those that cut into his path. Others that tried to attack him from either side met the whirled death of his blade or a flurry of punches and kicks that blurred with the speed and intensity of his movement.

It couldn't last, and Madigan knew she needed to get to

him and smack some sense into him. Still, as long as he could keep it up, it was impressive to watch. And to think that less than a year before, the kid had struggled to make his way out of the Zoo. He had heart and mind. The fact that he was so much of a geek stuck in an alien jungle and had still managed to hold his own on his first time in was one of the reasons why she had started to fall for him. But, as he grew more and more competent out there, she couldn't shake the feeling of pride. She had something to do with that.

Her and Madie. She remembered seeing the first plant he'd managed to get out of the damn place. Taking that blue goop stuff on a semi-regular basis had done wonders for improving his physique, reflexes, and durability.

And stamina. She couldn't forget the stamina. Not ever.

He moved out of her sight for a second as a powerful, burly ape creature barreled toward him. A flash of blood erupted. The color wasn't visible since everything looked green in her view, but the blade slashed wildly before he powered into the creature that had a full foot of height on him and used it as a body shield.

He roared and thrust forward, keeping the creature pinned with the sword while he fired relentlessly at anything that tried to step into his way. As he drew closer to the new team, he drove the monster to the ground, crushed a locust under its weight, and rolled. He stood smoothly to decapitate another of the mutants—a powerful, corpuscular fanged panther that was quickly pushed to the side as he jogged to where she stood.

"Did you think that would impress me?" Madigan asked

when he approached. As he walked, he cleaned his sword and sheathed it smoothly while his assault rifle reloaded.

"Honestly?" Sal asked, and from the tone of his voice, she could tell that he was smirking. "I don't care. It's fucking good to hear your voice again."

She chuckled and slapped his outstretched hand away. "No time for that yet, big guy. We still have a fight in front of us. How's your team doing?"

"Running low on ammo," he replied. He took his time and picked his shots efficiently and carefully to drive the creatures back and hopefully delay any thoughts about attacking again. "I have some American vets in there who will cover their asses fairly well. From what I saw, though, it looked like you guys could use a little extra juice instead. What were you thinking, bringing such a small team in?"

"Firstly," Madigan retorted as the enemy surged swiftly into another attack. She took her natural position at the point of the line while Sal and Courtney dropped to her flanks. "We came out here to save your sorry ass and I've not heard anything by way of a thank you. Secondly, we were in a rush, so we couldn't exactly put up a Zoo call in the bar and wait a couple of days to sift through the prospects. And thirdly, I don't need a thirdly because I'm still waiting for a thank you from you."

"Well, you'll get it once we're done out here." He chuckled.

"I missed you, Sal," Courtney interjected. "Although I have to say I'm with her. Some gratitude for us rushing out here to get your roofied ass out alive is in order."

"Way to blame the victim, guys. Besides, I had almost

everything handled until this fucking jungle went nuts on us."

"This is the gratitude we get," Madigan grumbled. She vented a little of the frustration when she kicked the legs out from under one of the apes and deposited the full weight of her suit on the exposed skull. "Un-fucking-believable."

Sal ducked to avoid a small chunk of tree that had been tossed at them and dropped to one knee as he drew his blade. He kept his shooting arm up as one of the millipedes rumbled closer and attempted to swing its stinger at Madigan. His push forward was quicker, though, and he ducked under her as she tried to bring her weapon to bear. He stepped into the chop and the blade jarred into his power glove when it found the tail and severed it smoothly. The beast hissed in pain, but he thrust his blade under the carapaces to put it out of its misery.

When the ground shook, Madigan froze and looked around. Flashes of color interrupted the seeming unending field of green in her view as lights flared to the west of their location.

"That... What is that?" Courtney asked. She stepped beside her friends and stared as they did.

"It looks like a mortar strike," Madigan pointed out. She tried to zoom in but all she could see were more flashes of explosives. The lights, however, reflected in crazy flickers and flares off suits of armor. A large number of them pressed forward in an organized formation and launched rockets at the creatures that had now turned to attack them instead. The Heavy Metal team, the Americans, and the kidnappers seemed to be set aside as lesser concerns while what looked like a solid group of humans advanced at a slow jog, their firepower battering the enemy with devastating results.

"What the fuck?" Madigan asked, her tone incredulous. "Who else would be out here? And in those numbers?"

"The suits look like Russian models," Sal said and zoomed in. "They are all the same too. But why would the Russians have this many people out here?"

"Attention all comm links." The voice crackled through the open lines, speaking English with a heavy Russian accent. "I am looking for a little man, a researcher. A specific one, of course. I didn't simply wake up this morning with a craving. He goes by the name of Salinger Jacobs."

Sal narrowed his eyes and pretended to try to put a face to the name. "Shit... Gregor? Is that you?"

"In the slightly bruised and very pissed-off flesh, my friend," the Russian replied with a laugh. "I heard you were in trouble and thought we could come in and help. If you don't think so, we can head off, no hard feelings. There are many monsters to kill elsewhere in the Zoo. This place has gone crazy over the past few days."

"You're telling me," Madigan grumbled and stared at the ranks of Russian soldiers who followed their old friend.

"Well, since you came all this way, it would be impolite to send you away without at least having a chat," Sal said with a chuckle.

"Excellent!" Gregor replied. "I would suggest you all take cover right now. And I mean everyone."

Sal was already moving by the time Madigan turned to ask him what that was supposed to mean. She knew better than to ignore that particular warning sign. Sal was brave enough, but he wasn't an idiot. When the time came to take cover, they took cover, dammit.

She grabbed Courtney and dragged the woman to one of the nearby trees, then glanced back to make sure Addams and Davis had done the same. They'd lost Xander already and damned if she would lose anyone else at that point. She dragged herself behind the massive trunk barely in time. The ground shuddered with far more violence than it had before, and the shockwave pounded hard enough to tumble a couple of the enormous trees.

By the time they managed to circle, a huge cloud mushroomed upward from the ground.

"What the fuck?" Courtney asked when she saw it. "That's not nuclear, right?"

"I doubt the Russians would trust their foot soldiers with nuclear weapons," Madigan pointed out. "That said, if that shit don't kill some Zoo creatures, nothing will."

"On the other hand, we might as well have plastered a neon sign for this location saying 'free meal, expect resistance,' to every monster and creature out there in the Zoo," Sal quipped.

She nodded. He made a good point. It looked like the payload's initial reaction had scared the monsters away, but they would be back and in force.

"Let's assemble the troops," she said and didn't bother to look at Sal before she jogged to where the mercs and the Americans struggled to regroup and determine what the hell was going on.

CHAPTER TWENTY-EIGHT

As the group gathered their equipment, Smythe watched the newcomers with real interest. Not the Russians, of course. He'd dealt with their kind before. They were pros but not the kind most people were used to. Cultural differences being what they were, he was well aware that there were differences in what was considered professional between countries and continents.

These days, he was all about keeping an open mind when it came to people who were competent. Jacobs hadn't struck him as the kind of person who could kick ass and take names when they first met him, and there he was. The kid probably had the highest kill count of the five of them.

Ditto the Russians, he assumed. They might be loud and abrasive to his sensibilities, but they'd dropped a bomb that annihilated more of the monsters than they'd killed all week. Frankly, they could be as loud and abrasive as they wanted if they came in with that kind of firepower.

No, he was worried about the two women who had joined their party and now snapped orders like they owned the place. From the way they moved and from what the crew had heard, he only needed one guess as to who they were. The infamous former sergeant Madigan Kennedy and the equally infamous Dr. Courtney Monroe.

They didn't seem to be focused on revenge at the moment, although that might change during their time in the Zoo. Things were happening out there. The ones he was most afraid of were encased in suits of armor, and that felt odd given all the monsters they had battled.

There appeared to be a break as they set up a few defenses that could be quickly abandoned on their way out. They also helped each other with resources, sharing ammo and making sure they knew what they had to fight with when they initiated the run for the exit.

"Do we have a count on the casualties?" Jacobs asked as he walked to where the two women stood.

"We're not talking about that right now," Kennedy replied. She marched over to him and only stopped when they were practically toe-to-toe.

"What are we talking about?" he asked and narrowed his eyes.

"Get your armor off," she commanded ominously.

"I don't think we have the time for that," he replied with a cheeky grin. "While the monsters were scared away by the big boom, they could come back at any minute now."

"Don't you get smart with me, Jacobs." Madigan pointed her mech finger at him. "You simply don't want me to deck you."

He nodded, apparently unashamed of the admission. "That too, yes."

"The two of you need to calm down," Monroe said and stepped between them.

"I don't know what you're talking about." Sal continued to smile. "I'm merely happy to see the two of you again."

"And don't think your sweet-talking us will get you out a world of hurt," Monroe said and suddenly turned on him as well.

Smythe narrowed his eyes. He'd been in his fair share of relationships, and the fact that he was currently single meant he knew how stressful they could be. In his mind, the fact that Jacobs was in a relationship with two women was proof of how brave and stupid he was at the same time.

A zippo lighter clicked to his left and he turned to see Diggs strolling over to him, a cigar in his mouth as he puffed away with a small grin on his face while he watched the exchange.

"Cigar?" the sergeant asked and offered one from his pocket.

"No thanks. I don't smoke."

"It's a cigar," Gregor protested. He strode closer and took the cylinder from the man's proffered hand and waited for him to light it before both men turned to watch the three Heavy Metal members still arguing.

Well, no, Smythe amended. It was more them shouting and Jacobs looking like he tried hard not to smile.

"Women," Gregor said with a chuckle and a shake of his head. "We should have brought popcorn."

His lament was interrupted when one of the powerful apes barreled out of the underbrush on a direct trajectory toward where most of the noise came from. The three people arguing amongst themselves didn't seem to be in the mood to be interrupted.

They drew their sidearms and, almost without any real effort to aim, pulled the trigger as one. The three rounds struck home in the monster's horned head and it dropped without a sound. None of the group looked like they would be distracted from their conversation, even with the jungle around them rife with mutants determined to kill them.

"And if you think we'll let you off easy because you're happy to see us, you have another think coming." Madigan picked up where Courtney had left off. "You have a whole ton of trouble coming your way and you won't wiggle out of it easily. I have half a mind to beat you within an inch of your life, Salinger Jacobs."

He nodded but before he could say anything, Courtney stepped in and interrupted him.

"We're not blaming you for what happened here, Sal," she said and looked a little less angry about it than Kennedy did. "And while yes, you could have made it a little easier for us to find you, I thought you would be dead when we finally caught up. I had all kinds of revenge all pent up. So, we'll take it out on you. I hope you don't mind."

"I'm only—"

"Don't say it." Madigan shook both her head and her armored finger.

"I'm happy to see you again," he finished and looked as serious as he could in the situation he was in. Smythe thought the man knew he couldn't smile and look like he wasn't taking them seriously, but he seemed genuinely elated to see them again.

Madigan's response was delayed. The expression he could make out was something akin to disbelief as she shoved Courtney out of the way and closed in on Jacobs. She was taller than him and the tank of a suit added more than a few inches to that when she stepped in close. He remained where he was and stared at her, seemingly unafraid when she caught him by the collar of his suit and hauled him close. She leaned down and pressed her lips firmly to his.

"Well... I just lost about a hundred bucks," Diggs grumbled, his expression disgusted as he took his cigar out of his mouth.

"Wait, why?" Gregor asked.

"Well, there were bets in the base about whether Kennedy and Monroe would murder Jacobs when they found him," the sergeant explained. "The odds weren't great, but when someone offers you ten-to-one odds on something as explosive as these three, you take action."

"In fairness, I too was afraid Kennedy would kill him," Gregor said with a chuckle and a nod. "It's half the reason why I brought this many people to come to his aid. I thought I would have to drag Kennedy off him, kicking and screaming. I am glad that it is not the case, though. They make a cute couple."

Smythe shook his head. He wasn't sure how a couple would extend to three people, but he wasn't in the mood to ask questions right now. Not when things were still volatile.

Monroe saw they were all staring, and she marched over to them.

"Don't you guys have anything better to do than stare at a reunion?" she asked, her head tilted defiantly.

"Not really, no," Gregor said with a chuckle. He stepped close to Monroe and wrapped her in a hug made awkward by the bulky suits both wore.

"How the hell are you, Gregor?" she asked with a smile and patted him affectionately on the shoulder when he stepped away. "The last I saw, you were in a hospital bed."

"Well, I was in a hospital bed. And then I wasn't. Too many times. A few life or death situations, and then we're here. I like it when life pulls shit like this."

"It's good to see you, either way, Gregor. And you should all be watching the jungle around us, you know? We're still out in the middle of an alien Zoo whose plants and animals want us dead. Yes, before you ask, even the plants. I've seen them, and you've probably seen the reports, so you know what I'm talking about. Let's keep our eyes open around here."

Smythe blinked and turned his back to let Kennedy and Jacobs suck face with a little privacy. Fair enough, they were in the middle of the fucking Zoo. It seemed like Monroe and Kennedy wouldn't come after him and his team for now. They were all in this shit heap together, so it made sense that they wouldn't have to deal with scientist-napping Jacobs and the consequences thereof until they were clear of the jungle.

He could still hear, though. Mostly the clicking and clanking of the couple's suits banging together. They appeared oblivious to anyone else watching them and were intent only on each other. Finally, they pulled apart and both of them gasped.

"I missed you too," Jacobs said with a chuckle and raised an eyebrow.

"Don't think you're in the clear yet, Sal." Madigan punched him gently in the shoulder. "You still have much more making up to do."

"And me," Monroe added. Smythe gave in to the temptation to turn to see what was happening as the leaner, smaller Dr. Monroe strolled back to the couple. "And speaking of, do you mind?"

"Be my guest." The other woman grinned and Courtney took the invitation to latch onto an already dazed-looking Jacobs and kiss him as ardently as Madigan had. Her smaller suit meant there was more room for closeness, which made an interesting contrast. Smythe tilted his head and tried to come to terms with what he saw. It didn't go unnoticed by Kennedy, who had made her way to where he stood.

"Hey, pervert," she all but snarled, and the edged tone snapped him back into reality. "Those two kissing won't eat your arm and shit it out later, but if you miss something out there, it might. Keep your eyes on the perimeter."

"Yes, ma'am," he replied, not quite sure why he'd called her that and didn't seem to care when she rolled her eyes. She turned away and headed to where the Russians had started the final stages of the process that would get them out again. There apparently wasn't a second bomb like the first one, and from the readings they received from the long-range motion sensors, the Zoo had used the lull to good effect. Even more animals had massed and now converged on the teams, no doubt with a thirst for vengeance.

Dutch, Murphy, and Campbell wandered closer to him, apparently as entranced by the sight of Jacobs and Monroe making out as he had been. He felt it was his responsibility to bring them out of it.

"Come on. They won't kill us yet, so let's keep an eye out for something that might," he said and kept his voice down as the other three had now directed their attention to him.

"Right." Dutch cleared his throat and inspected the repairs that had been put into his suit. "It looks like we have about forty people, what with the Russians, Americans, Heavy Metal team, and us, so we should be safe out here, right? It should be a cakewalk to get everyone out?"

"I doubt it," Smythe replied and shook his head regretfully. "I read up on it. Larger teams tend to attract greater numbers of the monsters, which means they're more likely to be bogged down in a battle until they run out of ammo. As it turns out, the optimal number of people to bring on a team into the Zoo is about a dozen."

"Huh." Dutch looked disgruntled. "So, this is great. We kidnap a guy with two women who shoot monsters like a damn Terminator, and he is fucking Zoo Tarzan or some shit. The military come out to save him, so he's important to the colonists, but not only them but to the Russians too. Does anyone else think this is FUBAR?"

Fucked up beyond all repair. That sounded about right to Smythe.

"We should get moving," Gregor called, and they all knew what the warning meant. Their borrowed time was almost up, and it would soon be time to fight again. Smythe stretched and rolled his neck. He needed sleep. He needed booze, a good meal, and maybe a good fuck too, but for now, to get all of those, he needed to survive. To do that, he needed to be on point and as focused as he could possibly be. There was a time when there were drugs provided to help him with that, but he was past that now. He needed to do it with good old humanity.

"Okay, ladies and gents," Jacobs called. The man looked invigorated as he pulled his helmet on and connected to the team commlink, which had about forty connections to it already. "Let's negotiate with the Zoo in a way that it understands. Heavy Metal Negotiations, bitch!"

He shouted that last line and damned if there wasn't some adrenaline attached to it. The Russians all cheered something in their own language, while the Americans stuck to a simple. "Hoo-ah!"

Smythe watched the monsters start to assemble at the edge of his motion sensors, and damned if they didn't look pissed to be there. The teams formed into lines, all focused on the march toward the edge of the Zoo, which was still a good distance away to the north.

Jacobs, Kennedy, and Monroe took point on the operation, and they had already engaged the monsters and launched a series of rockets at them. They opened fire as the rest of the group followed in a tight formation.

"Come on, boys." Dutch loaded a couple of the rockets he had been given by the Russians and dragged his teammates to join the nearest line. "Let's see how the Zoo handles these famous 'Heavy Metal Negotiations' and let's all get out of this one alive."

"Aye, sir," the others agreed, broke into a brisk jog, and

opened fire at the mutants that already swarmed with vicious intent.

"Fuck my life," Smythe grumbled under his breath when they started moving again. His comment, fortunately, didn't reach the open comms. There was no way to make this shit up and damned if anyone would ever believe it. Not that he would share this story with anyone. That would be plain embarrassing.

He rolled his neck again and locked his assault rifle in place as he picked up his pace. One problem at a time.

CHAPTER TWENTY-NINE

H e'd been around there for a while. Not as long as some but longer than most. That wasn't the kind of thing Sal tended to hold over people, of course. He was well aware of how difficult it was to survive in this place, and it definitely wasn't for everyone. It took a special kind of crazy to be willing to do what they did, and the thing that hurt the most was that many of the people there hadn't chosen to come but had been assigned.

His first time in, he'd dealt with attacks from bounty hunters, monsters attracted to the blood, those driven wild by someone plucking a Pita plant, and their reaction to the killing of one of the bigger dinosaur-like creatures. That had been his first time. There had been many other times, and at no point had he thought anything was as bad as his first time. Too much had changed, not only in himself but in the Zoo as well, for things to get that bad. He knew how bad it could get, and nothing would match the surprise and shock that came with his first trip into the Zoo.

Until now.

Sal had never seen the monsters this riled up before. So many different types and species had all gathered to attack as a group. The diverse species seemed like an army guided in a hive mind that he still had no way to understand. He'd put forth theories and speculated that the interference the trees and plants radiated due to the goop inside them was how the monsters achieved this collective mentality. In addition, he'd made himself something of a guinea pig and tried to determine if his interactions with the Zoo changed as he licked Madie more and more often.

Thus far, his results were inconclusive. His interactions with the Zoo had definitely changed, and he'd tracked the differences in his body over the months. They made him more effective in the Zoo, of course, and it was possible those changes were a result of the goop in his body giving him some kind of connection to the jungle.

Alternatively, they were merely a result of his body's changes and the training and conditioning he'd gone through with Madigan. He didn't yet know and needed to continue his tests.

That said, he was glad for the changes that came to him right now. Exhaustion seeped into his muscles. He hadn't had more than a couple of hours of sleep in the past seventy-two hours, and the fact that he was still on his feet was nothing short of a miracle in its own right. He could still shoot, fight, and keep them moving north thanks to the goop in his system. If it was still in his system at this point. It had been a while since his last dose. That interesting thought distracted him for a moment, and he had to will his focus back to reality.

The monsters ravaged the group's left flank the hardest.

The Russians shored the defenses on that side, and maybe the Zoo merely wanted payback for the big fucking bomb they'd unleashed. Sal moved to where their line had slowed and watched as the ticks counted down their return to the edge of the Zoo. It wasn't coming fast enough. Day was already close, and small pinpoints of light had begun to appear through the leaves at the top of the tree line. The faint and filtered light gave them something to see by, anyway.

The fact that there wasn't anything to see but trees and a veritable sea of frenzied, killer creatures didn't make the view much better.

He ducked and rolled under a trunk thrown at him by a particularly large simian. It tried to back away, but he pushed forward and bored two holes into the left side of its chest. It roared, fell in a tangled heap, and died almost immediately. He made a mental note that their heart was in the left side of their chest, which meant they were almost certainly based on apes found on earth. The fact that they hadn't seen any animals based on alien design yet was interesting. It made him wonder if there was any alien design behind the goop, or whether there was some purpose behind it he couldn't fathom.

It was...still unclear. There were too many unknowns. Sal jogged across the line and selected his targets carefully. A swarm of locusts hurtled in to attack the line. A couple of the men fell as tails flicked forward, punched through their armor, and released their poison. Their comrades caught the bodies and hauled them into the line.

When another cluster of the creatures surged into the attack, he drew the sword from his back, calculated a hasty trajectory, and launched it in a spinning arc at the creatures. The blade maintained its wheeling motion as it severed a couple of the outstretched stinger tails and finally buried itself almost to the hilt in the thorax of another monster.

It was an impressive throw, he had to admit. Even more impressive was the fact that he'd managed to avoid hitting any of his allies while in the middle of that kind of firefight.

"Lucky throw." Madigan yanked the blade free from the carcass, shook the blood from it, and hacked at a pair of hyenas that leapt from the underbrush. The weapon sliced them cleanly in half before she tossed it to Sal, who caught it smoothly and sheathed it.

"Can we get serious about this now?" Courtney asked as she stepped in, annihilated a couple of the monsters with a few choice shots, and helped a few of the wounded into the better-defended center of their lines.

"Wait, were we supposed to take this seriously?" Sal asked. Madigan shook her head, although he thought he could hear a hint of a chuckle from her as they worked across the line once more.

"Not even as a joke right now, Sal," she said firmly and followed the tracking on the mini-gun on her shoulder to eliminate the few creatures it hadn't aimed at. Sal kept pace with her, and they worked as their usual methodical team to deal death as efficiently and as rapidly as they could. The teams behind them seemed to have found some kind of cohesion as they pushed through the jungle, trying to maintain a steady pace and ensure that the horde found no vulnerable position to launch a frenzied attack against.

The monsters continued to pursue them in greater numbers than before, Sal noted. The smaller creatures began to withdraw after a while, which could only mean the larger monsters were inbound. Sure enough, one of the killerpillars bore down on the group while the lesser mutants hovered in readiness to bring up the rear.

"We need some momentum!" Sal yelled. Madigan nodded and waved her hand as a couple of rockets immediately fired from her shoulder. Sal sprinted toward her and the power-sections of his suit kicked in at full force. The lack of lag involved was something he could only marvel at as he careened toward Madigan and vaulted into a running leap when his right foot found her hand. She heaved him cleanly into the air, high enough that he almost worried about serious head injury from the branches.

He laughed when gravity kicked in and he hovered for an infinitesimal moment before he plunged downward again. As he gathered momentum, he projected and corrected his angle with a couple of thrusters connected to his back. In the final few seconds, he yanked his sword free and bellowed a challenge as he landed on top of the fifteen or so foot monster that trailed across the jungle floor like an anaconda with hundreds of poison-infused legs.

Sal brought the full weight of his suit and body to bear on the sword's point and found one of the gaps in the carapace once the monster stopped. It tried to shake loose the rockets Madigan had launched at it, which gave him the time to drive through the armor with the enhanced impetus of his landing. The creature released a hissing screech and the entire body writhed in an effort to shake him off, but he hung on and tightened his hold on the sword.

Courtney moved in with a grenade, already lacking the pin and lever, in her hand and she tossed it casually to him. He hoped she had given him enough time to work as he stretched toward it. He felt like a jock football player in the middle of a game as he snatched it and hauled himself up on the monster's body to shove the ordnance deep into the hole made by the sword.

He yanked the blade out quickly and dropped to roll away as far as he could. A dull thud echoed as the device detonated. It had most likely turned all the killerpillar's insides to mush and the monster flipped onto its back to writhe and roil until finally, it stilled.

Sal moved a couple of steps back and dissuaded any attacking monsters with bright swings of his sword. To simplify matters, he used the assault rifle on any that didn't take the hint.

"That's what I call teamwork," Madigan said with a grin and bumped his fist with hers. Both bumped Courtney's next. "Is there an appropriate Heavy Metal pun we can make?"

"Maybe something about how heavy our metal is when we work together?" he asked but instantly regretted it. That was seriously the worst.

"Nope. I don't think so." She shook her head.

He turned his attention briefly to the others in the group and studied the way they fought together. Despite the fact that most of them hadn't met before today, they appeared to work well as a unit. They obviously didn't show the kind of team spirit Sal, Madigan, and Courtney did, but they could always build up to that.

Gregor jogged to them, his watchful eye on the jungle.

"We've made good progress," he said and stopped beside Courtney and Madigan. "It looks like you've breathed fire into the boys, eh? I've been trying to do that ever since we set foot in this fucking place."

"Well, that's what happens when you lead by example, Gregor," Sal replied with a cheeky grin. He took a moment to reload his rifle but drew his sidearm to maintain his fire. "We're working like a Heavy Metal Militia out here, and you all might end up learning something."

"Heavy Metal Militia?" Gregor seemed to actually consider this. "I can't say the bosses back at the base would like that nickname, but I fucking do. I'm renaming the commlink now."

"What happens when one of your men is inevitably a spy who tells the commandant you've called your team by a name given to you by an American?" Courtney asked.

"The commandant on base likes you three," he reminded them with a shrug. "He'll turn a blind eye and forget to report it to his superiors in Moscow. The word will get back eventually, of course, but who the fuck cares what those *mudak* in their comfortable chairs think of what we do here?"

"The man makes a good point…" Sal left the thought unfinished, distracted by the unexpected retreat of many of the mutants. They appeared to have suddenly taken the notion to head back into the Zoo.

"What's happening?" one of the mercs—Campbell, from

the accent—asked. Sal assessed their group instinctively. There had been a fair share of casualties, fifteen by the looks of it. These were mostly Russians as they had borne the brunt of the attack. They had ten men down and a couple more wounded, while the Americans had taken casualties as well.

He returned his gaze to the Zoo, narrowed his eyes, and tried to make out what had happened. They were close enough to the edge that a little more light threaded in. Morning had arrived in full, which meant that along with the dreaded Sahara-level heat, they also had a better view of the somewhat startling shift in what had seemed a fixed pattern of relentless assault.

For whatever reason, the enemy had inexplicably veered from their attack course and now headed away again, deeper into the jungle.

"It's like they're being called somewhere else," Courtney said. She frowned as she leaned closer to make sure her sensors hadn't malfunctioned. "Maybe some other poor bastard is about to be heavily fucked by the monsters that attacked us."

"I can't really think of any other reason why they would suddenly abandon us," Sal said. "It could be that we're close enough to the edge of the jungle that they decided we're too chewy a meal and would let the Zoo spit us out again."

"You heard that when you were saying it, didn't you?" Gregor asked with a quick look at him, and Sal couldn't help a grin.

"I stand by my wording," he said with a staunch nod.

"It looks like we have a reprieve," Diggs said as he approached, his gaze wary as he looked around. "I don't want to stick around in this fucking jungle for a second longer than is needed, but we've endured the attacks for the better part of two days and I think we need a second to rest and attend to the wounded before we make the last push out."

Sal looked around. He could tell that Madigan didn't approve but in all honesty, he could use a breather himself. The fact that Diggs appeared to look at him for permission and Gregor also waited for his response somehow forced him into what appeared to be an uncomfortable position of command.

"Five minutes," he said finally and held his hand up. "Patch up those we can and collect the tags on those we can't. There's no telling if the monsters will change their minds, and none of us want to stick around this fucking place any longer than necessary."

The order was transmitted over most of the comm lines, and the group of now under thirty members hauled packs off and dumped them on the ground. The medics, assisted by Addams, started to treat the wounded immediately.

Those who had been poisoned were checked quickly for the type of venom used on them and thus present in their bloodstream, and antitoxin was applied directly into the vein. It wouldn't be a permanent solution as the poisons tended to stick around. Most of these men would develop some kind of kidney complication later on, which would have to be addressed at the hospital back on base.

Back on base. That felt like such a hopeful term, Sal thought with a small smile.

"What?" Courtney asked. She placed a hand on his shoulder.

"Dunno. This was one of those trips when I had some serious doubts that I would ever get back. Being trapped in here with a group that had no idea what they were doing, seriously outnumbered, and with the Zoo throwing a hissy fit for some reason I still have no idea about, there were doubts. And now the thought that we'll make it out alive… It feels sweet, you know? I think I'll sleep for a week. Have a nice, long, hot shower, and yes, sleep for a week."

"A couple of fucking sessions might get that sentimentality right out of you," Madison interjected. She ran a couple of checks on her suit, which Sal realized had taken a few hits and sported a couple of tears down the right side. It looked like a panther had dug into it.

"Fucking sessions of wha— oh, never mind," Sal said. The fact that he'd needed to think about her wording there for a second was all he needed to know about his current state. He needed rest. Proper, sleep-like rest.

Sal studied their most recent battlefield. The area showed little signs of fighting, though. Bullet holes in the trees were evidence enough, but as they tended to do, the monsters of the Zoo had recovered their dead and dragged them away, leaving almost no trace that any fighting had occurred at all. It was…unsettling. He assumed the bodies were eaten and assimilated into the Zoo, but that was only a theory. Too many theories with not enough concrete evidence. That was his main problem with this place from a researcher's perspective.

"Did you get any samples?" Courtney asked him. "While you were in?"

"Well, yeah, of course," he replied and patted the pack slung over his shoulder. "I have them all with me and more than enough data to bring home for a couple of dissertations. I'll write one up when I have the chance and sell the rest. Honestly, I want to be mad at those fuckers for kidnapping me, but the fact remains that we had planned a trip in anyway. This wasn't the best way to do it, but there is a bright side. I have all the data and will be paid besides."

"Since when do kidnappers pay you for the trouble of getting kidnapped?" Madigan asked with a militant scowl.

"Well, from what I could tell, they needed a specialist and didn't have time to go through the proper sources," Sal explained. "I don't agree with what they did, but they said I could keep this suit—or rather, I insisted on it—and they paid me up-front before we moved into the Zoo. Besides, they're not that terrible. For scientist-nappers, anyways."

Madigan shook her head, apparently unconvinced, but as the five minutes were almost over, they needed to resume the march. The bodies had been arranged neatly for easier transportation—being dragged along the jungle floor wasn't overly dignified, but it was better than being left behind to feed the monsters—while those who were wounded had been attended to as best they could. Anything more would have to be done when they got out. Given that their exit vector wasn't anywhere near where any of their vehicles had been left, they would probably have to wait in the glaring sun for a while.

Sal didn't mind. He could use a dash of sun on his face, simply to be reminded that it was, in fact, out there. After the dreary greens of the motion sensor slash night vision combo through which he had seen the Zoo over the past few days, he could live with a little glare.

Diggs glowered as Sal approached. The sergeant apparently needed his dislocated right arm put back into the socket. He cursed volubly, and Sal winced at the pop, but the patient was on his feet quickly, grabbed his pack, and looked at the group.

"It's time to hoof it." Sal connected to the living members of their group. "Team Heavy Metal, get your asses in gear, help all the wounded, and let's prepare to move out and get the fuck out of this fucking jungle."

A chorus of affirmatives, either sent through the comms or simply green thumbs-ups that appeared on his HUD, indicated the general willingness to be rid of this place for as long as possible.

He drifted to Courtney and Madigan as the column pressed on again in a much slower and more cautious approach than before. It made a pleasant change to a nightmare journey that had essentially been a sprint to the finish line.

"I didn't think that would work," Sal said on a private channel where only the two women could hear. "So, we're all Team Heavy Metal now."

"Hurray!" Madigan chuckled and raised a sarcastic yet triumphant fist in the air.

CHAPTER THIRTY

S mythe had never thought he could miss the sun this
much. Growing up in the south of England—closer to
Wales than he would ever admit—there had never been
much of an affinity between himself and the sun. It was
always hidden behind clouds and the light yet constant
drizzle that never seemed to end, except for the two days a
year when it came out and was sunny.

He could remember his parents all excited about the
sun coming out. They would make a whole day of it and
drag him and the rest of the family to enjoy a day in the
sun with all the insects and the drudgery, the mud that got
everywhere, and the uncomfortably muggy heat, all
because the sun was out.

Over the years, he'd spent his time in places that had
left him in the sun a lot. There wasn't much else in the
Middle East, after all, but he had never had an appreciation
for it. In fact, he had actually said on a few occasions that
he was descended from vampires and was allergic to

sunlight. Not garlic, though. Garlic bread would always hold a special place in his heart.

That said, he didn't think he had ever appreciated the sunlight as much as he did now. After three days under the heavy canopy of trees that made sunlight a rare, almost impossible sight, thinking he would die at every step of the way, to see the sun out in the open was an incredible relief. So much so that he would forgive how glaring and unbearable it was, especially there in the dunes.

They'd finally staggered from the jungle, and after a long moment of silent, disbelieving relief, decided they wanted as much distance between themselves and that fucking place as possible. The group had pushed on, all the way to where not even the tiniest smidgeon of life spreading from the Zoo could be found, and they continued to move until they were hidden from it by a massive dune. Only then did they stop. Out of sight, out of mind and all that.

That wasn't to say their position wasn't uncomfortable, of course. The sun was already beating down despite the fact that it was only nine in the morning, and it would only get worse over the next couple of hours. Thankfully, the Hammerheads the teams had used to bring them into the Zoo could be called remotely, and even now, their transports were speeding toward them. The best estimates said they would arrive in an hour or so and until then, they had nothing to do but wait for them to arrive.

Even in the blasting heat, Smythe had a hard time keeping his eyes open. The last few days had been spent mostly on the run, with a couple of pauses for sleep. He couldn't imagine how Jacobs felt at this point. The man hadn't slept almost at all since they'd started out. For himself, though, he dropped onto the sand. He let his suit absorb most of the heat radiating from it as he pulled his helmet on and lowered the shades so his eyes could slowly drift shut. He had time for a nap, right? It seemed to be what most of the other teams were doing since they apparently hadn't had much time for rest either.

"Get up!"

He shook his head. There wasn't much in the world that could make him move from where he felt even mildly comfortable. Men had set up to keep an eye on the jungle to make sure the beasts wouldn't return, so if there was fighting to do, alarms would be raised everywhere. Even then, getting up was an idea long since doomed to never happen.

"I said, get the fuck up!"

Smythe was about to ignore whoever it was a second time when a heavy boot collided with his side close to where his ribs were. Nothing broke, but he catapulted across the sand like a football kicked with real enthusiasm. Being attacked was one of the few things that would get him up and out of his dreamy state.

Still drowsy, he wasn't encouraged by what he saw as he heaved onto his feet. He had barely reached his knees when he turned the shades off on his HUD. This allowed him to see, after a brief adjustment period, the barrel of a massive assault rifle held to his face. The woman holding it, one former sergeant by the name of Madigan Kennedy, stood over him.

"Get the helmet off, numbnuts." She snatched him by the collar of his suit and dragged him to where Dutch,

Campbell, and Murphy were already assembled and pushed onto their knees. This...didn't bode well for them, he thought. With slow, measured movements, he removed his helmet and placed it gently on the sand beside him.

Madigan drew her sidearm and pointed it at Campbell's head where the dumbass knelt next to him. Dutch and Murphy had weapons aimed at their heads as well, these held by Courtney Monroe.

No, this definitely didn't bode well. The only person who might have been able to hold the two back from murdering the absolute shit out of the four of them in cold blood would have been Jacobs, but he was near the Russians, apparently coordinating a way to pay them for coming in to save their collective asses.

Which meant it was only the four of them, alone with the two women who wanted them dead most in the world. Smythe felt too tired to mount a resistance or try an escape. He merely wanted to sleep. If having his brains decorate the Sahara's sands would let him do that, so be it.

Besides, it wasn't like they would be able to take the two of them on anyways. Smythe had seen what they were capable of in the Zoo. The four Brits were scary as fuck in their own right, but this was not their turf.

"I don't suppose we can apologize?" Dutch said finally as the silence threatened to drag on interminably.

"Sure, go ahead," Courtney said. "Try to talk your way out of this one. I always like to hear that."

He looked at the sand and shook his head. "Look, the call was mine. We thought it was an easy jump in, but we lost our specialist on one of the trial runs. That left us in a lurch as we were on the clock, and when we saw the infamous Salinger Jacobs at the bar, it felt like he had fallen into our lap from the sky. We've paid him his share for the trip already, plus he took all the samples and flowers, so he's already been well compensated for all this."

Madigan dragged in a deep breath and looked like she considered his words for a moment. "You took what was mine." She hissed through clenched teeth for emphasis.

"And mine," Monroe added.

Kennedy stared at them for a moment, her expression hard before she seemed to relax, although she didn't lower her weapons. "If you ever set foot anywhere near him again, I will personally pump you full of more lead than is medically advisable. After that, I will take your bodies into the Zoo where you will never be found again and never be heard from again, do you understand me?"

Smythe nodded almost before she had finished talking, and he could see the other three doing so as well through his peripheral vision.

"Yes, ma'am," Dutch grumbled.

"The only reason why I've not done it here and now is because Sal told me you guys helped him and that you treated him well," Kennedy said and finally let her weapons lower to her sides. "Let's be honest, Sal is a little senti-mental about killing fellow humans. He only does it when he really, really has to, which means it would bother him if I offed you all here and now."

"If we offed them all here and now," Monroe reminded her.

"Right. Frankly, we need to get laid and we don't need a mopey partner in bed. So, get your shit assembled and get the fuck out of the Zoo. If you ever want to come back, you make damned sure you get my permission to touch down first. I don't care if you have a hall pass from the Secretary-General of the United Fucking Nations. I'll assume you want something with Sal again and I'll apologize to your corpses. Got it?"

"Oh, and be sure to let your bosses know my response to them will be a bullet to the head if they try to keep all their Pegasus material," Monroe added with a small nod. "So they can either leave it behind or they can die. It's up to them. They'll know what it means."

"Right." Dutch pushed himself slowly from his knees as Courtney lowered her weapons as well. "So…you're letting us go?"

Kennedy rolled her eyes. "You know what? You were right, I already regret this shit."

"Let it go, Madigan," Monroe chided her. "We're doing this for us, not for them."

The mercs scrambled to their feet and, after a quick moment to confer, moved hastily to the other side of where they had set up their impromptu camp. Madigan couldn't help a smirk as she watched them move away like they couldn't believe their luck.

"I almost feel bad for the motherfuckers," she said with a chuckle and shook her head once the men were out of earshot. "Almost being the key word there."

"Yeah, they still did scientist-nap Sal and drag our asses all the way through the fucking Zoo to save their lives," Courtney said with a shrug as they turned and started back to where Sal was still chatting to Gregor. "They needed a warning—not only for them but for whoever sent them."

"Anja's already working on tracking the people responsible," Madigan said softly.

Courtney looked at her. "And how do you know that?"

"Check your incoming communications," she replied. "Anja's been chatting ever since we got out from the Zoo's interference."

The other woman did as she was told, activated a commlink, and entered what sounded like Anja going at full speed.

"Anyway, I let Savage know that he had people coming for him and then— Oh, hi there, Courtney." The excited monologue cut off instantly. "I'm so glad to hear you guys got out. But it's sad to hear about Xander. Well, not really since I didn't know him, and from what I found out about him, he was an ass. Still, it sucks that he died."

Courtney smiled, having missed the off-beat Russian hacker who had held the home front since they had headed out into the Zoo. "It's nice to hear from you too, Anja. How many cups of coffee have you had today?"

"It's daytime?" She sounded perplexed. "Oh, well, I guess I pulled an all-nighter. Which means about...twenty cups of coffee? I might as well graduate to cocaine at this point, except it's almost impossible to get it out here. Not impossible, mind you, merely almost."

Courtney cut her mic's connection to the link, although she still listened to what Anja was saying.

"How long has she been talking to you like this?" She opened a private line with Madigan. Of course, the Russian could probably hack into the connection no matter how private it was, but appearances still needed to be maintained.

"She's gone full speed ahead since we left the interference," the other woman said with a chuckle. "She called me the moment we were out and went off like a damn machine gun. I think she's a little starved for human contact, that hacker woman."

"If I were stuck on a base with only Connie for company, I think I'd be a little starved for human connection too. I'll need to listen to what she has to say eventually, though. She's helped to run our operation on the Anderson front, so I'll need to know how that's going. Maybe not before a good meal and some sleep, though."

"I hear you there, sister. Although, again, I'll add a good, hard dicking to that list."

"You're really thirsty, aren't you?" Courtney said with a grin.

"A girl needs what a girl needs. I won't be ashamed of it," Madigan replied as Sal wandered to where they were chatting. She noted that he looked about five minutes away from collapsing himself, so she would probably have to wait to have her addition to the list satisfied. She wanted him healthy and hardy.

"What are you two ladies up to?" he asked and forced a smile as he moved between them.

"Well, we let the dumbasses over yonder live as long as they know that the next time we see them, certain bullets will be exchanged," Madigan said. "Also, it seems Courtney's getting an update on the Anderson front."

"Shouldn't we call it the Savage front?" he asked.

"Well, no, Anderson is still running the show," Courtney said. He shrugged and seemed like he wasn't in the mood for a debate, which was odd on its own.

"How about you?" Madigan asked. She slid her armored arm over his shoulders.

"Well, I've sectioned the data I've collected into what would work best for my dissertation and got some quotes on everything else." He shook his head. "I'll need second opinions, but there are many people who want to know about these new millipede creatures, so we could be looking at twenty grand from the data collected alone. That, plus some of the Pita flowers I managed to pick and the samples I collected. That's on top of the two hundred grand the mercs over there already deposited in my account, and we're looking at great profits on top of all the data I need for a dissertation. All in all...no, that was still a shitty trip into the Zoo. I think I need a couple of weeks off."

"You might get them too," Madigan said with a chuckle and patted his shoulder. "And the best news of all is our Hammerhead was parked the closest, so we'll be heading home soon. We'll give a couple of rides to some of our comrades and get them to the staging area."

"That sounds like fun," Sal said as one of the squat-looking vehicles came into view. He still wasn't sure how they'd fitted these government vehicles with auto-driver capabilities, but at that point, he really wouldn't look that particular gift horse in the mouth.

"I hope you don't mind, though, but I'll sit in the back," Sal said as they jogged to the vehicle. Davis and Addams joined them, along with Diggs and another couple of the survivors of the American team.

It would be a little cramped but at this point, he could

fall asleep on his feet. He would pay the others back for saving his bacon later.

CHAPTER THIRTY-ONE

Some might say they didn't even know why they were there. Dr. Anders didn't like being called into committee and only ever did so when he had some part in shaping the mind that would be celebrated with a doctorate. It always felt like such a waste of time otherwise, but the group who decided who was in charge of the committees tended not to care that he had bigger fish to fry—sometimes literally.

He looked up from his papers as the door to the conference room opened and a lean sixty-year-old strolled in. Anders recognized the man, of course. They weren't friends but some professional respect was shared between them. Maybe this wouldn't be such a huge waste of time after all.

"Any word from Tellisman?" Anders asked as he shook Dr. Friedman's hand firmly.

"He said he'll be a little late," the other man replied with a chuckle. "A little hiccup with his physical therapy."

"He got his injuries by going into the Zoo, right?" he

asked and scowled when his companion nodded with a somber look. "He should have known he's too old for that shit. It's a young man's game. He's lucky he got out of that crazy place alive."

"Speaking of the Zoo, did you see the dissertation presented by our candidate today?" Friedman asked as he placed his papers on the desk reserved for him.

"That's nothing," Anders replied with a shake of his head. "Did you see the video footage he used to support his findings? I've heard all kinds of crazy shit from inside the Zoo, but that's all it is. Merely…fabrications used by capitalist dumbasses trying to drive prices for their product up."

The other man chuckled. "I think we should deny candidacy on the grounds that he refused to come in and present it in person. I understand he's busy there in Africa, but the fact that he can't be bothered to take a break from it to come and have what could be the most important interview of his life? This is pathetic."

"And fake," Anders concurred. Both men looked up when the door to the room opened. The man who stepped through was an impressive specimen despite the heavy bandaging around his left leg and the cane in his hand to support him. Powerful, broad shoulders, a chiseled jawline, and what looked like a good amount of muscle beneath his tweed coat were plainly visible despite the gray that had appeared and spread from his temples.

Anders had always questioned why the man had elected to go into a STEM field when he could have chosen any other, but damned if he didn't have the brains to back his findings up.

He still remembered the younger man's dissertation like it was yesterday. It wasn't fair that someone as healthy, charismatic, and good-looking as Dr. Tellisman had the kind of brains he did. It had been a wash. A unanimous decision to grant him his doctorate hadn't been fair.

"You wouldn't happen to know where our candidate is waiting, would you, Peter?" Friedman asked, joking as he shook the taller, younger man's hand.

"I hear he might be looking around the botanical gardens," Anders added as he greeted the man as well.

"You've seen his work out there, right?" the newcomer asked and looked fixedly at the two other doctors as he dropped slowly into his seat with a groan.

"It's unverified," Anders retorted and shook his head. "There are no peer reviews on what's happening out there. Pure propaganda, well used to support his own budding startup in the area."

"Are you serious?" Tellisman asked.

"He's right. Much what he's put into his dissertation isn't verified and can't be verified until someone with real brains heads into the Zoo," Friedman pointed out.

"You two seem to forget something," Tellisman said and called up the data Jacobs had sent to them to support his dissertation. "I was there. I've verified everything this kid has put out."

Anders looked up from his folder and scowled, unsure that he'd heard correctly. "Surely, not...everything."

"No offense, Dr. Anders, but your head is so far up your ass you'll be able to suck on your own tonsils." The man laughed. "You too, Friedman. I've been there. I've verified basically everything he's sent us, and anything I haven't seen, I believe. I've worked with Salinger Jacobs, and while he's a little unorthodox, his methods are solid. I'm happy to put it on record that, despite the fact he's not here in person, I'll demand his doctorate be granted or I'll request another committee from the NSF."

"There's no need to be dramatic." Friedman had clearly run out of patience with his colleague. "We'll study the data, but you have to admit that what we've seen here is… fantastical."

"And yet it's real." Tellisman leaned forward, his expression somber and serious. "Denying the evidence in front of our eyes is something we leave to the religious studies majors."

Anders opened his mouth and glowered furiously as he tried to think of a retort to that, but he didn't have anything to say. He knew the other man well enough to know he wouldn't budge on the issue.

"Fine," he said finally but his brisk head-shake spoke his disapproval. "Let's look at the dissertation."

It wasn't like him to drink this much, especially with lunch. Things had somehow spiraled over the past couple of months. It seemed like everything they attempted ended up backfiring spectacularly.

Trying to get a regular team running into the Zoo hadn't had the best results, Randall thought as he dug into the filet mignon that had been placed in front of him a few seconds earlier. Everything had been poised for at least the start of a comeback. But no. They'd come away from that fucking place with their tails between their legs and not even bothered to return the money they had been paid, all jumbled within the context of two disparate things. The first was that they wouldn't go into the jungle ever again.

The second was a message from someone Randall had never thought he would have to deal with again, Dr. Courtney Monroe. The beginning of the end. That was how he had started to think of her, anyway. It wasn't too long ago that she was only the prodigal daughter of the man they could easily influence into padding everyone's pockets with the results of his findings. Now, she was in charge of everything, and the rest of the faithful in Pegasus were running scared.

Of course, he had never believed in Carlson's dream of world cleansing or whatever it had been. All he cared about was how many zeroes were behind the numbers in his Swiss bank account. And those zeroes were dwindling the more he fought back.

At least he still could still enjoy gourmet food, though.

He finished the steak, ignored the vegetables on the side, and placed his napkin quickly on the plate. He had declined dessert and chose instead to visit the bar for another drink before he headed back in to do damage control.

Randall drew in a deep breath as he moved to the bar. They would recommend the pina colada, but he happened to know their Old Fashioned was to die for. He raised his hand at the bartender and the man nodded to indicate he would soon finish with another client. The young woman was short, blonde, and all the right kinds of curvy. Exactly

Randall's type, coincidentally, and wrapped in a low V-neck, tightly-bound red dress.

"Good sir," he said and sidled closer to the woman and the bartender. He smiled and worked hard to look as charming as possible. "I'll take the bill for this lady's drink if she doesn't mind."

The woman chuckled. "That's very generous of you, Mr. Randall," she said in an oddly familiar voice. "But I don't think you have the money to pay for it."

He was about to voice his confusion, but all his questions dissipated instantly as she turned to face him and gave him a view of a face he was only too familiar with. He took a step back and yanked his hand away from the small of her back.

"Dr. Monroe," he said with a nervous chuckle and glanced around the room. "I didn't know you were in Europe."

"I make a point of not letting anyone know where I am at all times, Mr. Randall," she said with a charming smile. "It's a habit I picked up when I realized there were people in the world who wouldn't mind putting considerable money down to have me killed."

"Killed?" He took a hasty step away from her. "I…well, I never."

"I warned you, Randall." She maintained her calm and collected tone of voice. "Stay away, or you will get a bullet to the brain—paraphrasing, of course. I hope you have good insurance." She smiled by way of a farewell, left a couple of euro bills on the bar to pay for her drink, and took it to a table that had been reserved for her.

Randall didn't care. She could spend the rest of her day

there and he really hoped she would too. What mattered was that she was onto him. He didn't know how or why, but the fact remained that he needed to get out of the country.

As paranoid as he was, he hadn't bothered to leave his car with a valet. No, he'd left it in the charge of his driver-slash-bodyguard, who had parked it around the corner. He could buy plane tickets on the way. While he didn't know where, he honestly didn't care. Anywhere but there.

He hurried to the corner and forced himself to slow. Running in five-thousand-dollar shoes? How crazy was that?

It seemed to take forever to reach the car where it was parked in a nice little corner, easy to pull out of when they were in a hurry. And, dammit, they were in a fucking hurry. There was something wrong, though.

His driver sat at the wheel but his head was down against it like he was taking a nap. Randall was about to knock on the passenger window to yell at him to wake the fuck up when he saw the small hole in the glass.

There was a reflection too, which gave him a view of the rooftops above the car. He narrowed his eyes and tried to make the figure out. It wasn't easy, but as he turned to look, there was no doubt. Someone was up on the roof and aimed a scoped rifle at him.

Madigan thought there should have been some sense of satisfaction as she pulled the trigger on the rifle Courtney had given her, but she didn't feel anything as she watched the man's head explode like a damn watermelon.

Randall? Was that his name? Who could keep track these days anyway? She didn't appreciate being dragged into the corporate drama her friend was unfortunately a part of, but she owed the woman enough that she didn't even ask where they were going when she said they were heading out.

She drew back from the edge of the roof and took her rifle apart with deft and rapid movements before she retrieved her phone from her pocket. It took seconds to type a text message to Courtney.

Her groan was almost painful as she stared at it. Sal was having too big an impact on her if she even thought about doing this. Not a bad impact, merely an impact.

Heavy Metal injection completed, the message read. She rolled her eyes as she pressed send.

AUTHOR NOTES -
MICHAEL ANDERLE

MAY 21, 2019

THANK YOU for not only reading this story but these *Author Notes* **as well.**

(I think I've been good with always opening with "thank you." If not, I need to edit the other *Author Notes*!)

RANDOM (*sometimes*) THOUGHTS?

Question: Will the ZOO become a way for authors (both new and existing) from around the world to publish here in the US, allowing us to see how action adventure is thought of elsewhere?

Short Answer: Don't know.

Slightly Less Short Answer: ZOO still sparks the imaginations of those who see what we are doing. Viewing the artwork or the new video work as we endeavor to produce visuals that cause the imagination of authors from around the world to work overtime is working.

At least, so far.

There are more stories going into the ZOO, and I'm

excited to announce we are working with a contact in Sri Lanka to introduce the ZOO to authors in the Asia area countries. I'm wondering what a military ZOO story would read from those who know other weapons than what I'm familiar with.

Or, what kind of antagonist(s) will they dream up?

I've had to realize that the ZOO is a longer-term investment than I had originally thought. It's taking longer to pull it together, but we are getting there.

MORE BOHM?

So, I need some feedback (feel free to put it into a review, or say something on Facebook and tag me (Michael Anderle) so that—hopefully—Facebook will message me and let me know you have posted something.

Are you ready for BOHM to end and me to come up with another ZOO story, or do you want more of these characters?

AROUND THE WORLD IN 80 DAYS

One of the interesting (at least to me) aspects of my life is the ability to work from anywhere and at any time. In the future, I hope to re-read my own *Author Notes* and remember my life as a diary entry.

Cave in the Sky(™) Las Vegas, Nv USA

I just finished a meeting which included dinner at Javier's in the Aria Hotel with Mike Bray of Wolfpack Publishing. We were catching up on what we have done in the last week plus, and the ins and outs of the publishing industry.

If you had told me I would be excited to discuss the ins and outs of publishing events four years ago, I would have thought you were confusing me with someone else. Perhaps someone from a different industry.

Someone way sexier than me. (Yes, I consider the publishing industry pretty sexy. However, I love to read fiction.)

There are a LOT of changes going on right now. A major reason is technology that has produced the opportunities for small authors like me to grow and sell my stories have caused a crunch for publishers as their readers become our readers.

We have no overhead to speak of, and we can sell our books for a lower price for this reason, among many others. During this massive amount of change, it feels like we are watching sports events where sometime in the future, a few new publishing houses will rise from the ashes of the industry before us.

Here's to hoping LMBPN Publishing is one of those!

FAN PRICING

$0.99 Saturdays (new LMBPN stuff) and $0.99 Wednesday (both LMBPN books and friends of LMBPN books.) Get great stuff from us and others at tantalizing prices.

Go ahead. I bet you can't read just one.

Sign up here: http://lmbpn.com/email/.

HOW TO MARKET FOR BOOKS YOU LOVE

Review them so others have your thoughts, and tell friends and the dogs of your enemies (because who wants to talk to enemies?)... *Enough said ;-)*

Ad Aeternitatem,

Michael Anderle

CONNECT WITH MICHAEL TODD

Want more?

Find us On Facebook

https://www.facebook.com/Protected-by-the-Damned-193345908061855/

OTHER MICHAEL TODD BOOKS

PROTECTED BY THE DAMNED UNIVERSE

PROTECTED BY THE DAMNED*

8 Book series

WAR OF THE DAMNED*

8 Book series

DAMIAN'S CHRONICLES*

4 Book series

WAR OF THE ANGELS*

8 Book series

ZOO UNIVERSE

BIRTH OF HEAVY METAL*

10 Book series

APOCALYPSE PAUSED*

12 Book series

SOLDIER OF FAME AND FORTUNE*

12 Book series

TEAM SAVAGE *

3 Book series

Dungeon Core TV*

6 Book series

Dungeon Rails*

3 Book series

Hellspawned Chronicles*

3 Book series

The Sheva Chronicles*

6 Book series

Unlikely Bountyhunters*

6 Book series

House Drakonnen

The Accord

The Anchor's Inheritance Saga

* DENOTES COMPLETED SERIES

BOOKS WRITTEN AS
MICHAEL ANDERLE

For a complete list of books by Michael Anderle, please visit:

www.lmbpn.com/ma-books/

All LMBPN Audiobooks are Available at Audible.com and iTunes

To see all LMBPN audiobooks, including those written by Michael Anderle please visit:

www.lmbpn.com/audible